CHOPPER OPS

ZERO RED

CHOPPER OPS

ZERO RED

MACK MALONEY

SPEAKING VOLUMES, LLC

NAPLES, FLORIDA

2011

CHOPPER OPS

ZERO RED

Copyright © 2000 by Brian Kelleher

ISBN 978-1-61232-149-3

For my uncle Jack

1

December 20

It was a hot day in Murmansk.

A freak high-pressure area was melting ice throughout northern Russia. Temperatures up and down the Kola Peninsula had soared above seventy degrees for three days in a row. Waterways usually impassable by October were suddenly flowing freely again. Even the sun, which barely made it above the horizon these days, felt warm to the face.

The thirty-mile fjord leading into Murmansk harbor was bustling with activity as a result of the unusual weather. Fishing boats were moving in and out to take advantage of the surprising conditions. The docks at Murmansk itself were crowded with workers sorting through recently caught stocks of fish. Many men were able to work in their shirtsleeves.

Though pleasant, the unseasonable weather was considered a bad omen. Many Russians thought it unlucky to have the northern ice pack melting in the middle of winter. Not only was it a harbinger of some titanic storm to come, the harmony of all nature was thrown off. People felt out of sorts; farm animals became uneasy. Sea birds would gather in great flocks close to the shore and circle endlessly, sometimes for days. Even the fish acted queerly during such atmospheric shenanigans. Fishermen told tales of herring jumping right into their nets, confused by the warm weather. When this happened, it was considered very bad luck to eat the fish.

Not that anyone in Murmansk ever ate fish caught in the surrounding waters anyway; it was all shipped south for sale. There was a darkly logical reason for this: Six Naval bases of the Russian Northern Fleet were located within fifty miles of Murmansk. Nearly one hundred nuclear-powered submarines were docked at these facilities; three quarters of them were rotting away at their piers and leaking radioactive waste into the nearby waters. A meltdown of just one submarine reactor had the potential to kill a quarter of a million people in the region. In Murmansk, a city of 500,000, the citizens popped iodine pills like vitamins and kept gas masks in their closets.

They weren't foolish enough to eat the fish.

The largest docking facility along the Murmansk waterway was the shipyard at Shkval. Lying at anchor in the middle of its harbor was the enormous *Admiral Kuznetsov*. At 984 feet long, with 67,500 tons of displacement, she was Russia's only working aircraft carrier.

The massive ship did not present a glamorous sight. It was badly in need of a paint job. Its hull was more rusted than not. Its ski-jump bow gave it a distorted profile, as if part of the ship was melting. The gaggle of antennae, radar posts, and other paraphernalia poking out of its mast looked worn and beaten. Even the Russian Federation flag flying above the bridge was tattered. Yet the ship was barely ten years old.

Just how the *Kuznetsov* came to find itself in Murmansk was a bit of a mystery. The ship had glided into the harbor at Shkval thirty days before, unannounced, ostensibly to get its much-needed paint job. But ships never came to Murmansk to be painted. This was where Russian submarines came to die. Why then was the *Kuznetsov* here?

Rumors had swirled around Murmansk during the aircraft carrier's month-long stay. The *Kuznetsov* was on a secret mission, it was said. Nuclear weapons retrieved from the rotting subs of the Northern Fleet were being loaded aboard her for transport to safer areas in southern Russia. Nuclear-tipped missiles, torpedoes, depth charges . . . all were said to have been quietly moved to the *Kuznetsov* in the darkest hours of night and hidden away below its main decks. Indeed, figures dressed in bulky antiradiation suits had been spotted moving like ghosts on the carrier and on the restricted docks nearby.

But there were problems with this scenario. The *Kuznetsov* was in terrible shape, both inside and out. Its voyage up from the Black Sea had taken three times longer than expected. The ship's power plants had failed many times during the four-week trip, once leaving the massive carrier drifting for more than three hours perilously close to the Strait of Gibraltar. Was this really the vessel the government would choose to carry so many weapons of mass destruction?

The ship's company was a strange lot as well. The carrier had arrived in Murmansk half-staffed; a mass defection at Sevastopol had left it with a very skeletal crew. Those that remained were said to be a collection of hooligans, drug addicts, and thieves. Yet several dozen *Nahimoutsi*—junior Russian sea scouts—had been seen motoring out to the carrier during its stay. It was said these youngsters, some barely eleven years old, were being given tours of the ship. But once aboard, none of them ever seemed to return to land. Were these adolescents being used to plug holes in the *Kuznetsov*'s crew?

There was another odd thing: Rumored to be on board the carrier was no less than the godfather of the Russian Navy himself, Admiral Dimitri Kartoonov. A small fireplug of a man known for wearing his chestful of medals at all times, Kartoonov was said to have been brought over to the *Kuznetsov* soon after its arrival in Murmansk and ensconced in the captain's private suite. A case of vodka and several pounds of caviar were said to have made the trip with him.

Claims of Kartoonov being aboard the carrier created a schism among the rumormongers. One side said that the famous admiral's presence virtually guaranteed the ship was carrying a load of nuclear weapons because the Russian Navy would want its top man in charge of such a dangerous transshipment. But the other side said that, knowing the deteriorating state of many Russian warheads, there was no way the Navy would let its patron saint get within a hundred miles of such a precarious stockpile, never mind sail on the same ship.

Whatever the case, on this day when the temperatures climbed and people walked around hatless in the dead of winter, the *Kuznetsov* unexpectedly pulled up anchor and set sail just before noontime. With the help of six tugs, it clumsily negotiated the tricky turns of the Murmansk fjord, moving slowly past Sayda Bay and Gadzhievo, both thick with rotting subs.

Once it reached a point off Zapadnaya Litsa, the largest sub base of them all, the tugs finally set it free. With its propeller screws barely turning, the *Kuznetsov* moved slowly out into the deeper, misty waters of the Barents Sea, with only a handful of gulls in pursuit.

Fifty-five miles off Nord Kapp, Norway
Twenty-four hours later

The Russian scientific research vessel *Vilishynaya* was in the last day of a three-month voyage when it got the unusual call from Northern Fleet Headquarters.

The sixty-five foot converted trawler had spent the past ninety-one days sailing the lower reaches of the Arctic Circle, checking on dozens of underwater plutonium waste sites created by the former Soviet government more than twenty years before.

The data gathered by the research vessel was not good. Radiation leakage almost a hundred times higher than expected had been found in many cases. Since leaving the last dump site three days before, the vessel's crew had engaged in a program of continuously washing down the ship. But this was being done more for their own psychological comfort than anything else. Some things water and soap just couldn't wash away.

The crew was breaking for the noontime meal when the teletype message from Northern Fleet headquarters noisily clacked into the ship's radio room. The communiqué was in two parts. The first part asked that the ship's political officer be called to the radio room for receipt of the second half of the message, which would follow five minutes later.

The political officer was summoned, and after reading the first half of the message, requested that the radio room be cleared. The two communications men gladly left.

Once alone, the political officer sat down, lit a cigarette, and waited. Fifteen minutes went by. Then twenty. Finally the teletype began clacking again. The political officer read the second message as each word was typed out. It turned out to be just twenty-two words long.

The research vessel was being ordered to a new course, due north. It was to intercept the westerly course of the *Admiral Kuznetsov* and report any "observable aberration" in the ship's operation, specifically with the aircraft carrier's propulsion units or screws.

The political officer stared at the message for a very long time. What the hell was this about? Like everyone else, he wanted to make port and get off the contaminated ship as soon as possible. To change course as the Russian Navy was suggesting and sail to meet the *Kuznetsov* would add at least a day and a half to the already-grueling voyage, maybe more.

The political officer called one of the communications men back into the radio room, and without disclosing the meat of the message, requested he call Northern Fleet Headquarters for a confirmation of the missive. Another fifteen minutes dragged by, but then the message came back as confirmed.

The political officer then called the ship's captain and let him read the bad news himself.

The captain's face fell a mile.

"Why are they doing this to us?" he asked the political officer.

The man could only shrug.

"The *Kuznetsov* might be having a problem with its screws and they need a smaller vessel to get a look at them," he said. It was the only explanation he could think of.

"But that ship certainly has helicopters, or other means of inspecting their screws themselves," the captain replied. "Why involve us?"

The political officer stepped aside and indicated the teletype's keyboard. "Perhaps you want to ask Northern Fleet Headquarters yourself?"

The captain thought a moment, then shook his head no.

"We both know that will not help," he said.

With that he turned on his heel and started off for the navigation room.

The ship's new course was laid in five minutes later.

For the next eight hours, the *Vilishynaya* battled swelling seas and high winds, racing to a point 165 miles off the northern tip of Norway where it would intercept the aircraft carrier *Kuznetsov*.

Irritable and angry, the crew had ceased the washing-down operations. All nonessential personnel were locked in their cabins. The vessel's captain ordered the ship's video cameras to be recharged and made ready for visual inspection duties. Once they reached the *Kuznetsov*, his plan was to fall in behind the big ship, train his cameras on its stern, run off some videotape, and then head for home. If any abnormalities were found, he would radio Northern Fleet Headquarters, explain the situation as best he could, and let them take it from there.

The biggest problem with this plan would be the darkness. The long winter night had already fallen over the Arctic region. By the time the *Vilishynaya* reached the carrier, it would be nearly 2100 hours and inky black. The best the captain could do was mount four high-intensity arc lights on the bow of his ship and hope they would provide enough illumination to pick up any problems with the carrier's propulsion. Getting the screws on video would be impossible, of course—they were too deep below the waterline. But perhaps smoke or oil leaking into the ship's wake would indicate the problem, if in fact there was one.

They sighted the *Kuznetsov* at 2055 hours.

Its huge shape rose darkly above the eastern horizon, three dull red navigation lights piercing the night and providing an eerie silhouette of the massive warship.

Once it was spotted, the *Vilishynaya*'s captain made for the radio room and dictated a hailing message to be sent directly to the carrier: "We are under orders to assist you in any way our diminutive vessel can . . . please advise."

The captain ordered the radio man to send this immediately. Then he lit up a cigarette and sat down to await a reply.

Five minutes went by. Then ten. The *Kuznetsov* loomed closer to the puny research vessel. No sounding horns had been heard. And there was no radio reply from the carrier.

The captain asked the radio man if he was sure the

message had gotten through. The man replied all indications were the message had been received; the carrier was
simply not answering.

"Send it again," the captain said.

The radio man did as told, but once again, there was no
response.

The captain went out to the deck. The wind was gusting
at thirty-five knots and the seas were running up to fifteen
feet—the freakish warm weather had passed over this
point long ago. Firmly grasping the ship's railing, the captain stared out at the *Kuznetsov*, now just four miles away.
It seemed unnaturally dark. He raised his binoculars. Except for the three red lights, he could see no illumination
anywhere on the carrier's superstructure or along its deck.
Was this unusual? The captain didn't know. Maybe security dictated the carrier run only with the minimum
lights required by navigation law and nothing else. Maybe
this was why the ship was not responding to his messages
as well.

But maybe not . . .

The captain made his way up to the bridge and ordered
his ship to half-full ahead. The seas were getting choppier
now, the wind was up to forty knots, and it was getting
very cold. The carrier was moving at close to full speed;
the *Vilishynaya* had to be careful not to get into a collision
course with the oncoming monster.

The captain directed his helmsman to steer forty degrees
to starboard, and held on as the vessel lurched itself to the
east. The wind began battering their port side now, and
immediately the ship began drifting from its new course.
The captain barked out a series of compensation maneuvers, and the helmsman fought the steering column to
comply. When the captain looked up again, the carrier was
so close, it was taking up a huge chunk of the sky.

A quick order below sent the ship's video crew scrambling to the bow. Once the four arc lights were illumi-

nated, the captain called down for the video men to blink the lights several times. He wanted to let the carrier know they were close by and possibly get a blinking message in return.

But there was no response from the carrier.

The captain called down to the communications room. Had the carrier acknowledged their radio message yet? No, came the reply. Keep sending, the captain ordered.

The huge carrier was now just two miles away and coming on fast. Even the slightest deviation from its course would cause big problems for the *Vilishynaya*, if not from a collision, then from a close-in wake, which might conspire with the high waves to swamp the research vessel. The captain tried to light a cigarette, but his matches would not work. He told the helmsman to put a little more space between them and the carrier. The helmsman did so, but now the wind was actually blowing the research trawler toward the *Kuznetsov*, not away from it.

"Blink the lights again!" the captain yelled down to the video crew, who responded with a series of brief, intermittent flashes. The captain scanned the looming carrier for the slightest sign of acknowledgment. There was none.

The *Kuznetsov* was less than a mile away now and quickly bearing down on them. The captain ordered his engines to full speed. He needed forward momentum for the sharp turn to port required to place his ship on the carrier's stern. He intended to videotape the carrier's rear end for only a minute—no more. After that, the big ship would be on its own.

Thirty seconds passed. The huge shadow of the carrier blocked out any glimpse of the sky now—it was right beside them. The captain took the helm himself and called down to the video crew to switch on their lights and start taping.

The video crew did as told, and in the weird glow of the arc lights, the looming carrier looked positively otherworldly. The noise from its passing was deafening. The video crew, and anyone else on hand to see the vision, could not help but shrink from the sight. The captain cursed the Northern Fleet higher-ups who'd sent them on this mission.

"*Chtob ty zhoh . . .*" he murmured. "May you die like a dog."

It seemed to take forever, but finally the carrier went by them. The captain twirled the helm and the ship lurched wildly to port. Aided by the waves and the wind, the *Vilishynaya* suddenly found itself in a 180-degree turn. It straightened out no more than two hundred feet away from the carrier's massive stern.

"Start taping!" the captain yelled to the video crew, but they had turned on their equipment a long time ago.

It was strange now, because the trawler suddenly became very calm. Like being in the eye of the storm, riding the carrier's wake was actually easier on the *Vilishynaya* than the high seas and the battering winds.

It was a surreal calm, but a calm nevertheless. The captain gave steering back to the helmsman, then raised his binoculars again. He focused on the carrier's tail, but saw nothing unusual. There was no smoke, no oil trail, nothing at all deviant in its wake.

He called down to the video crew and asked if they were picking up anything unusual.

There was a slight delay in reply. But then one of the video men began screaming into his walkie-talkie.

"Skipper! You must come down here! Right away!"

It took the captain more than a minute to make his way off the bridge, down two sets of slippery steps, and along the icy, windswept railing to the bow of his boat. The first thing he saw on arriving was two video crewmen vomiting over the rail.

"Why did you disturb me?" the captain asked the man in charge of the video crew, shouting to be heard over the roar of the carrier's wake.

"There is something you must see, Skipper!" the man yelled back. His face was pale as well.

The captain spat angrily towards the carrier. "Don't tell me you actually found something wrong with this floating pig?"

The video man did not reply. He simply pointed down at the turbulent wash being left behind the carrier.

Water churning. waves crashing—this was what the captain saw. Nothing at all seemed unusual.

"You brought me down here to show me what I already know?" he barked at the video man. "That we were sent here on a fool's mission?"

Again the man did not reply. He did not move. His simply stayed frozen, his finger pointing at something in the carrier's wake.

It took the captain a few moments more—but then, yes, he saw it too. In the storm of white water being kicked up by the carrier's propellers, there was a thick rope dangling from somewhere up above.

"What is that?" the captain asked the video man.

"Keep watching, sir. Look there! See them?"

The captain squinted, and then saw that several objects were tied to the end of the thick line. They were being periodically kicked up by the churning waters in the carrier's wake.

At first the captain thought the bulky forms were potato sacks, probably filled with trash, the result of a garbage disposal duty gone awry. But after a few seconds, he realized these were not bags of trash flopping around at the end of the rope.

They were bodies. Eight of them.

The cigarette dropped from the captain's mouth. All of the bodies were headless and mostly without clothes. Their white limbs were grotesquely flailing this way and that, their bones broken from being battered by the carrier's wake.

It was a scene from a nightmare. The bodies seemed to

be beckoning to him. Suddenly the captain had to suppress the urge to vomit himself.

"What madness can this be?" he croaked.

"Look even closer, Skipper," the video man was saying. "Study the first one in line!"

The captain did, and after a few seconds realized that the first body was still wearing most of its clothes. But they were not of the type worn by an ordinary carrier seaman.

This headless body was clad in the distinctive blue uniform of an admiral of the Russian Navy, its torso weighed down by a chest full of medals.

2

Portsmouth, New Hampshire
The next day

It was 11 P.M. and Jimmy Gillis could barely keep his eyes open.

He was driving along Interstate 95, counting the exits until the one that would finally bring him home. On arrival, he promised himself a stiff drink and then right to bed. He couldn't remember the last time he'd felt so tired.

His busy day had started at seven that morning at Industrial Insurance Inc., of Portsmouth, New Hampshire, his place of employment for the past twelve years. Four meetings, two client presentations, two business lunches, with dozens of phone calls in between—it had been a typically hectic stint at the office.

He'd left work at 4:30, picked up his ten-year-old son Ryan at school, then retrieved his daughter, fourteen-year-old Kristin, from junior high. He'd dropped Kristin off at her cashier's job at the local supermarket, then brought

Ryan to hockey practice. Returning to his office, he'd made a batch of West Coast phone calls until six, when he'd left to pick up Ryan again. Supper for them was two McDonald's Big Macs and a large fries. Then the Christmas shopping began. For three hours, they plowed through the hordes at Portsmouth's mega-mall, spending a small fortune and leaving Gillis exhausted and Ryan sprawled in the backseat of their minivan, sound asleep.

Gillis's wife had been working since mid-October, and while they welcomed the extra money she earned as a part-time secretary, it was doing a job on both him and the van's tire wear. What's more, what his wife had made in eight weeks he'd just blown on Christmas presents for their two rather extended families. *What's the point of all this?* Gillis had wondered more than once that night. A vision of the family dog chasing its tail just would not leave his head.

Now, just three exits from home, Ryan woke up.

"Dad, can you keep a secret?"

Gillis hesitated a moment. "I've been known to," he finally replied.

"I have thirty-four dollars and sixteen cents locked in my bank in my room," Ryan told him. "I was saving it—to buy a really cool birthday present for Ma. . . ."

Gillis' wife's birthday was January 2nd, a rather inconvenient time for gift-giving. For years he had given her two presents at Christmastime, until she'd gently let him know that was not the thing to do.

"Because I'm out of school this week," Ryan went on, "I'm afraid that I'll spend the money before I can get something for her."

"I'll make sure you don't blow it, Rhino," Gillis said.

"Good," Ryan replied sleepily. He reached into his sneaker and came out with a small key. He pressed it into Gillis's hand.

"Just hold onto this until her birthday, okay? It's the only key to my bank. . . ."

With that, he lay back down and fell asleep again.

"Sure, Ry," Gillis said, reaching their exit at last. "Don't worry about it."

They pulled into their driveway fifteen minutes later.

Gillis woke Ryan up and after deciding to leave all the gifts in the van until morning, helped him unload his hockey equipment.

Walking up the front stairs, Gillis was too tired to notice that every light in the house was on. Revived, Ryan bounced up the steps, through the front door, into the hallway, and up to his room. Gillis dragged himself behind, hung up his coat and cap, and walked into the living room. The fireplace was blazing, the Christmas tree was alight.

And Marty Ricco was sitting on his couch, waiting for him.

Ricco was Gillis's closest friend; he was also his crewmate. Both men were part-time pilots for the New Hampshire Air National Guard. They'd flown aerial tankers together for nearly twenty years. In that time, they'd seen action during the Gulf War, had done tours over Bosnia, and had refueled countless numbers of military aircraft off the East Coast of the United States, many with fuel tanks running dangerously close to empty.

About a year before, though, their careers had taken a dramatic turn. Due to circumstances beyond their control, they were selected by the CIA, along with several dozen other military types, to fly to Iraq and destroy a rogue American warplane that had been wreaking havoc in the Persian Gulf region. During this ordeal, which became known as "Operation ArcLight," they saw real combat up close for the first time, almost got killed on several occasions, and wound up severely burned—all on top of being forced to fly helicopters, aircraft neither man liked or trusted. It had been a nightmare for them and their families, and neither wanted to revisit it ever again. In fact, in the year that had passed, they'd rarely spoken about it at all.

But while the secret mission had made them even tighter friends, it was very unusual for Ricco to visit Gillis this late at night.

"Jessuz, Marty," Gillis finally stammered. "What are you doing here?"

Ricco did not reply. Instead, he just glanced at his over-stuffed flight bag nearby.

Gillis saw it, and then started shaking his head.

"No way. I don't care if it's World War Three," he said. "I'm not flying anywhere. It's three days before Christmas. I'm tired. I've got twenty years in the Guard; they can't send me if I don't want to go."

Ricco just looked at the floor.

"This ain't for the Guard, Jimmy," he said quietly.

That was when Gillis looked into his kitchen to see his wife and Kristin leaning against the sink. Both were crying. Two men were standing beside them. They were dressed in stiff black business suits with highly starched white shirts and dark blue ties. Both had sunglasses on.

Spooks . . .

Gillis started shaking his head again. His hands balled into fists.

"No way," he said again. "No fucking way . . ."

One of the CIA men stepped from the kitchen.

"I'm sorry, Major Gillis," he said. "I really am."

With that, he handed Gillis a white envelope. It was sealed in thin red tape and stamped "Top Secret." Gillis ripped it open and read the top line: "For Your Eyes Only."

The letter was brief. It ordered Gillis to accompany the two CIA men and obey their instructions.

It ended with: "Best regards and Merry Christmas to your family . . ."

It was signed by the President of the United States.

Triple Shot Key
Off the coast of Florida
Midnight

There were thirteen bulbs twinkling on the small, scraggly
Christmas tree.

Six bulbs were red, six were green, one was black. The
three-foot tree was jammed in a hole dug deep into the
pearl-white sand. A long electrical cord ran from its lowest
branch back to a plug attached to one of the two house
trailers set up on the otherwise uninhabited beach. Every
so often, the plug would sizzle, causing the bulbs to dim
momentarily, giving the appearance that they were blinking.

Triple Shot Key was a string of sixteen tiny islands
located about halfway between Key Largo, Florida, and
the Grand Bahamas Banks. Covered with brightly colored
fauna and groves of palm trees, the key provided three
miles of uninterrupted beach, crystal-blue water, and
pleasant isolation.

It was also a fisherman's paradise. A pair of long poles
sticking out of the sand next to the Christmas tree provided
some evidence of this, but their lines had not been checked
in hours. A campfire nearby was also dying from inatten-
tion. Within its embers were the remains of a dozen beer
cans, four T-shaped steak bones, two cigar butts, and many
burned-out filter ends of a popular woman's cigarette.

The house trailers—both were twenty-four-footers—
had been on the beach for two days now. Though they
were equipped with rear axles and wheels; there were no
tire tracks around them. The trailers had not been towed
here. Instead they'd been dropped in place by helicopter.

They would be taken off the same way.

It was just a few minutes after midnight when the door to
the first trailer swung open and Jazz Norton tumbled out.
Thirty-five years old, he was drunk, disheveled, still smell-

ing of sex. So was the pretty blonde who followed him out the door.

They staggered to the beach, straightened the Christmas tree a bit, and checked the fishing lines. The hooks were empty, the bait long gone. Giggling madly, they rebaited the hooks with some leftover french fries and drunkenly cast them back out to sea.

"This is how the Brits catch fish and chips," Norton said, slurring his words badly.

They sat down next to the fire and opened a bottle of wine. Her name was Alex. She was smart, funny, a part-time model. They would be on this little piece of paradise for a total of five days. Plenty of booze, plenty of food, plenty of rubbers. The weather was good. The fishing was good.

Life was good. . . .

And judging from the squeals of delight coming from the second trailer, life was getting good for Norton's partner-in-crime, Bobby Delaney, too.

Delaney had been the mastermind behind this vacation. He'd located the trailers. He'd arranged for the helicopter. He'd arranged for the girls. His friend for the week was a Hooters-type named Mo. Big eyes, big lips, big every-thing, or as Delaney had put it earlier that day: "Fishing ain't never been this much fun."

This from a man who'd yet to bait a hook.

Norton and Alex moved closer to the fire now and stoked its embers. The night sky was incredibly bright with stars, and they spent a few minutes holding one an-other, gazing up at them.

Norton knew a few constellations, but Alex was a whiz at astronomy compared to him.

"See that group of stars?" she asked, pointing straight up. "That's Orion's Belt. Over there, that's the star Sirius. And that sort of faint image way over there, that's the Double Cluster of Perseus."

Alex knew which ones were stars and which were galaxies. She could tell Venus from Mars and Jupiter from Saturn. She even convinced Norton that if he looked hard enough into the Milky Way's band of light, he could see right through to the center of the galaxy itself.

A warm wind blew in off the ocean. Norton leaned over and kissed her long and hard. She was sexy right down to her toes.

Yes, life was good.

But not for long.

Norton stirred the coals again and refilled their plastic cups with wine. That was when he felt Alex's fingernails start slowly digging into his arm. Her grip became so intense, she was close to drawing blood.

She was looking across the bay, out towards the sea. "Look at that thing out there. What is it?"

It took Norton a few seconds, but then he saw it too. It was a bright light, definitely not a star, due south of them, a few degrees above the horizon. It was moving left to right directly over the last island in the Triple Shot chain.

The light would stop every few seconds, remain stationary for a moment or two, then smoothly start moving again—that was what was so strange about it. It was not an airplane; no fixed-wing craft could fly like that. But it was not a helicopter either. They were herky-jerky, inherently unstable, a constant battle to keep in the air. And very *un*-smooth.

What was it then?

"It's almost like it's looking for something," Alex breathed.

"Hey, partner!" Norton yelled for Delaney. "You busy?"

"Are you crazy?" came the muffled reply from the shuddering trailer.

"Come up for air and step out here, will you? Hurry . . ."

There came the sound of grumbling and a mattress

squeaking. Then the click of the trailer door and Delaney and Mo stumbled out.

"Did we catch something?" Delaney asked as they landed hard in the sand next to Norton and Alex.

"You've got a good eye for these things," Norton told him. "Look at that out there. What is it?"

Delaney looked across the bay and saw the strange light right away. "Well, damn. How about that . . ."

The light had moved about a quarter mile across the horizon by this time. It was acting very peculiarly. It would move fast for a few seconds, then suddenly stop on a dime. It would stay perfectly still, then start moving again, only to stop again after a few hundred yards and start the whole process all over again.

"Definitely not a chopper," Delaney agreed. "Not a fixed-wing aircraft either."

"We already figured that out, Einstein," Norton told him.

Suddenly the light swung around and started coming across the bay, directly at them.

Both girls jumped. Alex's fingernails went even deeper into Norton's arm.

"It's coming for us!" Mo yelled.

Delaney used his beer to douse the fire. Alex was holding onto Norton very tightly.

"You didn't bring that popgun of yours, did you?" Norton asked Delaney. Delaney was known to carry a huge .357 Magnum at times.

"Are you kidding?" Delaney replied. "Bring that hand cannon on a fishing trip? What do you think this is, the movies?"

This provided little comfort for them. The light was getting closer and growing brighter with every second.

"God, is it a flying saucer?" Mo cried.

"I knew we shouldn't have put thirteen bulbs on that damn tree!" Delaney whispered.

The light was just a few hundred feet from them now.

It was so bright it hurt their eyes. Suddenly it began to slow up again. Norton heard the noise and then he saw its profile.

Then he knew what it was.

So did Delaney.

"An Osprey?" Norton heard the words twirl off his lips.

"They have those things deployed?" Delaney asked, just as baffled.

It was a V-22 Osprey, a kind of half-airplane, half-helicopter that was the latest flying toy for the U.S. Marine Corps. The aircraft had a pair of huge propellers the size of two helicopter rotors mounted on movable, wing-tip nacelles. Move these props to the vertical and the plane would act as a helicopter. Move them to the horizontal and you had a medium-sized troop-carrying airplane, one that could go a lot faster and travel a lot farther than an ordinary chopper.

Any hopes that the strange aircraft was simply passing over were dashed when a small hurricane of sand began swirling around their heads. The aircraft's propellers were translating to its hover mode. The craft was painted dull black and looked sinister, like a gigantic bird of prey swooping down on them.

They hit the ground. The Christmas tree was ripped from the sand and blown away in the gale. The fishing rods went right after it. Norton was protecting Alex with one hand and covering his eyes with the other. The noise was tremendous.

But then suddenly, it got very quiet again.

By the time they looked up, the V-22 had landed about two hundred feet away.

The access door opened and two men jumped out. They were wearing black combat suits with no patches or insignia.

"This doesn't look good," Delaney murmured.

The two men stopped about ten feet away from the four of them.

"You Norton and Delaney?" one asked.

"Maybe," Norton replied. "What's all this about?"

"We've been looking for you two since sundown," the man said. "We have something for you."

The second man produced two white envelopes, both wrapped in thin red tape. He handed one to Norton and one to Delaney.

"You've got to be shitting me," Delaney cursed.

"Those are for your eyes only," the first man in black said, eyeing Alex and Mo.

Norton and Delaney walked a few steps away from the girls and by light of the V-22's landing beacon, ripped open the envelopes.

"Oh, God," Norton groaned. "Not again. Not now."

Delaney didn't even read his letter. All he looked at was the signature at the bottom.

"Damn, again with the President of the United States," he whispered bitterly. "I didn't even vote for this guy."

Norton just shook his head. "I did. . . ."

Alex and Mo were still trembling, still terrified. But now something else came across their minds.

Looking at the bizarre aircraft and then over at Norton and Delaney some twenty feet away, Alex turned to Mo and said:

"I *told* you they were in the CIA. . . ."

Chknk, Bosnia
0400 hours

Marine Captain Chou Koo's mind was finally at peace.

His weapon was up and humming. His Night Vision scope was delivering outstanding images. His hiding place, and that of his men, was as near to perfection as one could get in the art of ambush camouflage. A conveniently thick, early morning fog was providing even further concealment.

Chou's uniform was even beginning to dry. That would be a first in nearly twenty-four hours.

The young Asian-American officer was commander of the highly secret special operations unit known as Team 66. They were a unique bunch. Ostensibly under Marine command, they were actually a company of individuals who, for whatever reason, had just missed the cut for such high-profile special ops groups as Delta Force, the Green Berets, or the SEALs. There was a high percentage of flat feet in Team 66, for instance; lots of 20/40 eyesight too. Some guys were just a half inch over the permissible height; others might not have entirely aced their Academy calculus final. But by taking in those who hit triples instead of home runs, the U.S. Special Operations Command found in Team 66 a unit that more than made up for its minor shortcomings with tenacity, enthusiasm, and sheer balls. It also created a team that would pick up missions the brass-ass boys at Delta, the Green Berets, or the SEALs didn't want or couldn't do.

This current operation was just such a mission.

Chou checked his watch. It was now 0410 hours local time. In fifteen minutes, down the road that stretched out in front of them, a car bearing one Mlasavok Vutlchovik would travel. Vutlchovik—or the Vulture as he was called by anyone who had the misfortune of crossing his path— was a butcher. Literally. As commander of one of the most ruthless Serb paramilitary units, he'd been responsible for killing at least three thousand civilians over the past half-dozen years. Old men, women, young kids, infants, during the Bosnian War and since, Vutlchovik had slaughtered them all, many of them personally with razor-sharp meat cleavers. For someone like the Vulture, ethnic cleansing was a pleasure so perverse, even some hard-liners inside the Serbian high command had a distaste for him.

Ironically, it was not the Vulture's string of war crimes that was about to get him whacked. No, it was a piece of intelligence the DIA had come upon a while ago. It said that Vutlchovik was soon to meet with several ex-Soviet types who were to sell him a large quantity of a high explosive *plastique* material called Demex-4. Easily hidden, easily detonated, this explosive was to be used against soldiers in the American peacekeeping force in Kosovo. This could not happen. So it was deduced that the best way to prevent such a catastrophe was to get rid of the Vulture himself.

It was a mission that none of the other U.S. special ops groups wanted to touch. First of all, none of them wanted to work the Balkans. It was a messy, dirty place, where things usually went more wrong than right. Plus this mission involved too much legwork, too much exposure, too much skirting of the law when it came to cutting off the heads of foreign snakes.

Just the type of thing for which Team 66 was created.

It had taken four months of gritty undercover work, both on the ground and through monitoring the secret airwaves, to come to the little piece of knowledge that on this day, on this road, at this time, the Vulture would be traveling. Chou and his men were here, lying still in the fog and heavy shrubbery, to make sure that it would be the butcher's last day on earth.

That was why Chou was so at peace with himself. The long hours of spadework had paid off. Ambushing the Vulture's car was simply crossing the t and dotting the i. And then the world would have one less asshole to worry about.

He checked his watch again. It was now 0425. The fog was growing thicker. Chou went through his mental checklist. His men were set: Three were beside him, one was in the hedgerow across the road, and a fifth was in the tree overlooking the curve. They were all carrying M-16's equipped with HE grenade launchers. Everyone was locked and loaded. Once the deed was done, their egress route was all mapped out. It was a 1.2-kilometer run back to the beach from which they'd come. Three backup men and a rubber boat were waiting for them there. A mile-long paddle out to a waiting Navy sub, and they'd be in friendly hands by morning chow.

Chou checked his watch: 0426. Four minutes to go.

That was when he felt a tap on his shoulder.

He turned to see one of his backup men had slipped right up beside him without so much as a twig snap.

It was one of his sergeants. His name was Reaney.

"Why are you here?" Chou asked him, both surprised and agitated.

"We just got a flash message from the boat, sir," Reaney told him. "A Priority Six message. They want us to pull back—and I mean right now."

Chou just stared back at the man.

"What . . . what are you talking about?" Chou whispered urgently. "We're going to erase this guy in four minutes. We can't withdraw now."

Reaney was just shaking his head. "The message was very clear, sir. We gotta leave, right now. Get to the beach and get to the boat. The message said the security code for this is Eagle-Coronet/Alpha-Green."

Chou was baffled. This had to be a mistake. He whipped out his codebook and looked up Eagle-Coronet/Alpha-Green. He was not familiar with the doubled-up designation, so it took him a few seconds to find it.

But when he did, he felt his heart plunged to his feet.

Eagle-Coronet was code for an order made directly by the President himself. Alpha-Green meant that they were being withdrawn because another mission was about to take priority.

"Can we delay for a few minutes and then pull back?" Reaney suggested to Chou.

Chou considered this—for about three seconds.

"We have a direct order from our commander in chief," he told Reaney. "We do not hesitate one microsecond in a case like this. Kapeesh?"

Reaney lowered his eyes. He'd worked hard on setting

up this ambush; he'd been one of the men who put on the ground to track the Vulture early on in the mission.

"Kapeesh, sir," he finally replied.

With that, Chou sent out the signals to his men to start withdrawing. They all did, with only a moment's hesitation, just as he'd expect from them.

Within two minutes, the team had picked itself up and was running through patches of thick fog, back towards the beach, the rubber boat, and the submarine beyond.

Even as he was leaving, Chou could hear the sputtering of the Vulture's car coming down the road. The voices of three thousand souls were now whispering in Chou's ears. The devil would live to kill another day. *Why?*

"What could possibly be more important than this?" Chou asked himself, over and over, until he, like the others, disappeared into the heavy mist and became a ghost again.

3

It was the sound of hammers clawing wood that finally woke Gillis and Ricco.

Eight hours had passed since they'd been snatched from Gillis's house in Portsmouth. Driven to nearby Pease Air Force Base and put on an unmarked, all-black C-17 Globemaster cargo plane, within minutes they found themselves out over the Atlantic Ocean, heading east. By midnight, they saw the tip of Newfoundland pass from view.

The bad weather began soon after that.

First rain, then sleet, then snow, then ice. A massive storm that had been building over the Canadian Arctic for days was now spilling down into the North Atlantic, chasing away any semblance of mild weather at a frightening speed. The C-17's original flight plan called for flying just ahead of this fast-moving front, aiming for a rendezvous point way out to sea. But as conditions grew worse, the big plane's pilots had been forced to resort to a backup plan.

So, some nine-hundred miles out over the ocean, the C-17 had begun circling. Slipping out of night and into the next day, the airplane had burned up time and precious fuel waiting for a hole in what would become one of the biggest storms of the new century.

But rough as it was, Gillis and Ricco had slept through most of it. Sprawled across the three fold-down seats at the rear of the huge cargo jet—at six-foot-four Gillis took up two seats, while the diminutive Ricco needed only one—they had snored away the hours even while it seemed as if every bolt was coming undone on the circling airplane.

It was the racket being made by two of the C-17's crewmen that roused them. There was a large wooden crate strapped down near the rear door of the airplane. The crewmen were attacking it with hammers, noisily clawing off the sides, one plank at a time.

Once awake, Gillis and Ricco had little to do but watch the crewmen dismantle the crate. Inside was a conical object about ten feet high and seven feet at the base. It was painted in high-visibility orange. There was a small hatch with a tiny window at its center, and a ring of inflatable rubber bladders around its bottom. It looked like a modern version of an old NASA space capsule.

"What is this thing?" Ricco asked one of the crewmen.

"Are you familiar with the Wet Insertion technique?" the crewman asked in reply.

Both pilots shook their heads no. "Sounds kinky, though," Ricco said.

"Wet Insertion involves dropping personnel in this capsule into rough seas," the crewman explained, "It can be used for emergencies like ship repair, rescue missions, things like that."

Gillis yawned. "Looks dangerous."

"Not really," the crewman replied. "It goes out the back of the airplane, a chute opens, and it floats down. When it hits the water, the air bladders inflate, giving it immediate floatability. There are even provisions inside— should you drift off target. We don't expect that to happen, though, because from what I hear we're dropping you so close to the target that . . ."

Ricco and Gillis both held up their hands, stopping the man in mid-sentence.

"Wait a minute," Ricco said. "What are you saying?"

"Didn't they tell you?" the crewman asked.

"Tell us what?"

"That we're dropping you two, in this . . ."

Both pilots felt their jaws sink. Up to that moment, they'd just assumed the C-17 trip was a hitchhike, a quickie flight from one dry spot to another.

"Are you insane?" Ricco spit. "We're two old men. You can't drop us into the ocean . . . in *that* thing!"

The crewman just shrugged. "Those are my orders."

Gillis jumped to his feet.

"The hell with your orders," he bellowed. "I want to see the commander of this aircraft, *right now*. . . ."

Within a minute, the C-17's pilot had climbed down from the flight deck. He was in his mid-thirties, probably a captain. Like his crewmen, he was wearing a nondescript black flight suit.

"Problems, gentlemen?" he asked Gillis and Ricco.

"Who do you work for?" Gillis asked him.

"Beats me," the pilot replied. "We just do the flying. Beyond that, they don't tell us anything."

"Look," Ricco began slowly. "We're Air National Guard guys. Part-time tanker pilots. We're not Airborne, we're not SEALs, we're not Green Berets, or Black Berets, or any fucking berets. You really think it's wise to drop us in that can?"

The pilot looked at the orange capsule. "Well, those are the orders," he said.

"But suppose there was a fuckup in the orders. How would you know?" Gillis pressed him.

The pilot just shrugged. "I wouldn't, I guess."

"Our point exactly," Ricco said.

The pilot turned to his crewmen. "What are the operational requirements for that thing?"

One man retrieved a manual. "A general knowledge of parachute insertion," he replied. "One jump minimum."

The pilot turned back to Gillis and Ricco. "Ever jump out of a moving airplane?"

Both men wanted to lie, but couldn't.

"Yeah," Gillis said. "About twenty years ago . . ."

"Same here," Ricco added. "And it was just once."

The pilot clapped his hands together. "Well, that's all you need," he said.

He looked at his watch.

"Now I suggest that you saddle up. We've finally broken through the weather and we're approaching the drop point. . . ."

Gillis and Ricco were speechless.

"But . . ." Gillis sputtered. "We're out over the ocean. Where are you dropping us exactly?"

The pilot smiled wryly.

"Sorry," he said. "That's top secret."

Getting strapped into the insertion capsule was a painful affair for Gillis and Ricco.

Both were tied into their seats by way of six belts, with crash helmets jammed onto their heads that seemed too puny for what they were about to go through. The capsule itself was cramped and dark inside. It might have looked like an ancient Gemini spacecraft from the outside, but its interior held no controls, no handles or switches. There was just one lever, which locked the access door, and a big red panel light that contained a "blow button" for the hatch.

By the time they were sealed in, the C-17 had reduced its speed dramatically. Gillis and Ricco felt a hard turn to the left and then with little fanfare or warning, the crewmen released the tethers holding the capsule in place. It went out the rear door with a great *whoosh!* and began dropping to the sea below.

Its work done, the C-17 immediately turned west and disappeared back into the storm clouds.

Things started going wrong for Gillis and Ricco soon after that.

Upon leaving the airplane, the capsule began tumbling violently, its parachute lines entangled by the high winds.

It was a 1500-foot drop to the water, and even at full chute deployment, it was going to be a hard landing. Now, with the lines twisted, the capsule began falling way too fast.

There was nothing Gillis or Ricco could do, though; they were strapped in tighter than prisoners in an electric chair. Besides, their perilous drop would only last for a few seconds. It was just long enough for Ricco to yell: "I will kill the fuckers behind this!"

Gillis could not believe that just a few hours before, he'd been riding along the highway, van full of Christmas gifts, with his son sound asleep in the back.

"We'll kill them twice!" he cried out.

They hit the water two seconds later.

The capsule went in sideways, crashing hard into the wake of a twenty-foot wave. They went completely underwater, bobbed up, and went under a second time. Gillis and Ricco had been told to sit tight until the capsule stabilized and its flotation devices inflated and deployed. But there was no indication that these two things were happening now.

A succession of high waves began battering the capsule.

Looking out the small Plexiglas hatch window, all Gillis and Ricco could see was the raging white foam as each wave hit them.

"God damn!" Ricco kept spitting out. "Who did this to us?"

Suddenly the small red light above the blow button began flashing frantically. But neither man knew what this meant.

"Should we push it?" Ricco called out in panic. "Is that what that means?"

"Maybe it means *don't* push it!" was Gillis's jittery reply.

It was a moot point because two seconds later, the hatch blew itself. The first thing both men heard was the ear-splitting roar of the raging ocean outside.

Then the water started flooding in.

"*Sheet! This* is not good!" Ricco cried out

Gillis was already struggling with his restraining straps, but the ice-cold water was filling the capsule so quickly, his hands were becoming numb.

The capsule was now being pummeled by the stormy sea. Each time a wave hit it, water would pour in, sinking it a little bit further, allowing more water to come in with the next wave.

Within seconds, both pilots were fighting for their lives.

But then a strange thing happened: A man suddenly appeared at the opening. He was wearing a green flight suit and a large green helmet with the sunglasses visor pulled down. With surreal calmness, he reached in and undid Ricco's restraining straps. Once Ricco was free, he grabbed the National Guard pilot by his collar and simply yanked him through the hatch opening.

Gillis watched all this with a mixture of terror and hope. Ricco and the man in green disappeared from view; a moment later another huge wave swept into the capsule. The water was so deep now, it was up to Gillis's neck. He fought his straps again, but his unprotected fingers were too cold to even bend. He gasped, and took a lot of salt water into his stomach. Another wave came in and the capsule began sinking for real.

That was when the man in green appeared again.

Just as before, he simply reached in and disconnected Gillis's straps. Then, with considerable strength, he pulled the pilot out of the capsule and onto the partially inflated flotation collar outside. Gillis was astonished to see a helicopter hovering perilously close by. He could see Ricco's dripping boots hanging out of its doorway. They were not moving.

The downdraft from the helicopter's rotors was creating a wind of hurricane proportions. Gillis allowed the man in green to hook a harness around his torso; then his body was simply lifted up in the blowing wind. The next moment he was slammed hard against the landing strut of the helicopter. A hand reached out of nowhere and dragged him into the aircraft. He landed face-down on the floor. A moment later the man in the green flight suit landed right on top of him.

He heard voices shouting, and the helicopter started to move. Gillis threw up a stomachful of sea water. The noise in his ears was tremendous. The helicopter rose unsteadily, buffeted by the driving wind and rain. Gillis managed to keep his eyes open long enough to see the orange capsule fill with water and finally sink beneath the waves. Ten seconds later, he would have gone down with it.

Gillis barely remembered landing on the rusty, odd-looking ship. One moment he was on the helicopter, the next he was lying next to Ricco inside a ship's compartment with someone slapping his face. He threw up another bellyful of sea water, and finally got his breath back.

That was when he looked up to see that the two men in green flight suits who had just plucked them from the sea were leaning over him.

"Thank you," Gillis gasped. "Thank you for our lives."

"*Blagodariu . . . Nie stoit blagodarnostii*," was the throaty reply. "Don't mention it. It was our pleasure."

Only then did Gillis realize he was on a Russian ship.

4

According to NATO, the Russian Navy vessel *Battev* was designated an AURO—"auxiliary underway replenishment oiler."

At 450 feet long, and displacing forty thousand tons, the *Battev* could, theoretically at least, refuel two vessels simultaneously, plus transfer fresh water, food stores, and munitions, all while under way. Four heavy-duty cranes and a pair of cargo-transfer rigs made this possible, though even in its day, the *Battev* never lived up to expectations. Its engines never delivered the power that was required for full underway cargo transfer, and with dwindling resources to draw from, never once had the ship sailed with a full complement of crew.

The vessel itself was long and narrow; in some ways it looked like two ships joined at the middle. There was a substantial superstructure on its stern, as would be seen on most cargo ships. But there was another multilevel fabrication near the bow; this was where the bridge, main steering, officers' quarters, and navigation rooms were located.

The ship was heavily rusted—it had not been given a proper paint job in years—and really didn't look like a military vessel at all. Instead, it looked like a very large, very gangly tramp steamer.

The *Battev* had left the Black Sea port of Sevastopol about a week before. Carrying ten thousand pounds of fuel and half as much water, food, and other provisions, it was scheduled to rendezvous with the aircraft carrier *Admiral Kuznetsov* about one hundred miles east of Iceland. With these provisions on board, the carrier could complete the second part of its voyage to the Black Sea. Or at least that was the plan when the *Kuznetsov* left Murmansk.

At present, the *Battev* was nearing a point called Rockall Ledge, a deepwater trench 150 miles off the northwest tip of Scotland.

This was where the C-17 had found it, battling high seas, plowing its way north.

Gillis and Ricco had spent their first half hour on board the *Battev* shivering inside the ship's tiny sick bay.

They were being treated for exposure and hypothermia, which was ironic because the sick-bay room was so cold, they could see the condensation in their breath. They were given cups of hot tea by the Russian Naval medic and wrapped in aluminum-fiber blankets. Eventually they found the feeling coming back to their hands and feet. Once they were able to stand again, the Russian corpsman injected them with Vitamin B-12 and a mild narcotic. Then he pronounced them fit and healthy.

The two National Guard pilots were given new dry clothes—nondescript gray combat suits, leather fleece-lined boots, and woolen caps. Once dressed, they were led by another sailor down to the very bottom of the ship. Here they found a cabin with a sign on its door that read: *Sekretnaia Chasts Postoronnim Vhod Vospreshchen*—in English: "Intelligence Center. No Admittance."

The sailor opened the door anyway, motioned for the pilots to go in, and then left.

Gillis and Ricco took two steps inside the room and found a pair of familiar faces staring back at them.

It was Jazz Norton and Bobby Delaney. Fresh from their interrupted holiday off Florida, both men were slumped in folding chairs next to the doorway, looking tired and miserable, but not quite as chilled as the tanker pilots.

They knew each other; all four men had taken part in Operation ArcLight. But there were no handshakes, no warm greetings now. There was no love lost between these two teams.

Exactly why was a long story. Norton had been a top-rated test pilot when he was recruited by the CIA for the ArcLight mission. Delaney, his former F-15 squadron mate, who had been flying a backup plane for the President's entourage at the time, signed on to ArcLight at Norton's urging. At the very least the two ex-fighter pilots thought hooking up with the Company would eventually lead to unlimited hours of flying time. It was only later that they learned the CIA wanted them to fly not high-tech jet airplanes for the mission, but dreaded helicopters instead.

When they were asked to recommend some top-notch aerial tanker pilots, the names of Gillis and Ricco came up—and *this* was where the bad blood came in. One night during the Gulf War, the tanker pilots received an emergency radio call over Iraq. It was from Norton and Delaney, flying F-15's way down on the deck. An Allied pilot had been shot down; Norton and Delaney were providing cover for his rescue. Both were low on fuel, though, and Iraqi troops were moving in on the downed airman.

Norton demanded Gillis and Ricco descend and refuel them way below the allowable altitude for such things. Against their better judgment, Gillis and Ricco did so, and the rescue mission was a success. But a fistfight broke out after they all landed back at a friendly base, so dangerous was the thing Norton had ordered them to do. Thus the bad feelings were born. During Operation ArcLight, when each of the four men had displayed unquestionable valor and courage, these harsh feelings had softened a bit.

But not by much.

"Well, if it ain't Mutt and Jeff," Delaney cracked now as Gillis and Ricco walked in. "What kept you guys? Last-minute Christmas shopping?"

The tanker pilots ignored them.

Sitting at the back of the cabin were six more familiar faces. Still dressed in their combat camos from the pre-empted ambush, were Captain Chou Koo and five of his men from Team 66. They too had participated in Arc-Light—in fact, it could be said that Chou and his guys had saved the day. There was a series of courtesy nods between the National Guard pilots and the special ops troops. Gillis and Ricco had high respect for Chou and his men. Indeed, it was hard not to.

Sitting behind the small desk at the front of the room was one last familiar mug. It belonged to Art Rooney. He was a bulldozer of a man, with a sunburned complexion and a shock of white hair, and rarely did Rooney's mouth not have a cigar dangling from it. This time was no different.

Rooney was a CIA operations manager. During the hurried training for ArcLight, he'd been in charge of the unit's supersecret base off the southern coast of Florida, the place known as Seven Ghosts Key. Rooney had been instrumental in helping the four pilots learn how to fly choppers in preparation for the Iraqi mission. He also ran the secret base's officers' club, and was the chow-hall cook and bartender as well.

Though Gillis and Ricco didn't know it, Norton and Delaney had spent nearly a year on Seven Ghosts after the ArcLight mission. During that time, Rooney was usually the first person the pilots saw at breakfast every morning and the last one they saw at the bar every night. But about six weeks before, Rooney had disappeared—not an altogether unusual event on the secret island. Indeed Seven Ghosts Key was named after seven CIA agents who vanished from the island sometime during the sixties, never to be seen again.

Around Seven Ghosts, Rooney's disappearance was just assumed to be connected to some covert operation, even though at age sixty or so he seemed to be perpetually close to retirement. In any case, someone else took over cooking the eggs in the morning and pouring martinis at night. Life went on.

But now here he was. Wearing the uniform of a lieutenant in the Russian Navy. Stuck out in the middle of the Atlantic.

Just like the rest of them.

Gillis and Ricco both shook hands with Rooney.

"How long you been on this tub?" Gillis asked him.

Rooney spat out a few bits of his cigar. It was his way of ignoring the question.

"And did you get dropped into the ocean like us?" Ricco pressed him. "You don't look it."

"Just take a seat, boys," Rooney told them. "We're in a hurry."

The *Battev*'s Intelligence Center was smaller and colder than its sick bay. There was room for about ten folding chairs, the desk, and not much more. The ceiling was crisscrossed with pipes of all sizes, producing many offensive smells. A decidedly low-tech blackboard was hanging on the wall behind Rooney. Two pieces of chalk and a rag for an eraser completed the center's stock of intelligence equipment.

Gillis and Ricco retrieved two folding chairs, moved them as far away as possible from Norton and Delaney, and sat down.

Rooney relit his cigar, even though at least a few of the pipes running through the small room were carrying combustible fuel. Outside, the wind was howling.

"I'm glad you all made it here in one piece," Rooney began. "Sorry for the inconvenience. But something has come up, and the great thinkers who control our lives felt it best that we get you guys involved. The good news is, this mission will not take anywhere near as long as the last one."

A sigh of relief went through the room. The hellish ArcLight operation had taken nearly two months—anything less than that now would be considered a bargain. Rooney's comment defused a certain amount of tension as well. None of the men wanted to be here; that was obvious. It was only because the President himself had ordered it that they were present at all.

Rooney opened his briefcase and took out a folder full of black and white photos. With the aid of a roll of Scotch tape, he began hanging the photos on the blackboard.

The first photo showed a sprawling harbor identified as Murmansk. The next picture showed the profile of an aircraft carrier with a ski jump on its stern. The rest of the pictures depicted the big carrier from various angles, from aerial right down to below the surface. Obviously, some had been taken from submarines.

"British?" Ricco asked innocently.

"Russian," Rooney corrected him.

"Who knew the Russians even had an aircraft carrier?" Gillis said.

"Well, they do," Rooney said. "Just one. This is it."

Rooney checked his notes.

"This, gentlemen, is the *Admiral Kuznetsov*," he said. "Last known position was off the west coast of Norway, steaming at about twenty knots, southwesterly course.

"The carrier left Murmansk just about two days ago. It arrived there in late November and stayed for nearly a month. While in port, there were many rumors as to what it was doing there. Some said the Russians had loaded it up with hundreds of nuclear weapons taken from the de-

commissioned submarines of the Northern Fleet. Others
said it was only partially crewed, that only a few of the
ship's original company had made the trip up to Murmansk, and to fill in the holes, the Russians shipped aboard
a hundred or so sea scouts, many supposedly orphans.
There was also some intriguing speculation that Admiral
Dimitri Kartoonov was aboard the carrier. Now this guy
is as high as one can go in the Russian Navy. In their
eyes, he walks on water."

Delaney raised his hand like a kid in class. "Which rumors are true?"

Rooney drew on his cigar.

"All of them," he replied simply.

His answer raised a few eyebrows.

Rooney took a tape player from his bag and placed a
cassette into it.

"By the way, anyone here speak good Russian?" he
asked the group.

The question was answered by ten blank stares.

"That's what I thought," he said. Again he reached into
his bag and came out with ten sets of printed transcripts.
He handed them out and then pushed the tape recorder to
on.

For the next few minutes they listened to radio messages
that had been sent back and forth between the carrier and
the Russian Navy's Northern Fleet headquarters. As the
tape played, they followed English translations on the transcripts.

The communications seemed routine enough. Heading
and weather information. Reports on fuel consumption,
food and water stocks, minor problems with radar sets,
and so on.

But about six minutes into the tape, things got unusual.

They could hear a Russian officer at Northern Fleet
Headquarters asking the carrier's radio man to bring Admiral Kartoonov to the phone.

There was no reply from the carrier.

The officer asked again.

Still there was no answer.

He asked a third time—and for his trouble, got this chilling reply: "*It is my duty to inform you . . . that this ship is no longer part of the Russian Navy. If any Russian forces try to interfere in what we are about to do, we guarantee grave consequences . . . beyond Operational Order Number 362. There will be no more radio transmissions from this vessel to the Northern Fleet. Farewell, comrades.*"

At that point the transcripts read: "Transmission terminated."

Rooney clicked off the tape recorder. Everyone put down their transcripts. There was silence in the small room.

"Well, *that* was odd," Norton observed wryly.

"Believe me, we're just getting started," Rooney replied.

He began hanging up more photographs. They had been taken from the videotape shot by the crew of the *Vilishynaya* research ship. They showed the eight bodies being thrown about in the carrier's wake, performing a kind of grotesque water ballet. Each was missing its head. The way the corpses were flopping about, it gave the impression that they were waving at them.

A collective shiver went through the room.

"That's sickening," Gillis declared. "Who are they?"

"As best as anyone can determine," Rooney replied, "that's the senior officer staff for the aircraft carrier *Kuznetsov*—including the very famous Admiral Kartoonov. He's the one with all the medals."

"No wonder he couldn't come to the phone," Delaney said.

Rooney explained the origin of the photos.

"The Russians diverted this research vessel towards the *Kuznetsov* because it was the closest ship they had to go take a look at the carrier after receiving that kooky message. That they happened to get videotape of this—in the carrier's wake—was just dumb luck. Northern Fleet lied about something being wrong with the carrier's propellers, but I swear they sent that research ship up there just to see if someone on the carrier would take a shot at it."

Norton could not take his eyes off the pictures of the eight bodies strung out on the rope.

"Well, this all seems pretty obvious," he said. "Someone took over that ship. A mutiny or whatever. Right?"

Rooney just puffed his cigar.

"That's the million-dollar question," he replied. "There have not been any communications between Northern Fleet Headquarters and the carrier since then—yet the carrier seems to be proceeding on its mission as if nothing is wrong. It's on course. It's making the required heading adjustments. Staying in the sea lanes. All the normal stuff. But when we look at this videotape, it raises a question: How normal can things be?"

Delaney said: "Okay, so you've got a carrier that's full of nukes. You've got a message that might mean the ship has been taken over. And you got eight dead Russians doing the water dance. What does that have to do with us?"

"Simply put," Rooney replied, "we've agreed to give the Russians a hand with this one. They have no idea what's going on aboard that ship. They have no idea who made that wacky call, or who sliced and diced those guys riding the propellers."

A pause.

"So, the Russians are planning an assault on her," he continued quietly. "Spetsnaz, chopper-borne special operations troops. Real specialists. They'll shoot anyone in their way until there ain't anyone in their way no more. They intend to hit quick, kill the bad guys, and regain the bridge. And when they do, the ship will belong to Mother Russia again—mystery over."

"And us?" Norton asked.

Rooney lit his cigar again. "We need you guys to fly the Spetsnaz in," he said.

Dead silence. For ten long seconds.

Finally, Delaney broke the spell.

"Excuse me?" he asked. "Did you just say you need *us* to fly the Russians aboard?"

Rooney casually tossed his spent match into a nearby wastebasket. He'd expected this.

"That's right," he replied. "Get them down, let them do their thing. Simple as that."

But Norton and Delaney weren't buying it. None of them were.

"You brought us all the way out here just to fly some Russians from one boat to another?" Ricco asked acidly. "What the fuck is up with that?"

Norton piped up. "The Russians have chopper pilots— why involve us?"

Rooney walked over and made sure the cabin door was secured.

"Well," he said, his voice low now, "there is a *bit* more to this."

"There always is," Delaney cracked.

"Educate us," Norton suggested.

Rooney's normally bright face fell a little.

"First of all," he said, "when I said there were a lot of nukes on that carrier, I really mean *a lot.* . . ."

"How many?" Delaney asked.

"Most of what was once inside the operational submarines of the Northern Fleet," Rooney replied soberly. "Combined, in excess of one thousand megatons . . ."

His words hit like a small atomic bomb. A kiloton was the equivalent of one thousand tons of TNT. A megaton equaled a thousand kilotons.

"Damn," Delaney breathed. "Maybe we *don't* want to hear this."

"Well, you've got to now," Rooney said. "That ship is lugging around the equivalent of hundreds of hydrogen bombs. Tens of thousands of times the power of the bomb that hit Hiroshima."

A few whistles went through the room. "That's one big barrel bomb," Delaney said.

"But wait," Norton interrupted. "Are we talking about weapons or warheads? There is a difference."

"Well, that's the good news, if you want to call it that," Rooney replied. "For the most part we are talking about warheads, nukes that are not attached to any means of propulsion and therefore can't go anywhere."

"But?"

"Well, this is where it gets sticky," Rooney revealed. "We do know there are four workable, mission-ready nuclear weapons on board that ship. They are RMB-1750's, a relatively new type of sea-launched missile that was part of the carrier's weapons package even before it sailed for Murmansk."

"RMB-1750's? Never heard of them," Delaney said.

"Neither had we, until recently," Rooney went on. "The RMB-1750 is a very secret type of weapon the Russians managed to keep under wraps. We don't know a hell of a lot about them, but just imagine a medium-range ICBM launched from the deck of a ship instead of a submarine, and you got a good idea of what we're talking about. They are blockbusters, though; their warheads contain 150 kilotons apiece.

"What's the range of a weapon like that?" Ricco asked.

"Under the right conditions, nearly 1800 miles," Rooney replied. "Quite a shot from the deck of a carrier."

He hung up a map of the Northern Atlantic taken right out of a *National Geographic* and began marking positions. At the moment, the *Kuznetsov* was about 2600 miles from the East Coast of America. But it was damn close to places like Iceland, Scandinavia, the British Isles, and continental Europe.

"Has anyone on board the carrier actually threatened to use these weapons?" Gillis asked him.

"The answer is, we're not sure," Rooney replied. "We've been monitoring their on-board radio transmissions since this all began—transmissions that are not being broadcast on the usual Northern Fleet frequencies. Now I can't get into the specifics. . . ."

He looked around the small cabin. His message was clear—the place was probably bugged.

"But I can say this: Some of this radio traffic has been enigmatic, to say the least. For instance, this ship, the *Battev*, received a message from the carrier earlier today. It indicated that it was still intent on a planned rendezvous and supply transfer that had been scheduled long before the carrier left Murmansk."

"That's kind of weird," Delaney remarked.

Rooney just shrugged again. "They might be pretending that nothing is wrong, hoping they can get restocked. In any case, we're certainly not going to discourage that notion. In fact, we are counting on it doing that resupply. And here's why."

He returned to the map, took out a red pen, and drew an X designating the *Kuznetsov*'s present location. Then he took out a ruler and measured 1800 miles due north.

"If someone aboard that ship fires one of those missiles," Rooney said. "This is where it will go . . ."

The end of the ruler landed almost exactly on the North Pole.

"You're kidding," Norton said. "*The North Pole?*"

"Yep," Rooney replied with a puff. "Top of the world, Ma."

"But how do you know something so specific?" Gillis asked.

Rooney explained. "A few years back, the U.S. and Russia agreed to retarget their ICBMs away from each other's cities. Instead they were all targeted to fall into the sea. Do you remember that?"

A flurry of nods from the room.

"Well, the Russians did that with their Naval nuclear

warheads too. But instead of targeting them to fall into the ocean, some genius inside the Northern Fleet retargeted them to land in the Arctic under the ridiculous notion that a Naval warhead was already at sea and therefore could not be targeted there. So, according to records kept by the Russian Navy, the last known primary target programmed into those four RMB-1750's is the North Pole. That's what Operational Order Number 362 is all about. *That's* what we think whoever sent that last message was threatening: a nuclear hit on the North Pole."

"Wow," Delaney whispered. "Good-bye Santa Claus. And so close to Christmas too . . ."

"The hell with Santa Claus," Rooney snapped back. "Good-bye us, you mean."

He pulled a red sheet out of his briefcase.

"This is an environmental impact study made about fifteen years ago," he began. "We were able to lift it off the Navy's national security site last night. It says, in three simple sentences, that a nuclear explosion at the North Pole would have long-lasting, irreversible, and catastrophic effects for the whole planet.

"I quote: 'One: Any significant melting of the polar ice cap due to a nuclear detonation would raise tides and temperatures all over the globe. Two: Any significant radiation contamination of the polar ice pack would filter down into the Arctic food chain and eventually into the oceans' ecosystems as well. Three: Such a detonation would also deposit tons of contaminated ice particles into the atmosphere, all of which would eventually fall back to earth.' "

Silence fell upon the room. Outside, the wind was howling even louder.

"Now the effects of a nuclear hit on the North Pole might take some time to be felt," he concluded, "but as you can understand, a warhead hitting anywhere near there would be as catastrophic as one hitting a populated area, if not more so. That's what we are up against here."

Another puff from his cigar.

"And that's why we made the agreement with the Russians. They'll go aboard and retake command of the ship; you guys go aboard and disable those live nukes."

Absolutely no one liked the sound of that; even the taciturn Team 66 guys were squirming in their seats.

"But why can't the Spetsnaz do both things?" Ricco asked.

"Simple," Rooney replied. "As good as they are, we can't be absolutely sure what will happen when the Spetsnaz guys go in. They'll have the mutineers to deal with. So the Company wants a presence on board during the assault. The Russians can all shoot each other for all we care. We've just got to make sure those RMB-1750's are secured. And like I said, that's where you guys come in."

"Sure glad it's so simple," Delaney said under his breath.

More silence.

"Obviously this is a mission of the highest secrecy," Rooney said. "That's why you guys were picked. You know how to play by the rules—you did good during ArcLight. You know how to keep your mouths shut. And you know how to fly Russian choppers."

Another pause.

"Now I know this is a lot to dump on you," he went on. "But I'll guarantee you something. You get the Spetsnaz aboard and kill those nukes—damn it, you *will* be home by Christmas."

He checked his watch. "Okay, we have about two hours before we can actually give you the operational aspects of this. That's not much time, but you have two options on how to use it: You can either go catch some shut-eye, or get some chow. Your choice."

Some murmurs went through the room.

"But wait a minute," Delaney piped up. "You said that carrier is packed with nukes. How in hell will we be able to find four warheads among hundreds?"

Rooney just smiled. "When the time comes, we will give you good information where to look."

This comment raised eyebrows again.

"It sounds like you have some real hard intelligence coming from that ship," Norton said. "Almost as if you've got a Company guy stashed on board. . . ."

Rooney blew another cloud of smoke at the ceiling, then stubbed out his cigar.

"We do," he replied.

This comment stunned the group.

"You have someone *on board* that ship?" Ricco asked fairly amazed.

"That's right," Rooney said.

"Anyone we know?" Delaney asked him.

Once again, Rooney's eyes swept the room.

Then he winked.

"Sorry," he said, "but that's top secret."

5

Somewhere in the Nevada desert

"God, did he just tell them they'd be home by Christmas?"

"I think he did . . . we can run the tape back and check. . . ."

"Yes, that's what he said. And that guy Gillis—did you see his eyes light up when he heard it?"

"That was a totally irresponsible statement. Rooney is usually much more cautious than that."

"Well, at least he didn't mention the Zero Red Line . . . or that other 'small' problem we'd be facing if a nuke hit the Pole."

"God—if he had told them that, they might have laughed him right out of the room."

"Yeah, the poor bastards . . . little do they know . . ."

"But that's how it has to be. If they knew *too* much, it could screw up everything."

"But promising they'll be home by Christmas?"

"Well, they all might be . . . in boxes . . ."

*   *   *

Deep inside a mountain in the middle of the highly restricted Nevada Special Weapons Testing Range was a
large, man-made chamber known only as Level MQ.

It sat beneath a massive, hidden complex devoted to
ultrasecret military intelligence operations. A small army
of technicians manned hundreds of monitoring stations
within this complex, any one of which could, at the push
of a button, show with pictures and sound, via real-time
television, NightVision cameras, and/or heat imaging, just
about any part of the Earth. And anyone on it.

Seven men were sitting around a large oval table inside
the subterranean Level MQ at the moment. They were all
in their late sixties. Those not bald had gray or white hair,
overgrown to the shoulders in a few cases. They were all
wearing Western-style shirts, jeans, and cowboy boots.
And even though the room was dimly lit, they were all
wearing sunglasses.

Veterans of the deepest part of the U.S. military intelligence structure, they were known as the Seven Ghosts.

At the moment all of them were very worried. That was
the usual state of affairs inside Level MQ.

"We have those dimwits at Langley to blame for all
this," one man was saying now. "There was good evidence
things would go wrong with that ship long before it left
Murmansk . . . and they went ahead with their screwy plan
anyway. Now we're facing something that could become
much bigger than ArcLight."

"Are you kidding?" a second man asked. "If this thing
blows, it will make ArcLight look like a pillow fight. . . ."

Cigarettes and pipes were lit; coffee was poured. The
room became smoky.

"But I'm not sure what our role is here," the third man
said. "As always we're walking such a thin line. If we
start pushing lots of buttons, our lines of communications
might be discovered and just what the hell we've been

doing here all these years could be revealed. Now *that* would be a disaster."

"But we live with that possibility every day," a fourth man said. "Besides, doing nothing about this situation would be a much greater disaster than our being revealed."

"I agree," the fifth man said. "After all, our reason for being is not just to sit here and watch the world go by. We are here to act as a last resort. That's what we've done before. That's what we have to do now."

"Personally, I think we should have acted long before the damn ship even sailed," another voice said. "We should have told those assholes at Langley to back off and not complicate an already complicated situation for the Russians. Instead, they insist on getting someone aboard and stirring up the pot . . . and now this! It was a dumb thing for them to do."

This opinion was seconded by everyone present. The first man just shook his head and finally shrugged.

"Well, that's all hindsight now," he said wearily. "I just hope these chopper guys can pull it off."

"Well, they went above and beyond during ArcLight," another voice said. "If they were able to get through that, they can get through anything."

"It's the uncertainty of it all, though," another Ghost said. "I realize they're professional military men. But I just hate pulling their strings like they're puppets. They haven't got the faintest idea what is really happening and that's just not right. Just like before."

"And I say just like before it's better that they *don't* know," the first man said. "Just let them fly the mission. We'll give them what we can along the way. We can even have our seraphic friend look in on them if need be. Who knows? We might just get lucky and things will work out our way."

There was almost a laugh around the table.

"And in thirty-five years, just how many times have we got that lucky on the first try?" someone asked.

"I think I'll refuse to answer that question," the first man said.

More coffee was poured out. Pipes were relit. They all turned towards the huge TV screen that dominated one wall of the chamber.

"Can we see the target, please?" the first man said into a microphone.

The screen went black for a moment. Then it began filling with dark ominous clouds.

"The weather is going to be a big problem," someone said. "The storm that's coming might break records for the last two centuries and they'll be right in the middle of it very soon. Wouldn't you know it would be hanging over our heads just as all this nasty shit is about to go down."

"It means God is pissed at us," another voice said, adding: "Again."

"Can we get a heat shot, please?" the first man said into the mike.

The screen blinked again, and then an ominous blood-red image of a huge ship filled the field. Blurry with heat registrations, plowing through a cold black sea, it was the *Admiral Kuznetsov*.

"Is it me or does that thing look bigger?" one man asked.

No one replied.

"I'd say it's going about twenty-two knots," someone commented. "Same course. Same heading. Whoever is in charge apparently still knows what they are doing."

"Has there been any change in the on-board shortwave radio transmission?" the first man asked into the microphone.

"No, sir," a disembodied voice replied. "Same message. Same sequence."

"Shouldn't we at least let the chopper guys know about this shortwave radio thing?" the third man asked.

"For what reason?" the first man replied. "*We* don't

know what it is about. What good would it do for *them* to know?"

"Let's hear it again," another voice suggested.

The men all turned towards the radio speaker at the far end of the wall array. It had been picking up the same message from the *Kuznetsov* ever since the carrier informed Northern Fleet headquarters that it would no longer be communicating with them.

The strange thing was, the message, being sent over and over again, was coming through on a shortwave frequency used only by the Pentagon and the U.S. Navy during classified operations at sea. No one alive on board the Russian carrier should have known that frequency. Yet the message was still playing, obviously on a tape recorder set to loop, once every twenty two seconds.

It was the body of the message that was so strange—so baffling.

"Play it, please," someone said.

The chamber became filled with eerie static, and then the echoing squeak of an ancient reel-to-reel tape recorder, turning very slowly. Then the very odd little voice came on and said: *"Bitka . . . miachik . . . frukt . . . pinozhok . . . mats."*

Roughly translated: "Bats . . . balls . . . fruit . . . pie . . . mother."

What the hell did that mean?

The Seven Ghosts just didn't know.

The message played again and again. It sounded more haunting with every loop.

Finally the first man asked that it be turned off.

A very long silence followed.

"How far away is the carrier now from the Zero Red Line?" someone finally asked.

"About six hundred miles, or roughly one more day's travel if it stays steady."

"Do we want to talk seriously about contingency plans now? Or later?"

A grumble went through the room. No one was in the mood for contingency plans. They were only valuable if something was about to go wrong. Still, it would have been foolish not to consider that possibility.

"Let's just make the initial call," the first man said. "An inquiry as to what our other options are, and what could happen if we are forced to use them. Let's just hope that we don't have to."

Silently, the other six men agreed.

6

Aboard the *Battev*
December 23
1400 hours

Even Norton didn't know how he'd acquired the nickname "Jazz."

His full name was John Thomas Norton III. His father had been an ace fighter pilot flying F-4 Phantoms over Vietnam. His grandfather had flown Mustangs during World War II. His *great*-grandfather had flown Spads during World War I and had performed as a barnstorming pilot during the Roaring Twenties. Someone once told Norton that his great-grandfather's aerobatics act was called "All That Jazz," and somehow that was how he'd gotten his nickname.

But then there were some intriguing clues from his mother's side of the family. She had grown up in Hollywood, and had played surfer-girl-next-door roles in more than a dozen B movies. (Norton's good looks came from her half of the gene pool; his daring in flight was obviously a gift from dear old Dad. Both were now deceased.) In 1965, his mother appeared in a film called *Beach Blanket Jazz*. As her relatives told it, Norton was conceived in a dressing room on that movie set, thus his moniker.

Either way, the name was stuck on him at birth, which was ironic because he absolutely hated jazz music.

And at the moment, he couldn't get it out of his head.

He was sitting in the *Battev*'s officers' galley now; Delaney was across the table from him, staring into a bowl of soup. After Rooney ended their initial briefing in the *Battev*'s Intelligence Center, Gillis, Ricco, Chou, and his men had all opted to catch some sleep. Norton and Delaney went for the food, which turned out to be a big mistake for both their stomachs and their ears.

The galley was about one third full, and in one corner there was a battered tape cassette player bleating out some truly awful Russian jazz. It sounded so dreary, so unmelodic, so disconnected, it actually provided the perfect soundtrack for the battered Russian ship itself.

"Why can't those guys just stick to polkas?" Norton had said to Delaney more than once.

The *Battev* was simply the worst seagoing vessel either of them had ever been on. It was filthy; a thin layer of oil, soot, and just plain old dirt coated everything and apparently, everybody. The stink of acetylene vapor was everywhere—or at least Norton thought it was acetylene. The heads were squalid and unclean. Many of the lights did not work. The ship's PA system was a joke, as was its heating system. No matter where they went, the ship was freezing cold.

From what little they'd seen of them, the Russian crew looked like inmates of a gulag. Drab clothes, sunken eyes, sullen and unsmiling all of them. No one in the ship's company ever seemed to be doing anything of any special importance; they always appeared to be on their way somewhere, but never in any hurry to get there.

Most were young recruits, kids not yet up to shaving age; others looked like they were mere hours away from mandatory retirement—or even death. Whatever the age, no one took any special notice of Norton and Delaney, even though they were wearing the uniforms of American Navy commanders, bright blue and clean compared to the dirty gray Russian sailor uniforms.

"They don't *want* to know who we are," Delaney had said to Norton shortly after coming aboard the *Battev*. "We're spooks, remember?"

I guess we are, Norton had thought.

"Goddamn, what is this stuff I'm eating?" Delaney asked now, suddenly coming to life.

Norton stared down at his own untouched bowl. It looked like a mixture of vegetable soup and oatmeal, but it was ice cold.

"Like you said about these Russian sailors," Norton answered him, "you don't want to know."

"They could be trying to kill us, I suppose," Delaney said, examining his bowl of whatzit like a cop on a crime scene. "How would we know if they were putting poison or ground-up glass in here? We certainly wouldn't be able to taste it."

Norton dismissed Delaney's paranoia with a wave of his hand.

"Will you settle down?" he barked. "Take a look around you."

Delaney did, and saw at least twenty other people in the galley, Russian officers all, eating the exact same meal and apparently enjoying it.

Delaney finally just pushed the bowl away from him.

"I need to go on a diet anyway," he said, a funny comment as he was already rail thin.

At that moment, Rooney loped in. He spotted them and walked over, cigar puffing madly as always. He actually looked upbeat.

"What's with you?" Norton asked him. "Finally find some vodka on board?"

"Better than that," the CIA man replied. "I just got a piece of good news. . . ."

"We don't have go on this jerk-off mission?"

"Well, no, not quite that good," Rooney replied. "But something that might make it a whole lot simpler."

He looked at Delaney's untouched bowl of food.

"How's the chow today?" he asked.

"Fucking excellent," Delaney replied without a blink.

"Good, bring it with you," Rooney said. "There's someone you guys have to meet."

They walked toward the front of the ship and down two levels to a small barrackslike cabin near the anchor housing.

On arrival, Rooney was careful to knock politely on the cabin door. It took a few seconds, but the hatch finally opened. On the other side was one of the largest human beings Norton and Delaney had ever seen.

He was close to seven feet tall. Very Nordic-looking. Shaved head. A jaw of concrete. Gold teeth. Steely eyes. He was, in a word, frightening.

"Majors Norton and Delaney . . ." Rooney said by way of introduction. "This is Captain Yuri Krysoltev. Third Brigade. Spetsnaz Special Forces."

They shook hands with the Russian officer. The man grunted in return. His hands were like slabs of meat.

"I'm glad he's on our side," Delaney stage-whispered to Rooney. "He *is* on our side, isn't he?"

Norton and Delaney stepped into the cabin to find it was filled with Spetsnaz troops. There were six counting Krysoltev. All were dressed in distinctive black combat suits and berets. Each man was in the process of sharpening his combat knife. And while none of them were as enormous as Krysoltev, they looked like the cast of a *Road Warrior* movie nevertheless.

Simply put, the Spetsnaz was the Russian Army's equivalent of the Green Berets. They had a reputation for hard-nosed, ruthless professionalism, though in the eyes of the Western World they had nowhere near the operational experience of U.S., British, and other special ops groups. Like the troops in Delta Force, the SEALs, and the SAS, though, the Spetsnaz trained with many kinds of weapons and for many kinds of missions, usually operating in units no larger than a half dozen or so. And they did excel in one particular operation: resolving hostage-taking situations.

That was why Krysoltev and his men would be leading the assault on the *Kuznetsov,* Rooney explained. And while the other members of the American unit slept, Rooney wanted Norton and Delaney to get a first pass on the operational plans, seeing as they were the senior men for the American side of things.

The table at the center of the Spetsnaz berthing was cleared and Krysoltev laid out a diagram of the Russian carrier. His men gathered around like schoolkids.

Norton looked at Rooney. "Won't we need a translator here?"

Rooney grinned, and so did Krysoltev.

"Not unless you don't speak English," the enormous Russian said in a near-perfect Oxford accent.

Norton looked up at the Russian. His head was actually touching the ceiling of the cabin.

"I'll try to follow along," Norton said.

They got down to business.

"The key to retrieving the *Kuznetsov,* of course, is to gain control of the bridge," Krysoltev began. "Once we have it in hand, at the very least we can stop the vessel dead in the water. We will also gain control over the power systems. The propulsion. Communications. Weapons . . ."

He let that last word hang out in the air for a moment or two.

"As far as we know, there are only twenty or so assault rifles on the carrier," Krysoltev went on. "Plus some flare guns, smoke grenades, and a few pistols. We can estimate then that we will meet a maximum of twenty armed people. But in truth, we really don't expect them to put up much resistance."

"How can you be so sure?" Delaney asked.

Krysoltev gave a shrug. "Cases like this are very similar to hostage-taking situations," he explained. "The perpetrators are usually nervous, frantic, prone to panic. And while there is a chance that this whole thing was planned beforehand, how can one really prepare for such a thing as taking over a huge ship? They are really virgins in an unknown territory. . . ."

"If you say so," Delaney replied.

"So we really expect them to be·on edge, disorientated, plus tired and hungry as well," Krysoltev continued. "We'll descend on them with the element of surprise and thus secure a great advantage. Believe me, they won't know what hit them."

"Did you say there was a chance this thing had been planned, though? That it was not a spontaneous thing?" Norton asked.

Krysoltev glanced at Rooney.

"That's a bit classified right now," the CIA man said enigmatically. "Let's just call it speculation."

" 'Classified speculation?' " Delaney asked.

Rooney shrugged. "As good a phrase as any."

Delaney looked at Norton and just shook his head. One of the biggest pains about ArcLight was that the unit was never really privy to everything the CIA knew, even after they were sent into Iraq.

Rooney saw their concern.

"It doesn't really make any difference," he added. "Planned or not, they are still babes in the woods."

Norton decided he wasn't going to argue the point. If all the CIA wanted from him was to fly a chopper from this ship to another, then fly a chopper he would do. And if his involvement ended soon thereafter, that was fine too. Just like the guys in the Osprey who'd flown him and Delaney way the hell out here, stopping no less than three times on various Navy ships to refuel, if they played their minor parts well, then maybe, just maybe, he *could* get back to Triple Shot Key by Christmas—and before Alex got tired of waiting for him. Bottom line: Why get too involved?

But Delaney was a harder sell.

"But if you suspect this was a planned thing, then you must have a good idea of who will be waiting for you when you go aboard," he asked. "I mean, there are only so many people on board this carrier, right?"

Krysoltev thought a moment. "Let's just say we have an idea who is behind it," he said finally. "Known troublemakers among the crew. But they are amateurs. Below amateurs. And few in number. We really don't expect much fight from them."

"It's probably a *very* small number," Rooney said, jumping in.

"And again, they won't know when we are coming," Krysoltev added.

The conversation had gone full circle. Norton gave Delaney a nudge. Time to move on.

"Okay," Delaney said. "Just tell us what you want us to do."

"It's really very simple," Krysoltev said.

And it was.

By all indications of its course and speed, the carrier was still intent on its rendezvous with the *Battev*. Once the carrier came into visual range, the plan called for three Kamov choppers to take off from the replenishment ship. Chopper One would be flown by Gillis and Ricco. It would carry the half-dozen Spetsnaz troops. Chopper Two, to be flown by the *Battev*'s own pilots, would lug the Spetsnaz heavy weapons, communications gear, and extra

ammunition. Chopper Three, flown by Norton and Delaney, would carry the Team 66 guys.

They would be going in at night. Ideally, whoever was
running the carrier would be preoccupied with prepara-
tions for connecting with the *Battev*. Once down, the
Spetsnaz guys would assault the carrier's superstructure—
also known as the Island—racing up the five levels to
where the ship's bridge was located, and with their superior firepower mowing down anyone who got in their way.
Simultaneously, the Team 66 guys would go looking for
the armed-and-ready RMB-1750 nuclear weapons.

This would be the easy part, Rooney interjected, because the mysterious contact on the ship would lead them
right to the missiles.

"Plus let me give you one more twist," Rooney went
on. "It's the piece of good news we just received."

He looked at Krysoltev, who smiled widely. The glare
from his capped teeth was almost blinding.

"Now we know there are four RMB-1750 missiles on
board that ship," Rooney told them. "Four missiles, four
150-kiloton warheads fitted onto those missiles. However,
we just got confirmation that two of the warheads are duds.
They've been deactivated. So, do the math. Two work and
two don't. That cuts the chances of catastrophe in half."

Norton and Delaney chewed on this for a moment. Then
Delaney said: "But that still means a fifty-fifty chance of
a very big problem."

Rooney almost looked hurt. "Figures you'd see the glass
as half full, Delaney," he said.

"After having you as my bartender for the past year, I
can't see it any other way," Delaney fired back.

They moved on.

Rooney laid out a small diagram of the RBM-1750
weapon. It was a long cylindrical missile, twenty-four feet
in length, with a distinctive red nose cone. Once the weapons were located, the two live ones would be destroyed
by a very simple method. Just below the nose cone's seam

was a panel that could be removed by undoing two clamps. Within was the fusing system for the weapon; most prominent was an infrared light-sensitive device that provided the "sight-memory" for the warhead during the missile's trajectory. By shining a very simple laser pointer onto this device, the missile's electronic "iris" would be destroyed, fritzing the whole fusing system. Result: The warhead would not detonate on impact.

"If it takes you more than a minute to destroy both systems, it means you were taking your time," Rooney told them. "It's that simple."

This done, Team 66 would be loaded back onto Chopper Three, and returned to the *Battev*. The Spetsnaz guys would remain on the bridge until the *Battev* came alongside. Then the replenishment ship's crew would help secure the rest of the carrier until . . . well, by that time, the Americans would be out of it. So what happened next didn't make any difference.

"So? What do you think?" Rooney asked them.

"You were right when you said it was simple," Norton replied.

Compared to ArcLight, which had plans within plans, subplans, option plans, counter-contingency plans, this one *was* simple.

And he liked it that way.

But as always, Delaney had a question.

"How do we all keep in touch with each other once we're on board the carrier?" he asked.

Rooney smiled, reached into his bag, and came out with a small box.

"Ever hear of the POTS communications system?" he asked.

Both pilots shook their heads no.

He opened up the box to reveal within a half dozen very ordinary cellular phones.

"POTS stands for 'plain old telephone system,'" Rooney explained with some delight. "Each chopper gets a phone, each phone has its own phone number. We've programmed everyone's number into each phone and keyed it to speed dialing. You want to get a hold of someone after the landing, just reach out and touch them. Easy as dialing a phone."

Norton and Rooney took one of the cell phones and examined it. They were mildly astonished to see it was manufactured by Radio Shack.

"Wow, real cutting edge here, Rooney," Delaney said.

"If it works, then why not?" the CIA man said. "Remember, our objective here is to keep it simple."

Norton and Delaney just looked at each other.

"Yeah," Norton said, under his breath. "You keep saying that."

The briefing in the Spetsnaz room broke up about five minutes later.

The Russian troops went back to sharpening their knives; Rooney went to wake the other members of the American team to repeat to them what Norton and Delaney had just been told.

Meanwhile, the two pilots climbed up to the deck and made their way out to the bow to get some fresh air—and find a place where they could speak without fear of being overheard.

The view from this point of the ship was rather ominous, though. With every mile the vessel plowed northwards, the sea became more intense. The wind was shrieking now. They even saw the occasional snowflake go whipping by.

Even more disturbing, off to the northwest, poised like a huge tidal wave frozen near the shore, was the titanic Arctic storm, still waiting to pounce.

"When I was a kid in Kansas," Delaney said, "we used to go out in the field in the morning and see a thunderstorm way out on the horizon. And that thing would just build and build all day long, until finally, at the hottest point of the afternoon, it would just start moving like hell and come down upon us like the hand of God. It was scary."

"Well, we ain't exactly in Kansas anymore, Toto," Norton replied. "And I've seen some storm clouds in my life, but never that big. Christ, that thing stretches for a hundred miles."

At that moment, Delaney made the mistake of leaning against the chain railing. With only the slightest amount of pressure, the chain suddenly broke and he pitched backwards. If Norton hadn't grabbed him, he would have tumbled overboard.

"Jessuz!" Delaney cried. "This ship is such a piece of crap! Don't they do anything right?"

"Hey, the Russian Navy has been bankrupt for years," Norton told him. "I don't know how they manage to get anything out of port."

Delaney took a few deep breaths and calmed down a bit. Then they moved away from the broken railing and up as far as they could go on the bow.

"So anyway," Delaney began again, still a little shaken, "I don't know if I smell a rat here exactly. But at the very least I think I detect a filthy little mouse."

"Rooney's new and improved 'simple' approach, you mean?" Norton asked.

Delaney nodded. "He hasn't been this coy since he changed from Stoli to Fleischman's back at Seven Ghosts. Like we wouldn't know the difference between great and crummy vodka?"

Norton smiled grimly. "The same people who made that great vodka also built this ship," he said, indicating the broken chain railing.

Delaney shivered again. "Well, that's enough to stop me from drinking," he said.

Norton sucked in some of the cold sea air. He felt a million miles away from Triple Shot Key at the moment.

"It *is* very convenient that they already had a bunch of

Spetsnaz guys on board here," he said finally.

"Very . . ."

"And the fact that Rooney is practically part of the crew. At least now we know where he went after he disappeared from Seven Ghosts."

"Yeah—plus he's obviously getting updates on what's happening aboard the carrier from his man inside," Delaney pointed out. "I mean, why would the Company have a guy on board *before* the mutiny happened? Just a coincidence?"

"He's definitely holding about three cards back in a five-card hand," Norton agreed. "The question is, does it make any difference?"

"Meaning?"

"Well, consider the ArcLight mess for a moment," Norton said. "We were constantly trying to find out what the 'real story' was, constantly bugging them for more information. And where did it get us? It was still a nightmare from the word go—I think we knew too goddamn much by the end of it."

"And now, you don't want to know as much?"

"Maybe not," Norton replied with a shrug. "Look at it this way: I can buy the explanation of why we are here to do the chopper flying. For whatever reason, we proved during ArcLight that we can do the job and keep our mouths shut. That we can keep secrets."

"Yeah, well, that's been easy for us," Delaney replied. "We've been sitting down in the Caribbean for nearly a year—surrounded by CIA guys. Who's to tell?"

"Well, right," Norton said. "But Gillis and Ricco—they kept their mouths shut and they did a good job in Iraq. The Team 66 guys are experts at not talking. They barely talk to *us*. I guess that makes us all sort of a valuable commodity when it comes to stuff like this."

"So what are you saying then?"

"I say let's just do what they want," Norton told him simply. "Let's just fly the mission, drop the Russians on board this thing, fuck up those missiles, and scoot. Why worry about why Rooney was already here, and why the Spets are on board, and why that carrier still expects to get resupplied."

He paused for another breath of the cold salty air.

"I mean, everything that could have gone wrong during ArcLight did go wrong," he concluded. "Now call me crazy, but that leads me to think that in this case, everything just might go right."

Delaney thought about this for a moment. "Well, it would be damn refreshing if it did," he mumbled.

"Hey, he said home for Christmas," Norton reminded him. "I thought Gillis was going to pee his pants he was so happy."

Delaney yanked on his chin a bit. They both needed a shave.

"Well, you know, he's got kids and stuff. . . ." he said, letting his voice trail off.

Norton felt a slight pull in his throat. "Kids, family, Christmas . . . stuff that I ain't got."

"Me neither," Delaney said. "At least not anymore."

With that they walked back towards the forward superstructure, turning their collars to the bitter cold.

Five minutes later, the massive silhouette of the *Admiral Kuznetsov* appeared on the northern horizon.

7

Lieutenant Commander Andy Rogers gave his wife one last kiss good-bye, picked up his bags, and started up the gangplank to the USS *Skyfire*.

About halfway, he turned and waved, and saw her and the kids wave back. Then he held up two fingers and smiled.

"Two days," he mouthed the words to her. "See you then."

"Merry Christmas," she mouthed back.

Rogers smiled and then resumed his way up the gangplank.

The USS *Skyfire* was an attack submarine of the Los Angeles class. It was nuclear-powered, with a crew of 125, and its claim to fame was its speed. It was fast enough to keep up with most U.S. surface ships—specifically those within carrier groups—thus providing effective escort duty. Indeed, using its pressurized reactor to power a pair of steam turbines to turn one big propeller, the boat could do more than thirty five knots submerged.

The sub also came loaded for bear. It had four tubes holding the new Mk48/6A torpedoes—known as the "can't miss" weapon—plus a complete array of Harpoon antiship missiles and Tomahawk cruise missiles.

Rogers had been the executive officer of the *Skyfire* for eighteen months. Because of its speed and reputation, the submarine was occasionally called on to do special missions—snooping on Chinese naval exercises, eavesdropping on Russian underwater phone lines, testing North Korean shore defenses. A typical cruise for the boat might last five months. Sometimes they went out for as long as nine or ten.

But this late December cruise was going to be different. The boat was going out to test some new GPS gear—targeting hardware for the Tomahawks—and the specs said the mission could be completed within forty-eight hours.

Just two days . . .

If this proved true, and there was nothing telling Rogers at that moment that it wouldn't be, then the *Skyfire* would be back at Norfolk by December 25th.

And he'd be home for Christmas.

Rogers saluted on and went below to stow his gear. A few messages were left on his wardroom door, each one indicating that the *Skyfire* would be ready to sail on time in about one hour.

Rogers checked his watch; it was now 1600 hours. He synchronized it with ship's time, then put on his boat shoes.

Then he went to check in with the captain.

He found him sitting in his quarters, bent over his desk as usual.

He was Captain Jim "Chip" Bruynell, thirty two years in the service, most of it spent underwater. The *Skyfire* was his third submarine command, all on "special boats." Few would argue that there was a better submariner in the Navy.

Brilliant, quick-witted, and a hard-ass only when he had to be, Bruynell was the ideal skipper for the *Skyfire*. He held the respect of his men like few others. They knew they could trust him and in turn, he trusted them. Should any bad apples get under his command, Bruynell always made sure they were pushed out just as quickly as they arrived.

Bruynell absolutely loved sailing, and was usually in his best frame of mind right at this moment, just as the boat was going out for another voyage. And though this trip was scheduled to be little more than a blink compared to some of the marathon cruises they had undertaken, Rogers didn't expect his skipper's enthusiasm to be dampened a bit.

That was why he was surprised to find Bruynell looking so uneasy when he entered his cabin. Usually they shook hands and greeted each other happily at the beginning of a cruise. But not this time. Bruynell was poring over a message laid out in front of him, wringing his hands and rocking back and forth in his chair.

The first thing Rogers noticed was the yellow paper the communiqué was printed on. It had been sealed in red tape.

"Problems, Skipper?" Rogers asked when Bruynell did not immediately recognize his presence in the room.

Bruynell looked up, then stood and shook Rogers's hand.

"No, not a problem," he said, immediately returning to the yellow message paper. "Just a bit of a puzzle. Have a seat."

Rogers sat and waited for the skipper to look up again.

"We got this message about thirty minutes ago," Bruynell told him. "It came by courier, and the scrub who handed it to me had more bodyguards than the President."

"Who's it from, Skipper?" Rogers asked.

Bruynell just shook his head.

"I know it sounds crazy," he replied. "But I'm not sure. It's got all the right codes on it. The path seemed to have come through CIA at Langley. And it's a question of sorts. What I can't figure out is why we got it before they ran it through the assholes at ONI."

This was odd, Rogers thought.

On those rare occasions when the *Skyfire* had anything to do with the CIA, any message that might come their way always went through the long line of bureaucracy at the Office of Naval Intelligence first. To get a message directly from the CIA was unheard of.

"Well, what's the message?" Rogers finally asked. "What do they want to know."

Bruynell pulled on his chin a moment, a sure sign that he was getting stressed.

"That's just it," he said. "The question is so goofy, I'm wondering if it isn't some kind of a joke."

"Now, you've really piqued my interest, sir."

"Okay, then listen up," Bruynell said. "Here's their question. They want to know what would happen if we hit a ship with a spread of four Mk torpedoes at a distance of twenty thousand yards."

"That's an easy one, Skipper," Rogers replied. "The ship would sink."

"Let me finish," Bruynell said. "They want to know what would happen if we hit such a ship with four torpedoes and the ship was carrying more than one thousand megatons of nuclear weapons on board."

Rogers was stunned.

"What the fuck . . . ?" he mumbled.

Bruynell handed him the message. "That's what it says."

Rogers read the communiqué, and then checked its security lineage. Everything seemed to be in order. And yes, that was exactly what the question was—along with a request to send the reply, in code, back to a certain CIA computer site, one that was definitely *not* located at Langley.

"Who would want to know such a thing?" Rogers finally asked.

"I don't have the slightest idea," Bruynell replied, shaking his head. "And I really don't know the answer to the question. Do you?"

Rogers had to think a moment.

"Well, if the weapons were not yet fused, I'm not sure either," he replied. "I mean, I suppose it's possible that if our torpedoes hit a certain area, like the magazine, it might be enough to set off a chain reaction. I mean, a bunch of things would have to go just right—or maybe I should say, 'just wrong'—for one of the weapons to detonate on its own. But you know what it's like with nukes, sir. Anything can happen."

Captain Bruynell pondered this answer for a few moments, then furrowed his brow darkly.

"All right, let me ask you another question, one that isn't on this message," he said. "Say we did hit this hypothetical ship that is carrying one thousand megatons of nukes. Say we're twenty thousand yards out and our torpedoes trigger one of those nukes to go off, and say they *all* go off. Where does that leave us?"

Rogers felt his jaw drop.

Twenty thousand yards was about eleven miles away. That was perilously close to a one-megaton explosion, never mind one a thousand times more powerful.

"We'd be fried, sir," Rogers answered finally. "The hypothetical ship would vaporize and we'd go up right along with it."

That was when Bruynell's face became ashen.

"I don't know why I am feeling this, Andy," he said. "But something is telling me that's exactly what someone wants to happen."

8

The *Battev*'s helipad was a scene of barely controlled chaos.

Somehow the ship's crew had managed to fit all three of its Kamov helicopters onto the flight deck, even though the pad was obviously built to hold two at the most.

Scrambling around the helipad, dressed in heavy-weather gear, yanking on thick cables here, pulling guy wires there, about twelve crewmen were doing their best to hold the three helicopters in place and keep them from falling off the rolling ship.

It was not an easy task. All three choppers had their double rotors spinning, creating a mighty swirl of rain, sleet, snow, and spray. Added to this were the wild sea conditions, with waves up to fifteen feet crashing up onto the helipad from three sides and an absolutely blistering wind. It was no surprise the flight deck was becoming thick with white foamy ice, all of it shimmering weirdly beneath the harsh glare of two-dozen halogen lights.

It was now 1900 hours—seven in the evening. Out on the western horizon, sixteen miles to port, barely visible through the stormy darkness, was the *Admiral Kuznetsov*. It was still heading southwest, its speed still about twenty knots. Had this been a normal resupply rendezvous, the *Battev* would be due to make a 180-degree turn to port at 1915 hours, a course change that would bring it up beside the carrier by 1925 or so. There had been no communications with the *Kuznetsov* in the past twelve hours, and none since the lone message confirming the high-seas supply meeting received earlier in the day.

So it was a bit surreal then; everything aboard the *Battev* was moving ahead as if nothing was wrong. Cargo was being packed, cranes pulled into position. The ship would make the arc maneuver precisely on time. And it would find itself pulling up alongside the carrier within a half hour.

By then, though, the *Kuznetsov* would be back in friendly hands.

Norton and Delaney arrived on the helipad stuffed inside flight suits usually worn by Russian Naval Aviation officers.

Lime green, overly bulky, with emblems of the Russian Navy running down the sleeves, they made the men look more like cosmonauts than chopper pilots. Their helmets were twice as large as the bone domes they were accustomed to wearing in fighter planes. There were a half-dozen wires hanging from each helmet, yet neither man had the faintest idea where any of them plugged into or why.

Their boots were thoroughly Russian as well: They were made of heavy black leather with fleece inner linings and metal toes and heels. It was nearly impossible not to clomp

around in them. Norton figured their Russian gear added
at least twenty pounds to their weight. With the sea spray
soaking them immediately after stepping onto the helipad,
that number went up at least another fifty percent.

In the thirty minutes since the rogue carrier had been
spotted, Norton and Delaney had been able to have a quick
meeting with the rest of the American team. All were in
agreement they would simply fly the mission as Rooney
and Krysoltev had laid it out for them, all the while striv-
ing to keep their participation to a minimum. This meant
no heroics, no improvising, no grandstanding.

The incentive of this *modus operandi* was simple: They
all wanted to be on their way to somewhere else before
Christmas arrived. Gillis and Ricco back to their families
in New England; Norton and Delaney back to their lady
friends hopefully still waiting on Triple Shot Key; and
Team 66 back to the Balkans to try another shot at whack-
ing the Serbian Vulture. If Krysoltev's notion was true that
those who'd commandeered the carrier would not put up
much resistance, then there was no reason this quickie mission could not be pulled off. Delaney had thus christened
the whole affair "Operation KISS"—for Keep It Simple,
Stupid.

The American team agreed it was the perfect name.

"Doolittle had more room on the *Hornet*," Delaney declared as they watched the *Battev's* crew balance the three
Russian choppers on the smallish helipad.

It was the halogen lights that made the whole thing look
so odd. With a thin coating of ice on everything and everybody, the helipad looked as if it was caught in a starlight
camera lens. Even more bizarre, the many different colors
gleaming in the false-warm glow lent a peculiarly festive
look to it all. Reds, greens, gold.

Very strange . . . Norton thought.

A crewman materialized out of the spray and pointed
Norton and Delaney towards their aircraft. It was the chop-

per stuck furthest back on the crowded flight deck, the one with twice the number of wires and cables attached to it. Chou and his Team 66 were just loading aboard. The aircraft appeared to be already warmed up and ready to go.

All three helicopters were known to the Russians as Kamov Ks-27's; their lesser-used NATO code name was "Helix." The Kamov was built as an antisubmarine platform, but could be called on as a search-and-rescue aircraft too. (Indeed it was one of the Kamovs that had pulled Gillis and Ricco from the sea.) Though the chopper did not hover well, had a clunky dual-rotor system, and was known to be frighteningly unstable at low altitudes, its powerful engines usually compensated for these shortcomings. It was ugly too; it resembled a huge breadbox with rotors on top, and on the face of it, this was not good. After all, the rule of thumb was: "If it looks ugly, it flies ugly." But like all Russian choppers, the Kamov was built solidly, and carried a reputation of refusing to go down without a fight. Flying pretty had little to do with it.

Even more important, the controls for the Kamov were not much different from those found on a Hind gunship, the Russian-built chopper that Norton and Delaney had flown during the ArcLight operation. The same was true for Gillis and Ricco, who had flown a Russian chopper nicknamed "Hook." Theoretically, then, none of the four pilots would have any trouble doing a quick study on the Kamov and then getting it to fly. Or at least, that was the plan.

Now, as they fought the wind and spray and the whirling rotors of the other two choppers, Norton and Delaney began moving across the very crowded helipad. Avoiding the scrambling crewmen, stepping over cables and wires, they soon found themselves in front of Chopper One, the aircraft being piloted by Gillis and Ricco. Both National Guard pilots were already sitting in the chopper's cockpit, studying their controls. Delaney skidded to a stop, stood at attention right off the chopper's nose, and gave them a mock salute. It was all the National Guard pilots could do to resist flipping him the finger in return—but that just wouldn't do in front of the Russians. So both men gave Delaney a sarcastically weak salute in return, and then went back to their preflight checklist.

Norton and Delaney had resumed jogging to their own aircraft when they suddenly collided with another huddled figure who was dashing across the helipad from the opposite direction.

He was bundled up in the same heavy flying outfit as they were, and both pilots were amazed to discover it was Artie Rooney. He was climbing aboard Chopper One, an AK-47 assault rifle strapped across his back.

"Hey, where the hell are you going?" Norton yelled at him.

"You don't think I'm going to pass this up, do you?" Rooney yelled back over the scream of the chopper engines. His oversized helmet looked comical jammed down on his thick white mane. "This is going to be too much fun."

"But it might get hairy out there," Norton warned him—but Rooney waved him off.

"The ride out will be the bumpiest part," the CIA man yelled to them. "I got to have *something* to tell my grandkids about."

Norton noticed that there was a bright yellow box stuffed into Rooney's breast pocket. He lifted it out a bit; it was a Kodak disposable camera.

"Always be prepared," Norton said, tapping the camera back down into Rooney's pocket. "Just get me in a few of those pictures, okay?"

They turned to leave, but then Delaney stopped Rooney just as he had one foot aboard the Kamov.

"I just thought of something," he yelled loud enough for both Rooney and Norton to hear.

"What is it?" Rooney yelled back, a bit perturbed. "We went over everything. . . ."

"Are there any airplanes on that carrier?"

Suddenly it was as if everything just stopped. The wind ceased blowing, the choppers' engines ceased screaming.

"Airplanes?" Rooney said, asking himself the question. "God . . . let me think . . ."

Norton was amazed. They had gone through two intensive briefings about the rogue carrier and what the situation might be aboard her. Yet incredibly, in all that time, no one had brought up whether there were any warplanes on board the ship.

"I really don't know," Rooney was finally forced to reply. "I hope not!"

"Yeah, me too," Delaney yelled back.

The racket of the helicopter engines and the screech of the wind came crashing back again. Rooney finally climbed up into the Kamov. Gillis was at the left-side controls, and glancing back, he too was surprised to see the CIA man dressed for combat, packing the Russian assault rifle, stepping aboard his aircraft.

Ever the priss, Gillis yelled back to him: "Do you have clearance for this?"

Rooney gave Gillis the old Italian hand-to-the-elbow salute.

"Here's my clearance!" he shouted up to the pilot. Gillis simply saluted him off and went back to praying over the Russian's copters controls.

At that moment, the Spetsnaz troops appeared on deck and quickly ran to their aircraft. The monstrous Captain Krysoltev was the last to climb aboard. Norton could see Rooney shouting urgently in the Russian officer's ear—he was sure it was about the possibility of airplanes aboard the carrier. The huge man's face suddenly turned into that of a confused schoolboy. Obviously, the subject had not come up on his end either.

Now both Rooney and Krysoltev began shaking their heads no. It wasn't clear, however, whether they were telling Norton and Delaney that no, there were no warplanes aboard the carrier—or no, we don't know if there are.

Delaney wanted to rush back and question the Russian officer directly. But before he could take another step, Gillis and Ricco hit their throttles and the Kamov shot off the helipad. A moment later, Chopper Two, the one with the Spetsnaz heavy weapons and ammo on board, went off like a rocket as well.

Caught in the vicious, combined downwash, Norton and Delaney turned and resumed running to their own aircraft.

It was time to get going.

The clouds of the gigantic storm were now stretched from one end of the horizon to the other.

They were a mixture of absolute black and dark swirling gray. The illusion that the storm was actually a huge, frozen ocean wave was enhanced by the thick line of cumulous clouds that topped the storm at around twenty thousand feet. Only now, the wave looked bigger and definitely closer.

For Norton and Delaney, flying at one thousand feet, the massive storm cloud just about filled their field of vision. Even with all they had to do in the next few minutes, they could not stop themselves from staring at it, jaws agape.

"That's one more reason we should do this as a slambam," Delaney said. "I'd prefer not to be around when that baby finally hits."

It was their chopper, the third Kamov, that was carrying the heaviest load. Not only were Norton, Delaney, Chou, and his five men on board, so was all the equipment for the Team 66 guys. And if there was one thing the Kamov was not made for, it was troop-carrying. As it was, the Team 66 guys barely fit inside the cargo bay with all their gear. Unlike the Spetsnaz, who had the luxury of carrying just their personal weapons with them while Chopper Two lugged their heavy stuff, Chou's men were crammed into the rear of the Kamov with two weapons apiece plus a lot of ammunition, grenade boxes, two portable rocket launchers, and other sundry equipment.

They were wearing Russian uniforms too—not Spetsnaz, but those of Russian Marines that Rooney had cooked up somewhere. Each man appeared to be very uncomfortable in his new outfit. Nothing seemed to fit right when it came to Russian combat suits. Chou's outfit, especially, looked several sizes too big for him. Their helmets looked childish too.

Takeoff from the *Battev* had been normal enough—that is, if lifting off in a howling rainstorm from a ship that was pitching mightily in heavy seas could be considered normal. And the Kamov's controls were similar to those of the Hinds Norton and Delaney had flown in Iraq as well—but only to a point. The Hind's controls had been placed in a very confusing manner all over the cockpit. Oil-pressure gauge here, auxiliary oil-pressure gauge way over there. The Kamov's control panel was designed the same way, except the controls were scattered about in an entirely different pattern.

But luckily, the two pilots knew enough about Russian choppers to figure out the main controls—throttle, steering, the universal—to get off the ship.

Once airborne, though, the flight wasn't without its drama.

"This thing drives like a freaking truck!" Delaney yelled—it was also extremely loud inside the cockpit. "Why don't these guys ever build anything smooth and quiet?"

But Norton did not hear him. The rough ride and the earsplitting scream of the engines were not foremost in his mind at the moment. The huge carrier looming on the horizon was. He could see its three red running lights cutting through the blowing sea mist. He studied it. The ship looked ominous, oddly dark, haunting—the massive storm clouds behind it completing the unsettling scene.

"Keep it simple," he kept telling himself. "Fly on, sing a song, fly off. Home by Christmas."

As these thoughts went through his head, Norton was also doing everything he could to keep sight of Choppers One and Two in front of him. They were all running without any navigation lights or any illumination at all. As they passed in and out of the fog and rain squalls, the first two Kamovs would suddenly vanish from Norton's view, only to reappear several hundred feet in front of their previous positions a few heartbeats later. It was all Norton could do to see their blurry outlines in the growing sheets of rain.

"I'm reading no weapons radar emitting from the carrier," Delaney reported, watching the Kamov's tiny air defense radar screen. "Assuming this toy works, that is."

But again Norton was not listening. He'd lost Choppers One and Two again. He increased throttle and after a few tense seconds, caught a glimpse of both Kamovs flying about five hundred feet below him, and no more than two hundred feet off the water.

Their orders were to stick together. And while it was certainly more dangerous to fly close to the ocean's surface, it also gave them more stealthiness.

So Norton pointed out the choppers to Delaney and indicated they were going down. Taking his cue, Delaney yelled over his shoulder to the troopers in back: "Hang on, guys. We're dropping a couple floors."

With that, Norton put the Kamov into a steep dive; the aircraft shuddered mightily in response. Pulling up only after they reached two hundred feet in altitude, he was soon moving up on the tail of the second Russian copter again, fighting the controls to stay steady.

"Well that sure as hell woke everyone up!" Delaney yelled over to him at the conclusion of the violent maneuver.

The carrier was now just two miles away. Norton was catching fairly clear glimpses of it through the low clouds.

Its deck appeared completely empty. No airplanes, no humans in sight. The radars atop its mast were not turning; there were no flags hanging anywhere on the ship.

"Is there anyone even aboard that tub?" he thought out loud.

"After all this, there better be!" Delaney yelled back.

They were now about five hundred feet off Chopper One's tail, with Chopper Two right beside them. As usual, Gillis and Ricco were dancing to their own drummer. The plan was for the Kamovs to fly to the ship together, go in together, land together. But Gillis and Ricco were really pouring on the coals and speeding way ahead of Norton and Delaney, with the Russian weapons copter in close pursuit. From the looks of it, the National Guard pilots had their aircraft open at full throttle.

"Jessuzz, what's their frigging rush?" Delaney called out.

"Those two really *do* want to get home by Christmas," Norton replied.

Norton pushed to full throttle, and felt the bump of all the troops in back colliding as a result of the sudden acceleration. The last thing he wanted to do was to land separately and not all together as planned. Yet Gillis and Ricco were now pulling far ahead.

"Do those two ever do *anything* right?" he yelled over to Delaney.

"Nope!" was his partner's simple shouted reply.

They were now just a mile away from the *Kuznetsov*— still there was no sign of activity on the carrier. No signs of life at all.

That was when a strange notion crossed Norton's mind. Maybe everyone on board the carrier was dead—by their own hand. Or maybe, it was just a huge Flying Dutchman. Maybe they would find no one was home. Food still hot, coffee still brewing—but not a soul on board.

He shivered at the thought.

"I can't wait to get this over with," he murmured.

They were a half mile out from the carrier now, with a massive rain squall in between. Gillis and Ricco started to climb a bit; so did the ammo chopper. They were both getting ready to slip into their landing profile. Norton knew it would be wise for them to do the same.

"OK, showtime in two minutes, boys!" he yelled back to Chou and his men. "You ready, Joe?"

"We are always ready," Chou replied with typical élan.

It was at that moment that Norton felt Delaney tug on his arm.

"I just had a strange thought," his partner yelled over to him. "These uniforms. These aircraft. Do you think we could be shot as spies?"

It was a typical Delaney question. Something that seemingly made some kind of perverse sense, but in the next blink, did not.

"Anything can happen within the next few minutes, partner," Norton replied. "Anything . . ."

As if to prove himself correct. Norton looked up to find he'd lost both Kamovs in the rain and clouds again.

Suddenly, they were flying all alone.

Jimmy Gillis was getting mad.

It was bad enough that he knew so little about the Kamov; he hated helicopters to begin with, and this one was hard to fly, hard to steer, hard to keep on course. But on top of all that, the cockpit flight computer, which ran all of the important aspects of the Russian chopper, was a real dog. It had started acting up shortly after takeoff. Its screen would display a field of information—important things like speed, altitude, pitch, and fuel consumption—only to freeze up every few seconds, essentially leaving them blind in the midst of the extremely ugly weather.

Purely out of frustration, Gillis began banging on the readout screen trying to free it up, just as someone might bang the radio in their old Chevy to get it to come on. And to his amazement, this solution worked.

For a while.

But just as they were 2,500 feet out from the *Kuznetsov*, the flight computer failed altogether—and no amount of pummeling could revive it. So Gillis finally reached over and hit the manual override. Suddenly he and Ricco were flying the Kamov for real.

At two thousand feet out, Gillis yelled to the Spetsnaz troops to get ready for their drop. Krysoltev gave him a confident thumbs-up in return. Now Gillis and Ricco had to concentrate on their landing approach in earnest.

The huge carrier was pitching like a toy in a bathtub. The seas were at least twenty-five feet high and the wind was getting even more ferocious. Except for the three navigation lights, there was still no illumination on the carrier, and certainly no signs of life on its deck or Island superstructure. The ship *did* look like it was empty and adrift.

Fifteen hundred feet out now. Gillis glanced behind him and could just barely see the Russian weapons chopper back in the squall. Norton and Delaney were nowhere in sight. He looked over his other shoulder to see Rooney, squeezed in between two huge Spetsnaz men, trying to read the directions on his disposable camera. Where did Rooney intend to send the camera to have his pictures developed? he wondered. *Fotomat*?

Nine hundred feet out. What they had to do now was very clear in Gillis's mind: land parallel to and slightly forward of the carrier's superstructure, allow the Spetsnaz troops to disembark cleanly, and then sit tight and keep the motor running.

If all went according to plan, the Russian special ops troops would retrieve their heavy weapons and ammo, enter the Island, and take immediate control of the bridge. Once they were in place and the ship under their control, he and Ricco would see if Norton and Delaney needed help. If all was well with them, and the four warheads had been destroyed, then the fighter pilots would give Gillis a go-message. At that point, he and Ricco would take off and return to the *Battev*, which would be only a few miles away by that time.

Gillis vowed to drink a whole pot of tea once he got back on the Russian supply ship. Then he would demand that he and Ricco be picked up by anything remotely American and flown back home, their duty done again.

Five hundred feet out . . .

The carrier was pitching even worse than the *Battev*, if that was possible. Gillis knew they would have to time their landing perfectly so as not to damage the Kamov's landing gear. The last thing anyone wanted was to get stuck on the monstrous Russian flattop.

Three hundred feet out . . .

Then two hundred . . .

Now one hundred . . .

Suddenly they were over the carrier's stern. Gillis jammed the throttle back and lowered the Kamov to ten feet. The squall had enveloped the ship by now, and it was all he could do to keep the chopper steady. They sputtered along, nearly scraping the deck at one point, until they reached a spot about fifty feet from the Island. That was when Gillis yanked the front of the chopper up, further draining his airspeed. The engines sputtered defiantly in reply. Once even with the Island, he pushed the nose down and went into a hover.

Now all they had to do was wait for the carrier to pitch up again. . . .

"Steady . . . steady . . ." Ricco was yelling, looking down at the deck from his open window. "Okay . . . go down . . . *now!*"

Gillis pushed his controls forward and gave the throttle a goose. Two seconds later, they hit the carrier's deck with a thump. Considering the conditions, a perfect landing.

"Okay, guys!" Gillis yelled to the Spetsnaz troopers. *"Time to jump!"*

But there was a problem. The chopper's side door would not open—its clasp lock was jammed. Krysoltev began banging on the handle with his rifle butt, but the door would not budge. Two of his men started wrestling with the handle, alternately prying it and pushing it. But in the tight quarters of the packed cargo bay, their attempts to free the door almost became comical.

As this was going on, a handful of figures suddenly burst from the Island's deck-level doorway. Gillis spotted them first and quickly alerted Ricco. It was very hard to see in the rain and the darkness, but there were at least five figures running towards the chopper, waving their hands frantically, all wearing heavy rain gear.

"Looks like we've got company!" Rooney yelled from the back.

"Load weapons!" Gillis heard Krysoltev order his men in Russian.

After some slipping and sliding, the five individuals finally reached the chopper. Gillis caught a good look at them as they ran past the cockpit.

And in that moment, everything seemed to change.

Much to his relief, these weren't drugged-up sailors or crazed mutineers coming to greet them.

They were kids. The Nahimoutsi sea scouts put on board at Murmansk. None of them much older than his own son.

Gillis felt a huge weight lift off his shoulders. Maybe everyone had got it wrong. Maybe *nothing* was askew on the carrier.

The five children reached the side of the Kamov just as the Spetsnaz troops finally solved the lock and slid the access door open.

And that was when the nightmare began.

The next thing Gillis knew, his ears were filled with a very disturbing sound.

Pop! Pop! Pop-pop-pop!

He turned and saw streams of blood flying everywhere.

Pop! Pop! Pop!

He couldn't believe it.

The Spetsnaz had opened fire on the five kids.

Now came screaming, crying, grunting. One by one Gillis saw the bodies fall to the deck.

"Jessuz! Stop shooting!" he yelled. *"They're just kids!"*

But no one was listening. A grenade went off somewhere, knocking the Kamov sideways. The gunfire continued—suddenly it was all around them. Another grenade went off, knocking the Kamov back to its original position. More gunfire. More screams. Finally the Spetsnaz soldiers jumped from the chopper and began running towards the Island.

Gillis and Ricco looked back and saw Rooney, in shock, staring down at the five dead children. There was blood on his hands.

"No one can know about this!" he screamed.

He reached in his pocket, took out the disposable camera, and crushed it between his fists.

"No one . . ." But before Gillis could absorb what had happened, another frightening sound pierced his eardrums.

Coming right over their heads was Chopper Two, the Kamov carrying the extra Spetsnaz weapons and ammunition. It was on fire. From its midsection to its twin tails, the aircraft was engulfed in flames.

It went over so low, Gillis and Ricco could see the pair of Russian pilots struggling with the controls. For a moment it looked as if they had the situation under control and were going to set down. But then streams of tracer fire suddenly erupted from the top of the carrier's Island. In an instant at least a dozen unseen gunmen were pouring gunfire into the burning chopper.

The Russian pilots attempted to pull their aircraft back— but it was no use. The barrage of tracers caught something combustible inside the burning cargo bay and detonated it. The helicopter blew apart in midair, the wreckage slamming onto the carrier deck not fifty feet in front of Gillis and Ricco. One of the Russian pilots was ejected through the glass canopy. On fire, cut horribly, he rolled right off

the ship and into the stormy sea below. The other pilot
somehow managed to crawl from the wreckage, his left
arm missing, his hair aflame. The torrent of red tracers
from the top of the Island turned on him. He was riddled
with a fusillade so intense, his body began hopping across
the deck, until it too finally went over the side.

Only then did the gunfire stop.

Krysoltev led his men through the sheets of freezing rain,
running low, slipping and sliding across two hundred feet
of open carrier deck.

They were programmed to focus only on the matter at
hand, and the fact they that they had just mowed down
five young boys had not quite registered yet. Their only
objective at the moment was to reach the cover of the
Island superstructure, and this they were trying desperately
to do. But gunfire had suddenly erupted all around them
too. Bullets seemed to be coming from every direction.
Yet the weather was so intense, it was hard to tell the
bullets from the pelting raindrops.

Still, they kept running.

Krysoltev was the first to reach the superstructure.
Scrambling mightily, he slammed himself up against the
steel bulkhead, heart beating, weapon up, ready for anything. His men slid up right beside him, all in a row, his
sergeant first, followed by the two corporals and the two
privates. At last, things were going as planned. They
would wait here for the supply chopper to come down.
Then they would retrieve their extra ammo and heavy
weapons and begin the assault on the Island.

Within seconds of reaching the superstructure, though,
there came a blinding flash of light through the pouring
rain. The Russian soldiers were suddenly caught in a storm
of hot metal sparks. They dropped to the deck, instinctively covering their faces. Only after the fierce wind blew
the smoke and flame away did they realize the ammo
chopper had crashed not a hundred feet away from them.

The resulting explosion had been enormous. In seconds, all of their heavy weapons and extra ammunition were gone, rising through the rain in a ball of fire.

Krysoltev watched the small mushroom cloud ascend and felt his heart sink.

This is not good, he thought.

They would have to take the Island with the weapons they had in hand, a much tougher task.

But not an impossible one.

"Forward!" he then cried.

But before they could move, another barrage of tracers began pinging all around them.

"Pasha!" Krysoltev yelled to his sergeant. "Where is all this gunfire coming from?"

The sergeant looked in all directions. It did seem that bullets were bouncing off the bulkhead and the deck at the same time.

"It's coming from everywhere!" was his shouted reply.

"Then this is not the smart place to be!" Krysoltev bellowed into the wind.

He reached over and tried to open the hatchway door leading to the first deck of the Island. It was locked tight.

"Niki!" he called out to his explosives man. "Do your job!"

Corporal Nikolev Boshei came forward, deftly attached a piece of plastic explosive to the hatchway handle, stepped back, and fired a burst from his AK-47 into it. There was a quick explosion and the door was blown off its hinges.

Boshei immediately took up a position on the other side of the opening and peeked in.

"Clear!" he yelled.

Krysoltev checked the clip in his rifle. His men did the same.

"We do not stop until we reach the bridge!" he declared.

With that, they all rushed inside.

• • •

Just seconds after Krysoltev and his men disappeared into the Island, bullets began bouncing off Chopper One once again.

The wind and the rain and the darkness made it extremely difficult for Gillis and Ricco to see where the gunfire was coming from, but most of it seemed to be hitting the rotors.

"What should we do?" Gillis yelled over to his partner.

"It's either stay here and get shot at, or take off and leave the Kry-man and his guys on a hook!" Ricco yelled back.

"We stay until our lives are threatened!" Rooney shouted from the cargo bay. "Stay cool . . . stick with the mission!"

A moment later, the gunfire stopped.

But then, by the light of the burning ammo chopper, Gillis saw something else. About two dozen dark figures had climbed over the railing on the port side of the carrier deck and were now slipping and sliding their way towards the Kamov.

Ricco and Rooney saw them too.

"Who the fuck are *these* people?" Gillis heard the CIA officer yell.

"They sure ain't kids!" Ricco cried in response.

It was true. These weren't kids. They were grown men, sailors armed with pistols, meat cleavers, kitchen knives, and fire axes. They quickly reached the side door of the chopper and began to rip it from its hinges.

"Jessuz, get us out of here!" Rooney started yelling now.

Gillis began to do just that. He revved the engines and lifted the control stick. But then the side door came halfway off. Suddenly the wind and rain was swirling inside the chopper. Rooney opened fire. So did the mob. Next thing they knew, bullets were flying all around the Kamov's cockpit.

Rooney began screaming fitfully: *"Take off! Take off!"*

There was shouting, sickening groans, the *pop-pop-pop* of gunfire. The mob was not attacking the chopper. They wanted to climb on it—and *get off* the carrier. Gillis looked back in horror. The mob was fighting each other to get into the chopper even as Rooney was emptying his rifle into them and pushing them out. Some who were shot were pressing their faces up against the cockpit window; bloody smears were suddenly everywhere. The roar of the Kamov's engines, the whipping of its rotors, the cries of men fighting, killing and being killed. It was bedlam—all in the space of just a few seconds.

And then, in the middle of all this, Gillis's cell phone began ringing.

"Take off!" Rooney was still screaming. *"Jessuz! Go!"*

Gillis gunned the engines again, lifted his controls, and the Kamov began to ascend. But by now some of the mob had grabbed onto the chopper's landing struts. They were bleeding, some were horribly wounded, but they were fanatically holding on.

Gillis managed to get the Kamov about ten feet off the deck, but the weight and instability of the men hanging off the chopper prevented him from getting any more altitude than that.

Everything was happening so fast, Gillis didn't have time to think. He gave the Kamov full power again—but it was no use. The chopper just would not go up any further.

More men appeared. They too jumped up to grab a piece of the helicopter. Now they were hanging from the landing struts, the door handles, the needle-nose antenna, even the belly-mounted sonar dome. They were slowly pulling the Kamov back down to the deck. Gillis and Ricco were fighting the controls madly. The engines were screaming in protest. They both knew if the copter touched the deck again, it would be for the last time.

And still, Gillis's cell phone kept on ringing.

Then a strange thing happened. A fusillade of tracers suddenly rained down from the top of the carrier's Island and began hitting the chopper all over. The windshield in front of Gillis and Ricco shattered, throwing shards of glass in every direction. The radar dome exploded and blew away in a thousand pieces. All four landing tires were instantly shot out.

But then the men who were trying to pull the chopper back down began falling too.

As each one fell away, dead and dying, the Kamov became lighter. The lighter it got, the further up it went. Finally they made it up to twenty-five feet.

Ricco was yelling: "God damn, that was close!"

That was when Gillis looked over his shoulder and saw the most horrible sight of all: Rooney was lying on the floor of the copter, a huge butcher's knife sticking out of his chest.

"Oh, Jesus . . ." he was murmuring. "Oh, Jesus . . ."

Gillis slapped Ricco on the shoulder and screamed at him to look in back. Ricco saw a stream of blood gushing out of Rooney's chest.

"Christ—Artie hang on!" Ricco yelled back to the CIA man.

But Rooney could not hear him.

Ricco tore off his seat belt and crawled back into the bloody cargo bay. He grabbed the knife with both hands and pulled it out of Rooney's chest. This only caused a larger torrent of blood to come gushing out.

"Hang on, Artie!" Ricco kept screaming at him. But Rooney was hardly moving now.

Gillis had to make a quick decision. It took him all of two seconds to do so.

Giving the Kamov full throttle, he climbed up and away from the carrier and headed back to the *Battev*.

• • •

By this time Krysoltev and his men had reached the Island's second level unopposed. But they had come up against an unforeseen obstacle within the superstructure: darkness.

It was pitch black inside the Island. All of the passageways' lights were out; the emergency lighting system had been turned off too. The Spetsnaz troops didn't want to illuminate themselves for fear of presenting too good a target. Yet time was slipping away from them, and every second they wasted walking in the dark meant their ascent to the bridge would be that much more hazardous.

Finally Krysoltev pulled out his flashlight and attached it to his rifle's muzzle. His men did the same.

"When they see us coming they will run away," Krysoltev said as rationalization. "I guarantee it."

With that they began running down the passageway.

Thirty seconds later, they reached the ladder up to the next level. Krysoltev went up alone, only to be greeted by a stream of tracer fire. He immediately ducked back down the ladder, then poked his gun high over his head and fired off an entire clip, shooting in every direction.

The tracer fire stopped.

He climbed back up the ladder more carefully this time. There was no return fire.

"You see?" Krysoltev roared. "They run like rabbits!"

They resumed their charge. Up the ladder and through the next dark passageway, flashlights bobbing madly, the sound of gunfire in their ears, yet not around them.

Running full out now, Krysoltev turned a corner and stumbled over something, sending his massive frame into a bulkhead. He picked himself up and directed his flashlight at his boots. They were covered with blood. He pointed the light five feet behind him to find it was a body he'd tripped over. That of a young boy. He'd been shot between the eyes.

His men kept on running; Krysoltev was now in the rear.

One of his corporals went up the next ladderway, firing his rifle ahead of him. There was a huge explosion and more gunshots popping. The corporal came back down the ladder missing half his head.

The second corporal went up next, firing his rifle over his head. There was another explosion—the corporal fell back to the deck, his chest cavity blown away.

Krysoltev pulled them from the ladder well, tossed a magnesium grenade up to the next level, and took cover. There was a brilliant flash, a chorus of screams. Then came a cloud of smoke, thick with the stench of burning flesh.

Krysoltev and the three remaining troopers went up the ladderway, firing wildly. Three bodies still aflame were lying next to the open hatchway. Already they were burned beyond recognition.

The soldiers jumped through the fire and kept on running.

Up the next ladderway, Krysoltev was in front again. He threw two magnesium grenades ahead of them. More explosions, more screams, another cloud of burning flesh. Krysoltev climbed up and saw two more dead bodies, smoking guns in hand, faces missing. His men followed. A second later, one of the bodies exploded—the enemy had been carrying explosives with him. The shrapnel perforated Pasha, Krysoltev's first sergeant. The man let out a gasp, then chunks of yellow tissue came spewing out of his mouth. He fell over with a huff. Krysoltev picked up his weapon and kept on running.

Now there were just three of them and they still had two more levels to go before the bridge. The passageways were still absolutely dark, and they missed the illumination of flashlights that had been carried by the three dead squad members.

Still they pressed on. Krysoltev reached another hatchway—taking a right hand turn here would lead them to the ladderway that would bring them right up to the entrance to the bridge itself.

He stuck his AK-47 around the corner and let off a burst. It came back at him tenfold. The storm of tracer fire lit up the passageway for its entire length on both directions. Krysoltev and his two troopers hugged the wall until the storm finally subsided.

"Give up, comrades!" Krysoltev yelled. "We have fifty men waiting for you out here. You cannot win. . . ."

There was a long silence from the other side of the hatchway—the unseen gunmen were contemplating Krysoltev's offer. This was just what the Spetsnaz commander wanted.

On his signal, he and his men tossed their last three magnesium grenades through the hatchway. There was another roll of explosions. The flash was blinding. But there were no screams this time. Just the stink of burning skin and bone.

Another spray from their AK-47's brought no return fire. Krysoltev peeked around the corner and saw yet another pile of burning bodies on the other side.

"Reload, my friends," Krysoltev told his pair of troopers. "The final climb awaits us."

They jumped over the pile of bodies and reached the last ladderway. But just as Krysoltev grasped the first rung, he was thrown across the passageway by a massive explosion. He fell face-down on the deck, breaking his nose and shattering four of his front teeth. His hard landing saved his life, though—a stream of tracers, fired from behind, tore apart one of his remaining troopers. The man's dead body landed with a thud right next to him. His throat and jaw were gone.

Krysoltev managed to roll over and send a stream of fire back down the pitch-black corridor, chasing away the gunmen. Then he got to his knees, picked up his remaining trooper, and pushed him up the ladderway.

Suddenly they were out in the open air again. At last they'd reached the gangway that led right to the bridge's main hatch. Gunfire and explosions were going off nearby.

The fierce wind and rain were stinging their faces. Both men were soaked in other people's blood. But they kept on moving.

They dashed along the railing and scrambled up to the bridge hatchway. The lone trooper jumped to the other side and Krysoltev yanked the door open. The trooper stuck his weapon inside.

But he did not open fire.

Instead he just stood there—frozen. As though what he was seeing inside the bridge did not make any sense.

"Pull your trigger, comrade!" Krysoltev yelled at him— but it was too late. The man did not fire, and as a result was quickly cut down by a hail of bullets coming from inside the bridge.

Krysoltev felt his heart thump five times in rapid succession. There was such rage within him, he thought it would burst right out of his chest. Five of his best men, dead in less than two minutes! And he with a broken nose and four very expensive busted teeth.

He'd been a fool to think this was going to be so easy. . . .

Jamming a fresh clip into his AK-47, he pulled the bridge door back and raised his weapon.

But then he too froze. He looked inside the bridge and just could not quite believe what he saw staring back at him.

"How . . . can this . . . be?" he gasped.

At about the same time Krysoltev and his men were entering the Island, Norton and Delaney were just landing on the *Kuznetsov*.

Lost in the rain squall, they'd missed the carrier on their first approach, necessitating a dangerous fly-around, before finally setting down just twenty feet away from the bow of the ship.

They were only barely aware of what was happening up in front of them. The rain, the sea spray, the wind, and

the darkness all conspired to cut visibility down to almost
zero. But obviously things weren't going well. They'd
seen the ammo chopper go in just as they began their
second landing approach. It had been hit with a hail of
gunfire coming from the Island as soon as it appeared over
the deck—and Delaney swore he'd seen a missile of some
kind slam into the chopper as well. In any case, they'd
watched it crash and then seen flashes of gunfire coming
from the carrier's Island, riddling the flaming wreckage.

At that point, Delaney began frantically calling Chopper
One's phone—but there was no answer.

"So much for the smooth sailing!" he had yelled, slamming the phone down.

"I just hope the Spats can do what they have to on half
their ammo!" Norton had yelled back.

It took nearly a half minute of jockeying, but at least
their Kamov had come down where it was supposed to,
just a few feet behind the rear aircraft elevator, and a
stone's throw from the ass-end of the carrier itself.

No sooner had they touched the deck than Chou
slammed the Kamov's door open and the Team 66 guys
piled out. They went into a protective ring around the
chopper, guns up, ready to fire at anything that moved.

That was when Norton began unstrapping from his seat.
The plan called for him to go with Chou and his men as
the senior officer while Delaney stayed up top with the
Kamov, keeping its engines running, ready for the quick
takeoff.

"You okay, pard?" Norton asked him.

"As much as I'll ever be," Delaney replied.

"You better try calling up ahead to Frick and Frack
again," Norton suggested. "I'm sure they need a diaper
change by now."

Ricco pulled out his cell phone again and turned it on.
It was at that moment, though, that they saw Gillis and
Ricco's Kamov coming at them through rain. It roared
right over their heads.

"Where the fuck are they going?" Norton yelled. "They're supposed to stay until they get our okay. . . ."

"Are those pansies running away?" Delaney yelled back. "I can't believe it. . . ."

"Get them on the phone!" Norton roared. "Hurry!"

Delaney hit the speed dial for Chopper One again. He got a beeping tone in response.

"It's fucking busy!" he cursed.

He tried the phone again. Still busy.

"Can you believe those guys?" Delaney bellowed. "I'll strangle those two with one hand. . . ."

Norton shared Delaney's sentiments, but knew he couldn't delay any longer.

"The hell with them," he yelled. "We got our own shit to do. . . ."

With that, he tapped Delaney on the helmet, then quickly went out through the side door.

"Just don't stop for tea!" Delaney called after him.

Landing hard on the deck, Norton scrambled around the rear of the chopper and found Chou and his men ready to go. They had already located the metal staircase that ran along the outside of the ship and down two decks to the carrier's aircraft hangar.

It was at the bottom of these stairs that they were supposed to meet the mysterious contact. This insider would then lead them to the RMB-1750 warheads and help destroy them.

They began moving quickly. Chou and Norton were in the lead, the five Team 66 troopers following behind. They went down the stairs and found themselves peering into the vast hangar bay whose huge dividing door had been pulled half shut. This side of the hangar was hardly empty, though. It held five Russian fighters, three navalized MiG-29's and two Su-33 Flankers. They were all loaded up with missiles and bombs, unusual for airplanes sitting inside a ship.

Just as soon as they reached the hangar, the Americans

heard a distinct popping sound coming from the other side
of the aircraft bay door. Then there was a flash and the
orange flame of an explosion. Norton and the Team 66
guys hit the deck, weapons up and ready.

Suddenly bullets were flying all around them, bouncing
off the steel walls, the grimy floor, the loaded-up fighters.

"Who the fuck is shooting at who?" Norton yelled over
to Chou, who had taken cover beneath a white and blue
MiG-29.

"I have no idea!" he yelled back.

Another explosion went off—another spray of gunfire
ricocheted around the hangar bay. Voices trying to out-
scream each other in coarse Russian echoed off the walls,
always to be followed by another spray of gunfire.

Clearly this was not a smart place to be.

The small group began crawling along the fuel-drenched
floor, heading for a ladderway located behind the MiGs.
Norton was the first one to reach it.

It was there that he met their onboard contact.

And the strange thing was, Norton actually knew the
guy.

It was Gene Smitz.

Smitz was the young CIA contact who had run the
ArcLight operation a year before.

At that time he was a low-level spook more at home
counting paper clips than directing covert operations over-
seas. But the mission to Iraq had changed him, as it had
changed them all. Smitz went through the thick and thin
with them, and at the mission's climax, virtually executed
four renegade CIA agents without so much as blinking an
eye. What he'd been doing since then, Norton had no idea.
But for some reason, it made a crazy kind of sense that
he would be the man the CIA had somehow smuggled
aboard the *Kuznetsov*.

Smitz even looked different from the last time Norton
had seen him. He was bulkier, and his tortoise-rim glasses

were long gone, as was the look of a perpetual college student that Smitz had had during Operation ArcLight.

His hair was long and cut very unevenly now. His face was carrying a five-day beard. His clothes—dark civilian pants, weather-beaten black turtleneck, jean jacket, heavy construction boots—were nowhere near the preppie L. L. Bean clothes he'd worn at Seven Ghosts.

In a word, Smitz looked . . . *Russian*.

They shook hands—a strange act as another spray of gunfire started popping all around them.

"We still on the mark?" Norton asked him.

"You bet, Jazz," Smitz replied. "Let's go. . . ."

With that they began to run down a series of ladder-ways, spiraling into the bowels of the carrier.

Smitz seemed to know where he was going. Turning left, going right, flying down this ladder, jumping over that one.

While they were running, he was yelling over his shoulder to Norton and Chou. But with all the clanging of boots and the sounds of gunfire bouncing off the walls even way down here, they were hard pressed to hear what he was trying to tell them.

"It's been screwed up on this boat since Day One!" was one phrase Norton managed to hear him say.

"So there *was* a mutiny then?" Norton yelled ahead to him.

Smitz suddenly skidded to a stop, causing a mass collision of bodies. He looked back at Norton and Chou quizzically.

"You mean they didn't brief you?" he asked them.

Norton and Chou both shook their heads.

"They didn't tell us much of anything," Norton replied. Smitz couldn't believe it.

"I'll really have to fill you in once we get off this tub!" he told them.

Then he started running again.

•   •   •

Down they went, deeper and deeper into the huge carrier.

Just when Norton didn't believe they could go any further, Smitz came to a halt before a huge steel door. It was painted yellow and covered with Cyrillic writing. Norton didn't have to read Russian to know this was a very restricted area they'd come to.

"Behold the nuclear weapons bay," Smitz told them. "The holy of holies."

He began working on the gigantic combination lock.

"At least they told you about the RMB-1750's, right?" he asked Norton.

"That's why were here," Norton replied. "Two live ones, two duds."

"Duds because I've been working on making them duds," Smitz replied. "But of all the damn luck, my laser pointer ran out of juice, and I could not find anything on board here to take its place. You guys brought some with you, right?"

On cue, Norton and all six Team 66 guys pulled out their laser pointers and blinked them in Smitz's face.

The CIA man shielded his eyes. "Well, at least you came prepared," he said.

"So all this is really because you ran out of batteries?" Norton asked him.

Smitz just shrugged. "I guess you could put it that way," he said.

Norton rolled his eyes. "God, don't tell Delaney that."

Smitz finally solved the combination lock. With a mighty effort, he swung the huge door open. They all looked inside.

Norton nearly lost his breath. The bay was overflowing with hundreds of weapons—all of them nuclear.

"Okay, guys," he joked. "No smoking . . ."

They began walking through the jungle of missiles, bombs, torpedoes, and depth charges. The men became hushed, and each footstep sounded like a whisper.

"You sure all this is crap is unarmed?" Norton asked

Smitz in a very low voice as they slowly made their way through the dim chamber.

"Un-fused is a better word for it," Smitz replied. "A nuke can't go off unless it's been fused properly. Now don't ask me how they did it, but the Russians defused all of these weapons before they were put aboard at Murmansk."

"All except four . . ." Chou pointed out.

"That's right," Smitz answered over his shoulder. "They are part of the carrier's onboard weapons package. Different from all this."

They reached the end of the bay, and here they found a large black wooden box with hay sticking out of it.

"This is it," Smitz said. "Four warheads—two disabled, two armed. I've been able to sneak in here twice, but like I said, my pointer died before I got to the third and fourth weapon. I tried to fiddle with some wires, but then I thought, shit, I could blow one of these things up. So I decided against that. It's been kind of no-man's-land down here since the ship left Murmansk anyway—it was pretty hairy just trying to get in to do it."

"Are you saying they keep this place unguarded?" Chou asked. "With all these nukes around?"

Smitz stopped for a moment. "In some ways, guarding this place was the least of everyone's worries on here," he said.

"This has got to be one hell of a story you're going to tell us," Chou said.

But Smitz was now back to concentrating on the storage box and especially its combination lock. The faceplate was missing.

"I think we'll have to force this lock," he said. "I must have screwed it up the last time I was down here."

Chou waved to his men, and two came forward and started to pry open the box. But to everyone's surprise, it was an easy job. In fact the box was not locked at all.

"That's odd," Smitz murmured.

The troopers easily lifted up the box's lid and stepped back for Smitz to look inside.

He did, and his face dropped a mile.

"Jessuzz . . ." he breathed.

"What?" Norton asked him. "What's wrong?"

Smitz just stepped back and said: "Take a look."

Norton did.

The box was empty.

"Damn . . ." he whispered.

"You're sure this is where they were being kept?" Chou asked Smitz.

"I came down here to goof two of them," Smitz replied testily. "I *know* they were here. . . ."

At that moment, Sergeant Reaney ran up to them. He addressed Chou directly.

"Sir, we might have an even bigger problem here," he said.

"And how's that?" Chou asked him.

Reaney led them over to a spot in the magazine about twenty feet from where they were standing. He pointed to the floor. There was a coil of thin yellow electrical wire running past a pallet holding several nuclear-tipped torpedoes.

Without speaking, they followed the yellow wire and saw that it ran up one side of one torpedo, through its warhead, and out the other side. The yellow wire then ran the length of the second torpedo, through its tip, and like the first one, out the other end. Then it went on to the third and fourth torpedo as well.

Now all of the Team 66 troopers were following the wire.

"It leads over here, sir," one man called out.

"And it runs through here, sir," another reported.

"And through here, and here," a third chimed in.

That was when everyone just stopped and froze in place.

Not only did the wire run in circles around the entire magazine, it was connected in some fashion to every warhead in the place, before finally disappearing in a massive entanglement up through the ceiling of the weapons chamber.

"My God," Smitz whispered. "When the hell did they do this?"

"Never mind that," Chou said. "Can an electrical current set off a nuclear warhead? Do you know?"

The young CIA man was suddenly perspiring. They all were.

"I . . . I have no idea," he stammered. "But it sure looks like someone on this ship thinks so."

"Jessuz," Chou breathed. "There's more than a thousand megatons of nuclear warheads in here. . . ."

"Yeah," Norton said. "And it looks like every last one of them is wired to blow. . . ."

The cell phone was ringing madly as Gillis swung the Kamov around to the rear of the *Battev*.

He had no time to answer the phone, though. He was too busy trying to line up for a landing.

It would not be easy. Battered by huge waves and vicious winds, the old cargo ship was still being tossed around crazily. The helipad itself was awash in ice and water and listing madly to port. Two crewmen were huddled near the edge of the platform. One was using two flashlights to guide the chopper in. The other was holding onto his shipmate's leg, a human anchor so he would not be washed overboard.

The Kamov somehow aligned itself with the stern, then went into a very shaky hover, its engines straining against the gale. Smoke was pouring out of its exhaust tubes; crucial parts within the power plants had been shot away. The helicopter was emitting a frightful screech, howling in agony above the forty-knot winds. It was only through their combined strength that Gillis and Ricco were able to prevent the chopper from pitching right into the ocean.

The crewman with the flashlights waved his arms frantically. His shipmate was screaming at him to hurry, get the damn helicopter down before they were swept off the deck.

The Kamov finally did come down, slamming onto the helipad once, then twice, before banging in on its flattened tires for good. The Russian crewman immediately dropped his flashlights—they were gone in a gust. He and his shipmate ran to the securing cables attached to the side of the helipad and then rushed across the platform. They somehow managed to hook the cables to the bottom of the Kamov's landing struts. Then they locked them into the platform itself.

Only then did the helicopter's side door fly open. The crewmen rushed forward and helped unload Rooney. A stretcher appeared. They placed Rooney onto it, and ran him into the nearest protected area, which was the ship's aft equipment storage bay.

Gillis and Ricco were quickly at Rooney's side. The ship's doctor appeared. He took one look at Rooney's sucking chest wound and grimaced. Taking out a hypodermic needle, he injected a massive quantity of a yellow liquid into Rooney's leg. It was obviously a painkiller.

Then the doctor turned to Gillis and just shook his head.

"Say good-bye to him," he whispered in thick English. "And don't be slow. . . ."

Gillis and Ricco knelt beside the CIA man. The color had completely drained from his face.

"I fucked up," Rooney was gasping. "My last goddamn mission and I fucked it up."

"Don't be so dramatic," Ricco told him. "You're okay. You just need a Band-Aid or two."

Rooney managed a weak laugh. "Look, we can't let any more of this happen. There's more shit going on aboard that carrier than anyone knows."

He coughed heavily, spitting up some blood.

"Get into my PC . . . it's in the boardroom on this ship. . . ." he went on. "Try to figure out the message there.

Someone on that carrier has been sending it out on a very secret Pentagon shortwave frequency. It must be the key to what they want."

More coughing. More blood.

"My PC's password is . . . Grand Dad."

They could both feel him slipping away.

"Okay, Artie, will do," Ricco said.

Rooney grasped at Gillis's sleeve.

"And don't leave those guys out there," he said very weakly. "If they get stuck on that ship, they'll become very expendable."

Rooney's clutch weakened.

He looked up into Gillis's eyes and said: "And one more thing, Jimmy . . . take good care of your son. Promise?"

"Yeah, Artie. I promise. . . ."

Then Rooney closed his eyes.

And was gone.

Back on the flight deck of the *Kuznetsov*, Bobby Delaney was getting very antsy.

He'd been watching events unfold up ahead of him and madly speed-dialing Chopper One's cell phone at the same time. But every time he got no reply.

The ammo-laden Kamov was still on fire next to the carrier's Island. There were a few bodies lying near the wreckage. There was another pile of bodies about four hundred feet away from him—some of them were still moving.

Delaney had watched gunfire coming from all over the Island, and from the opposite side of the deck. At one time, he'd thought a few stray rounds might have even hit the top of his chopper, but he was very reluctant to go out and check. The rotors were still spinning, and that was all that mattered to him.

It was strange, though. To Delaney's ears, the amount of gunfire he was hearing almost sounded like more than would be expected for a battle between the half-dozen

Spetsnaz and twenty or so of . . . what? Mutineers?

Maybe there was a battle going on before *we got here. . . .*

Now that was a bizarre thought.

A string of explosions around the Island startled Delaney out of his daydream. More gunfire sprayed the deck. Smoke was now pouring out of a bulkhead at the bottom of the superstructure. He could feel explosions going off below the carrier deck too—even through the vibration of the Kamov's twin rotors turning, his bones were rattling with aftershocks of something big going off down below.

He checked his watch. Norton and the Team 66 guys had been gone for almost five minutes. How long did it take to find the RMB-1750's and fuck them up?

The ship shuddered once again. More smoke began pouring out of the Island. Another check of his watch. Six minutes now.

Where the hell are those guys?

More waves crashed over the side of the carrier. The sky was so black and ominous, it looked like something from a bad dream. Delaney reached down and retrieved his AK-47. He made sure his clip was full.

"Hurry up, Jazz. . . ." he began whispering. "Maybe I'd like to get home for Christmas too. . . ."

That was when he looked to his left and was startled to see a face pressed up against his side window.

It was Norton.

He didn't look happy.

Delaney slid the window back. "Jessuz, what took you so long?"

"They're not there!" Norton was screaming.

"What's not where?" Delaney shouted back.

"The fucking warheads . . ." Norton yelled over the racket of the rotors. "They are not there. *They're gone.*"

Delaney was confused.

"Well—where the hell are they?"

Norton did not reply. He looked more agitated than Delaney had ever seen him.

"Hey, does this mean we came all this way for nothing!" Delaney yelled, finally realizing the ramifications of what had happened.

"Not only that," Norton yelled back. "The whole fucking magazine is wired to blow. There are hundreds of nukes down there. Anything—a stray bullet to a torpedo to someone throwing a switch—and this whole ship goes up. And we go up with it. . . ."

Delaney was dumbfounded. This was way too much bad news to be taking in at once.

"So what are we going to do?" he asked Norton.

"There's only one thing we can do," Norton replied grimly. "We gotta stay—and find those missing warheads."

Delaney just stared back at him.

"*Stay?* You mean on board. *Here?*"

"We got no choice!" Norton yelled at him. "Those four weapons are somewhere on board. Two of them are still alive. We can't leave until we find them. . . ."

Delaney just couldn't believe what he was hearing.

"Christ, Jazz," Delaney yelled back. "This boat is enormous. Where the fuck could they be?"

At that very moment, the entire carrier shook from one end to the other. They heard a whooshing sound so loud, it blocked out the scream of the storm and the roar of the chopper engines.

Then, from the forward end of the ship, they saw an orange ball of flame rise up into the stormy black sky. It was an RMB-1750 missile, trailing a long stream of white smoke, heading towards the northwest. It quickly entered the low clouds and was gone in a blink.

"God damn," Norton breathed. "Please tell me I just didn't see that. . . ."

Delaney's eyes were transfixed on the remains of the missile's smoke trail, eerily blowing in the wind.

"I wish I could, partner," he said. "I wish I could. . . ."

9

NORAD headquarters
Cheyenne Mountain
Colorado

U.S. Air Force Captain Richard Kennedy had just come on duty when the world began to end.

In his seven years as a senior technical officer inside the vast underground vault that served as the eyes for the U.S. military's air defense system, rarely had he seen such anxiety, such confusion, such plain old nervousness among his colleagues and aides.

The reason: A weapons shoot had been detected by the Big Board, the enormous TV screen that dominated one wall of the NORAD center. It was identified as a medium-range missile, and the Board was indicating that the shoot had originated from a point in the North Atlantic and had traveled more than a thousand miles to a target very close to the North Pole.

By all indications, the shoot was a ballistic weapon with

a nuclear warhead attached, and according to the Big Board, was most likely Russian in origin.

Other than that, little else was known. Exactly where the missile came down, and what happened on impact, could not be ascertained at the moment.

It was now Kennedy's job to put together a quick chronicle of events and flash-wire it to both the Pentagon and the White House. And he had to do this in less than thirty seconds.

But what had happened exactly?

Was the shoot the opening volley of a Russian attack on North America that had fallen short of its mark? Or was it a single missile launched by a Russian submarine, maybe by mistake? Or could it have been a mistakenly identified missile fired by a friendly power that had somehow gone astray?

Or was it simply a software glitch inside the Big Board itself?

That last possibility was Kennedy's biggest fear. He knew whatever he put in his flash message would have far-reaching ramifications, including raising all U.S. nuclear forces to high alert, and possibly even triggering a retaliatory strike. If this was all just a software glitch, the effects could be devastating.

That was why he had to word his message so carefully.

He sat down at his keyboard and, as his fellow officers gathered around, began banging out what he knew. As he was typing, one aide came over and whispered something in his ear. Because of the missile's very high arc and unusual atmospheric conditions, this man said, its flight and descent in all likelihood would have been seen by many people in New England and northeast Canada. And at that moment, the aide reported, phones at all major air bases in those areas were ringing off the hook.

Kennedy let out a long slow breath. At least that answered one question: The shoot was not a glitch inside the Big Board.

"This one looks like the real McCoy," he told his colleagues. "We've got to push it up to a Level Six priority."

A hush came over those crowded around Kennedy's desk. Level Six was an internal classification that meant the U.S. was just one step away from war.

Kennedy finished typing his message and grimly read it over one last time. But just as he was about to send it, the red phone at the side of his console began ringing.

This startled them. The red phone never rang. Never once in Kennedy's seven years at NORAD had it come alive. It was known as the "override line." A phone to be used only if something extremely unusual had happened, such as a training exercise in which some high-security launch codes were inadvertently used, or a U.S. missile that was fired by mistake.

But the red phone was ringing now, and it was up to Kennedy to answer it.

As his aides and fellow officers gathered closer around his console, he picked up the phone.

The conversation was brief. Kennedy identified himself and then listened wordlessly for thirty seconds.

Then he hung up.

"Call off the internal alert," he told the other officers. Instantly all the whistles and buzzers inside the control room stopped.

"What happened?" one officer asked him. "A mistake? A firing from one of our own ships?"

The truth was Kennedy didn't know. The voice on the other end had simply given him the security code for the day and then ordered him to disregard anything that might have been seen on the Big Board in the last twenty minutes. The U.S. was not coming under attack—end of conversation.

When Kennedy checked the code given against his security sheet of the day, he saw it was of the highest clearance possible, indicating the disregard orders had come from the White House itself—or possibly someplace even higher.

He finally managed a nervous grin.

"They said it was someone trying to whack Santa Claus," he explained. "I guess he's been having trouble with the elves."

Portsmouth, N.H.

Ryan Gillis had seen the light.

He'd been in his room, lying on his bed, staring out at the stars, as he was known to do in his less rambunctious moments.

It was December 23rd and his dad had been gone since the previous evening. Ryan hated when his father was away. He knew his dad had an important job with the Air National Guard. He knew just about everything a ten-year-old kid could know about air-to-air refueling, and how his father and his Uncle Marty had serviced many Air Force fighter pilots on cold stormy nights when their fuel tanks were running low.

But a year before, when Ryan's father had gone away for nearly two months, he'd been afraid for him every day. He'd been most worried that his father would be killed in a plane crash. But there'd been more anxiety than that. When he'd told some of his friends that his father was on a secret mission for the President, a story that Ryan had made up, they'd teased him unmercifully.

But then his dad came home and everything went back to normal.

Until now.

Now he was gone again, and Ryan could feel those pains in his stomach return. Like there was a load of rocks in there or something. His dad was in danger, he just *knew* it—yet he could not tell anyone what he was feeling. He couldn't tell his mother because he didn't want her to worry any more than she was already. He certainly couldn't tell his sister Kristin, because she would just call him a little mook and tell him to leave her alone. And there was no way he was going to tell any of his friends at school. He'd learned that lesson last year.

No, Ryan had determined that if he was going to worry about his dad, he would have to do it alone.

That was exactly what he'd been doing when he saw the strange light in the sky.

It had appeared suddenly just above the horizon. It was moving too slow to be a meteor entering the atmosphere. Yet it did not look or act like an airliner leaving contrails.

What really freaked Ryan out was that just seconds before, he had actually whispered a secret prayer to God; he'd asked to be shown a sign that his dad was okay. And just like that, the strange light had appeared in the sky.

Ryan had stared at it, not quite believing what he was seeing, as the reddish light arched up and went back down again, all in the space of about twenty seconds.

Then just like that, it was gone.

But no sooner had it disappeared than Ryan found himself back on his knees, praying again, thanking God for giving him what he had wanted.

That night, he would sleep peacefully for the first time since his dad went away. Suddenly everything in the world seemed all right again.

At least for a little while.

In the Nevada desert

There was also some praying going on inside the Nevada mountain where the ultrasecret Level MQ was located.

This was *not* the usual state of affairs within the darkened chamber. The seven men who lived here were not particularly religious, even though they had had to sweat out more than a dozen world crises in their nearly forty years of solitude, half of which had come close to apocalyptic proportions.

During those uncomfortable times, when these seven men had more or less pulled the invisible strings that, on each occasion, swayed things towards a peaceful resolution, nary a word about prayer had been uttered. But prayer was on the minds of more than a few of the seven men now.

The last few hours had not gone well. Thanks to their network of omnipresent electronic eyes and ears, the seven men knew more than God about what was happening aboard the *Kuznetsov*. They knew the Spetsnaz assault had failed miserably. They knew that most of the American team was stranded aboard the carrier. They knew Rooney was dead.

They also knew that the RMB-1750 fired at the North Pole had been a dud.

But this was not necessarily a good thing.

"If a nuke goes off in the Arctic and no one is around, does it make a sound?" one of the men asked now as they watched a big TV screen similar to but infinitely more elaborate than the one installed in Cheyenne Mountain.

The men were studying a real-time video broadcast of a piece of the Arctic located very close to the North Pole. Across a formerly pristine field, of snow and ice there was now a huge black scar that stretched at least a half mile in every direction except south. This was where the RMB-1750 missile had come down. Even with its deactivated warhead, the destruction was widespread.

"We were so lucky this time. . . ." one voice said. "A minute later and those NORAD boys would have been having kittens."

"Yes, but that just means we won't be as lucky *next* time," a second voice replied. "We know that one was a dud. If they launch another missile, then the odds it will be carrying a real warhead just went to two-to-one . . . against us."

"Obviously things are crazier aboard that carrier than

we ever imagined," said a third. "We should have taken action sooner. We should have sent in a more lethal force."

"Hindsight is always twenty-twenty," a fourth voice intoned. "But in this case, you might be right. The chopper guys are good. There was no reason to believe they couldn't have done it again. But as far as those Spetsnaz troops, that's where we screwed up—putting faith in them."

"My God," another voice said. "What would have happened if that had been a *real* nuke on the tip of that missile?"

"That's what we don't want to find out," another replied. "I think it's time we look at the more unpleasant options."

"The 82nd?"

"No, another assault on the carrier would just mean more lives lost—not to mention being very messy. Plus the weather just won't allow it. That's our biggest enemy here. As it is the atmospherics are already screwing up the chopper guys' cell phones. Busy signals. Dead air."

"Are you saying those Radio Shack phones are no good?"

"No, I'm saying our multi-billion comm-sat system can't handle heavy weather."

"What are our options then?"

"We really only have two choices—sink the carrier with torpedoes or air-launched cruise missiles."

"Well, we've already made the preliminaries on the torpedo scenario . . . and for some reason, that seems to be the quietest way to do it, if torpedoing a ship carrying a load of nukes can be done quietly."

"And what will the Russians think of us sinking their most capital Naval vessel?"

"That ship has one thousand megatons of nuclear bombs on board, and God knows what else. The Russians have certainly lost control of it—that much is certain now. They're already past the Red Zero Point and in less than

three days, they could be sailing into New York Harbor—
whether they shoot another missile at the Pole or not. So,
you tell me—what *is* the alternative to sinking it?"

The question hung in the air like the cigarette smoke.

"It will take the sub another twenty-four hours to get
into position. Maybe in that time something will happen
on board—"

"Something like a miracle, you mean?" a voice interrupted. "Because that's what it's going to take now for
this thing to be resolved."

Silence.

"But what about the people we have on board? The
chopper ops guys and our other assets? With the weather
about to get really nasty out there, I can't imagine how
we can get a rescue team out there to get them off before
the sub arrives. So what happens to them?"

More silence.

"Well, we can dispatch our winged friend to get a closer
look at the situation. But we all know there is no way he
can get involved."

"Send him anyway,—" several men said at once.

A button was pushed, a call was made, and it was done.

"But we have to look at reality here. The sub will be in
position this time tomorrow. It will have to act as soon as
it arrives."

"So we strand our people out there then? Leave them
helpless? Along with the sub crew? That's our decision?"

Now came a much longer silence.

It was a question that needed no answer.

At the very bottom of the secret mountain facility, there
was a small dormitory.

Though it held bunks and provisions enough for four
people, usually only one person stayed there.

He was now asleep in the first bunk, a book on ad-
vanced astrophysics laid across his chest. He'd been reading a chapter on space-time warping when he drifted off

to sleep several hours earlier. He was still dressed, his T-shirt featuring an imprint of two feathery wings on the back and the inscription "Angels Do It Forever" on the front.

The buzzer on the console beside his bunk rang just once. That was all it took to wake him.

He picked up the phone and had a brief conversation with someone on the other end. He checked his watch.

"I can be ready to go in thirty minutes," he said into the phone. "You can tell them to start warming up the Chevy."

Twenty minutes later the man had showered and drained a cup of coffee.

He was now dressed in an all-white flight suit with a pair of black Converse sneakers and a baseball cap that read: "Not all Angels Are Good Angels," across the bill.

He stepped out of his dormitory into the hallway and pushed the elevator button. The lift appeared, he climbed in, pushed another button, and the doors closed. He was soon hurtling straight up through the mountain.

After fifteen seconds, the elevator stopped with a hiss of air and the man walked out.

"Morning, boys," was how he greeted the pair of technicians manning the small hangar at the mountain's summit. "It *is* morning, right?"

The techs just shrugged. "How would we know?" one replied.

The man walked over to the ancient refrigerator located in one corner of the hangar and retrieved a small bottle of Coke. The bottle was made of thick green glass of the type sold back in the 1950's. In fact, that was exactly when the bottle had originated.

He sipped the Coke—it was a tradition of his before any flight—then burped and nodded to the techs. "Okay, let's see if we can get back before dinnertime."

The techs began pushing buttons. On the floor before

them a seamless door opened and a small elevator rose. It was bearing a very strange aircraft.

At first glance, this flying machine looked very plain, if out of the ordinary. Pancake-flat, triangular in shape, it was the size of a sports utility vehicle flattened out. Like a bad flying saucer from a bad science fiction movie, was how someone had once put it.

But it could fly very, *very* fast.

The only identification that could be found on the odd craft was written in very small gold leaf letters right below the cockpit. They read: *Aurora-6/h-M*.

Another button was pushed and the canopy hatch opened. The man finished his Coke, carefully placed the bottle in the bin next to the icebox, then climbed the ladder and sat down inside the aircraft. One of the techs followed him up.

The man took off his cap, shook his longish hair, then took the crash helmet offered by the technician.

"You checked the oil? Put some water in the radiator?" he asked as he put on the helmet.

"Done and done," the tech answered by rote.

Meanwhile, the other tech attached a pod behind the vehicle's front landing strut. It contained a huge reel of blank videotape, hundreds of hours' worth. In reality, this strange airplane was supposed to be a recon vehicle. Nothing more.

But sometimes, reality could blur.

One tech told the pilot: "Remember, if you break anything this time, don't blame it on us, okay?"

"I promise," the man replied.

The pair of techs returned to their control board and began an orgy of button-pushing and keyboard-clacking.

"The inertia dampener is still overloading a bit," one said. "We'll have to check it on the comeback."

"That gyro buffer is getting crazy too," the other reported, reading a constant flow of diagnostic numbers on one of the many screens facing him. "But it'll hold up for another flight. Let's unzip. . . ."

The first tech hit a button and the roof of the station slid open. It wasn't morning at all. It was late afternoon. The sky was blue. The sun was blazing in the west.

The second tech keyed his microphone.

"Okay, bring it up and scoot before the whole world sees you."

With that, the strange aircraft began to slowly ascend. There was no smoke, no exhaust, no engine whine in the least. In fact, the aircraft made absolutely no sound at all. Nor were there any outward signs of propulsion.

It took about ten seconds for the aircraft to pass through the opening in the station's roof. Then buttons were pushed and the roof closed back up again.

The aircraft hovered over the station for a few seconds. Then it began to vibrate slightly, its pearl-white hull taking on a bluish hue. The whole aircraft also began sparkling along its outer edges.

Then it shot forward.

One minute later, it was a hundred miles away.

10

Aboard the Kuznetsov
2200 hours

"Ever hear of a Russian submarine called the *Okerzo*?" Gene Smitz asked.

Norton, Delaney, and Chou just shook their heads no.

"It was the only sub the Russians built in the so-called Tornado class. In many ways, it's the real reason we are all here."

"Here," at the moment, was a small electrical storage compartment adjacent to the weapons magazine at the bottom of the *Kuznetsov*. This place was nicknamed the Fuzski or "the Fuse" because past crews joked that if they really wanted to end their service aboard the trouble-plagued carrier, all they would have to do was start an electrical fire in the compartment—"light the fuse"—and the ship and everyone on it would go up in a cloud of radioactive cinders.

On Smitz's advice, it was here the stranded Americans

had come to hide. This was based on his belief that no
one else aboard the rogue carrier wanted to come anywhere near the wired-up nuclear weapons bay anytime
soon. Or as Smitz had put it: "Sometimes the safest place
to be is on the pin of the hand grenade."

Two hours had passed since the failed helicopter assault.
The last remaining Kamov—Chopper Three—was still up
on the flight deck, but it was discovered that the gunfire
Delaney had felt while waiting for Norton and the Team
66 guys to return had actually punctured the chopper's
main hydraulic line. Without the hydraulics to run the controls and work the engines, the aircraft could not fly. And
this meant they could not get off the carrier now even if
they wanted to.

They had no food, no water, barely rudimentary first-aid
kits, no other weapons besides their Kalashnikov rifles, and
only limited ammunition for them. They had exactly three
flashlights between them, two with batteries running low.
Everyone was soaked to the skin, tired, and miserable.

Even worse, they were completely cut off from the rest
of the world. They had no idea what had happened to the
Spetsnaz troops—they were last seen going into the Island,
guns blazing. Gillis and Ricco had apparently fled back to
the *Battev*, though again no one knew why. And no one
had any idea where Rooney was.

So for more than an hour, Norton had sat in one corner
of the Fuzski desperately trying to reach someone—anyone—on his cell phone. And though he continuously
punched the speed dial for both Krysoltev and Gillis, all
he got were busy signals in return.

Clearly, their situation was becoming desperate.

The Team 66 guys had staked out a defense perimeter
of sorts around the Fuzski. Two men were guarding the
ladderway to the left of the cabin, two more were stationed
at the hatchway to the right. The fifth was keeping watch
two levels up in the aft section of the aircraft bay. Despite

the fact that the nuclear weapons magazine area was highly dangerous, they all knew it was just a matter of time before some unseen enemy would descend upon them. Then what would they do? Surrender? Or defend their position and have gunfire pinging off hundreds of nuclear weapons nearby? It wasn't much of a choice either way.

So while Norton kept hitting his redial button, Delaney, Chou, and Smitz were crouched next to the door of the Fuzski, dividing up their remaining ammunition. And as they were doing this, Smitz explained to them how he'd become mixed up in the carrier's travails in the first place.

It was not a simple story.

"Anyway this sub, the *Okerzo*, was built in the seventies," he was saying. "It was a prototype, about two thirds the size of a Typhoon-class sub, hence the Tornado name. The Russians spent a lot of rubles putting it together; that's why there was only one of them ever built. But it was money well spent. This sub could dive nearly twice as deep as other Russian subs, plus it was made to be super-quiet, and even had a crude but effective coating of sonar-absorbing paint on its hull—or so they say."

"But what does this have to do with us being stuck here?" Delaney asked impatiently.

"I'm getting to that," Smitz went on. "When the Soviet Union collapsed, the *Okerzo* was out at sea somewhere, up to who knows what. By the time it reached its home port again—which was a secret base way up near Russkiy Island in the Arctic—there was no more Soviet Union. The *Okerzo* was such a secret vessel, even some higher-ups in the Russian Navy weren't aware of its existence. So, when the Soviet Union went down, the sub was able to slip away without being accounted for. God knows where it went. But it reappeared about nine months ago and was sold by its crew to some black-market arms dealer—a middleman with a lot of money and connections to an old friend of ours."

"And who might that be?" Norton asked.

"Would you believe the Great Zim himself?" Smitz replied.

The mention of this name stunned them.

The Great Zim was the Middle Eastern billionaire who'd owned the American AC-130 gunship that the chopper team destroyed during Operation ArcLight. An Osama bin Laden type, Zim had been a super-terrorist/ arms dealer extraordinaire until the American unit had bombed his fortress deep in the hills of Iraq at the climax of ArcLight.

"The Great Fucking Zim?" Delaney fumed. "I thought we greased him when we greased his headquarters last year."

"We thought so too," Smitz replied. "But either he or someone who took his place is still in the arms business. In fact, they are expanding into new areas: that is, buying nuclear weapons."

"I guess it's not that much of a surprise that Zim or his people bought a Russian submarine," Chou said. "I mean, he bought a gunship, so why not a sub?"

"Exactly," Smitz said. "But this is a sub that can shoot nuclear weapons—and be very hard to find before or after doing so. We know the *Okerzo* was not carrying nukes when it disappeared. But now that it has some new owners, they want the weapons."

That was when it all started to make sense to Norton.

"So they hear that the Russians are moving a lot of nukes out of Murmansk," he began. "And figured this was their big chance."

"You got it," Smitz replied. "Because after all, this may be an aircraft carrier, but look at the weapons it's hauling: missiles, depth charges, torpedoes. Weapons taken off subs; weapons *made* for subs."

"Son of a bitch," Delaney breathed. He was starting to

get the picture now too. So was Chou. "This asshole Zim has come back to haunt us."

"But how did he make the connection to the Kuznetsov?" Chou asked.

"Simple. His people got to people here, in the carrier's crew," Smitz went on. "Top dogs, seven senior staff officers and a dozen or so senior sailors. It was not hard to get them to play footsies, from what I heard. Once in bed together, they hatched this plan. They would meet the *Okerzo* somewhere between here and Murmansk, unload some of the nukes, get some cash, and then keep on going. It would have been the perfect weapons transfer—way out at sea, at night, with no one else looking. What was going to happen once this ship got to Rostov is anyone's guess. But we figured that about twenty people in this crew—the original officers, and their confederates in the lower ranks—would be walking off the ship with about fifty million dollars to split among them."

He paused for a somber breath.

"It would have been the biggest black-market weapons deal in history," he concluded. "At least that we know of . . ."

"So how did you get involved?" Delaney asked.

"The Company got wind of the deal and we told the Russians," Smitz explained. "But because we figured it would be just too difficult to track down the *Okerzo,* both sides agreed it was best to just go ahead and let the arms deal play out, but be close by when the weapons transfer actually took place."

"So *that's* why the Spetsnaz were already aboard the *Battev* then," Norton observed. "That's why Rooney was there too."

"Exactly," Smitz said. "We were going to catch them with the goods, in the act."

"So all this was really one big sting operation?" Delaney asked, cutting to the quick of the matter.

"You could say that," Smitz admitted. "Although now, in retrospect, a very dangerous one."

Norton, Delaney, and Chou just shook their heads.

Smitz continued. "Because you see, the whole deal got fucked up when this Kartoonov guy came aboard. He was the monkey wrench no one thought of. With him on the ship, the conspirators—who included the carrier's captain, by the way—couldn't just stop in the middle of the Atlantic and start off-loading nukes. So when the ship sailed, the plotters and their cohorts had to engineer a takeover to get Kartoonov out of the way. . . ."

"Wild," Delaney breathed. "Like a movie."

"Yeah, a bad one," Norton observed.

"Well, here's a little more plot intrigue for you," Smitz said. "Though Kartoonov was a big hero in Russia, he was about to get his ass deposed. Seems he did some very questionable stuff during the Soviet heyday. He wasn't a spy exactly—but not a true Commie either. Real enamored with America. Loved hot dogs, they say. Played Elvis records. A real Pepsi man. These things tend to piss off the hard-liners in the Russian Navy even these days. So the ax was finally going to fall on him when he got to Rostov. And he probably knew it. . . ."

"Well, that ax got to his neck a bit early," Norton said.

They went back to reloading their rifles.

"But you're still not explaining how you got on board," Delaney said to Smitz.

"I was put on by the Russian Intelligence Service, at the insistence of the Company, just in case the whole she-bang went really haywire, which it has, obviously," Smitz replied. "They told everyone I was a meteorologist, but as soon as we sailed, I found a place to hide and stayed there. I was told to remain in my berth at the bottom of the ship and be on hand in case we had to get the U.S. military involved.

"When things started to go wrong, I had to go to my contingency plan. We knew there were four nuke-capable warheads on here—the RMB-1750's this ship would be carrying anyway. I had to defuse them—and only got to two before my laser pen went kerplunk. That's when the call went out for you guys."

He began cleaning the chamber of his rifle.

"I'll tell you something, though," he went on. "The first forty-eight hours on this ship were wild, man. I started hearing gunshots nonstop just one hour after we left Murmansk. And even though I was told to stay put, I was forced to move around a lot—I never knew who was coming down the passageway to get me. Then I saw the eight bodies hanging off the back end and I knew things were fucked up. I mean, killing Kartoonov? To the ordinary Russian seaman, that's like killing the pope."

He finally paused and looked up at them.

"I can't believe Rooney didn't brief you on all this," Smitz said.

"Apparently there were a lot of things he chose not to tell us," Norton replied. "We were just supposed to be pilots on this one. Taxi drivers."

"Well, he *must* have told you about the environmental report, right?" Smitz asked. "The four things that might happen if the North Pole was nuked?"

"Four things?" Chou said. "I thought there was only three."

Smitz held his hand out and started counting off one finger at a time.

"One, affecting tides and temperatures around the world. Two, affecting the underwater food chain. Three, throwing billions of contaminated ice particles into the atmosphere. And *four*, how a nuclear blast could upset the planet's rotation, maybe even throw it off its axis . . ."

The three men just stared back at him.

"What?" all three seemed to say at once. Their faces registered absolute disbelief.

"Throw it off its axis? What sci-fi movie did that plot come from?" Norton asked.

Smitz just shook his head. "I know it sounds crazy," he said. "But that's how I was briefed, over the phone, by Rooney himself. The Navy did the study and that's one of their conclusions—a top-secret one, for sure. But even throwing off the Earth's rotation by a millionth of a degree could disrupt everything. Tidal waves. Earthquakes. Massive flooding. God knows what else."

"Will someone pinch me, please?" Delaney said holding out his arm. "I just gotta be dreaming here. . . ."

Smitz jammed a full clip into his AK-47 assault rifle. "Don't bother," he said, displaying his own bare arm. Indeed there were a number of red marks up and down the length of it. "I've been trying to wake up for days."

There was a long silence now, broken only by the sound of gunfire coming from the forward part of the ship.

"Well, if we are stuck here, is there any way you can at least lay out the situation on board right now?" Chou asked.

Smitz shrugged again.

"Well, I'd say we own this little piece of the world," he said bemused. "And whoever is actually running the ship owns everything from the Island forward, I'd guess. But there is someone else as well."

"A third party?" Delaney asked. "Fighting on board, you mean?"

"There has to be," Smitz replied. "Like I said: I've heard gunfire ever since leaving Murmansk. Even after the eight bodies went over the side, there was still fighting on this boat. So I have to assume there are at least two factions in play—and that one of them wired up all the nukes."

Further inspection had confirmed that the miles of yellow electrical wire running above, over, and through the nuclear weapons in the magazine ran up through the vent system to somewhere higher in the boat. It was, then, like one gigantic time bomb—and no one dared to cut the wires, for fear of setting off an explosion of apocalyptic proportions.

"I'd also have to guess that whoever wired up the mag-azine are the same people who activated the RMB-1750's," Smitz said. "We just have to pray that the one that went off the deck was a dud."

Indeed, a moment of silence passed between them.

"Two sides still fighting each other for control?" Dela-ney said, breaking the spell. "Well, I have to admit, it did look pretty weird up top when we first came aboard. It seemed like there was gunfire coming from everywhere, but . . ."

"But maybe what really happened was we dropped into the middle of an ongoing battle," Norton finished for him.

"That's my conclusion," Smitz confirmed. "But who's fighting who? I just don't know. . . ."

"Maybe the original bad guys and a new gang in town are slugging it out," Chou said. "Fighting for control of the nukes . . ."

". . . which we hold here," Smitz said. "And which they'll eventually come looking for."

Norton and Delaney shook their heads on cue.

"What a mess," Norton said. "We're stuck here, on a floating battlefield, waiting for two guys to strangle each other before one of them comes to strangle us. How do we get ourselves involved in these crazy things?"

"We needed some excitement in our lives," Delaney said. "Don't you remember?"

Smitz checked his watch, then asked: "Did Rooney at least tell you about the Zero Red Line?"

His question was again met by three blank stares.

"Do we want to know?" Delaney asked.

Smitz chuckled grimly. "Probably not," he replied. "On this one I can agree with Rooney for holding back the information from you."

He bent down and, using the grimy dust on the Fuzski's floor, drew a very rough approximation of the Atlantic Ocean, with the U.S. on one side, Greenland at the top,

Europe to the right. Then he drew a line a few inches to the right of center.

"This is the Zero Red Line," he explained. "It's been around for decades and it means exactly what it says."

"And that is?" Norton prompted him.

"That no Russian warship carrying nuclear weapons that is not completely under control of Moscow gets past this line," Smitz said starkly. "It was instituted back in 1965, after there was a brief disturbance aboard a Russian submarine about five hundred miles off of Virginia. Though it was more like the crew went on strike than a mutiny, for about an hour or so, the nukes on that boat slipped from Moscow's control. When the U.S. heard about it, they laid down the law to the Russians. If it happens again, no matter what the circumstances, we're sinking the offending ship. No warning, no second chances."

He pointed to his crude oily map.

"The Zero Red Line is exactly two thousand miles from the eastern most tip of the United States," he said. "And the last time I checked, we were pretty damn close to it."

"Well, ain't that peaches and cream?" Delaney said bitterly. "No wonder Rooney never told us. I, for one, might have been just a little reluctant to fly a mission knowing if it got fucked up, my own country would then be looking to ice me."

Smitz smiled grimly. "Well put," he said. "But to tell you the truth, that's why I'm pretty sure that the missile they shot off was one of my duds. Because if it had been the real thing . . ."

"We'd be dust by now," Norton finished for him.

"Simple as that," Smitz replied, adding: "Which in no way means it still isn't going to happen. If they launch a live missile at the Pole, or if and when we cross that line, this ship is going down one way or another, and sooner than later."

"Christ, any idea where the hell we are now?" Delaney asked. "In relation to the line, I mean?"

Smitz could only shrug. "Let me put it this way," he said. "If all had gone right on this voyage—that is, if the arms deal was going to be made—the meeting point, as we came to know it, was about two hundred miles on the wrong side of the line.

"Now, despite the fucking nuttiness on board, assuming this ship stays on course, we're dead meat in about . . ."

He checked his watch.

". . . well, less than twenty-four hours, I'd say."

"Christmas Eve," Chou murmured.

"Perfect . . ." Norton said. "Just fucking perfect . . ."

At that moment, there was a sharp knock at the Fuzski's door.

Two Team 66 guys came in. Both looked worried.

They had a hasty whispered conversation with Chou, then departed.

"This does not sound too good," Chou said, grabbing his rifle.

"What is it?" Norton asked.

"Come on and see for yourselves," Chou said, grabbing his rifle and hurrying out the door. "And you might want to bring your popguns with you."

They rushed up two levels.

This was the hangar deck, but it was still cut in two by the huge fire door. This movable barrier was a necessity of safety. Should a fire break out on the hangar deck, with all its fuel and bombs exposed, the first procedure would be to close the big door, protecting at least half of the ship and hopefully isolating the situation.

But now this door had become a border of sorts. Just after the chopper assault failed, someone had closed it and locked it tight. Now the American team was stuck on the aft side of the door, while someone else controlled the area on the other side. And it was noises coming from that other side that Chou's men had just alerted him to.

One item from Team 66's bag of tricks that they did

bring along was the combat equivalent of a stethoscope. Electronically powered, it was usually used to detect on-coming vehicles or for general eavesdropping purposes. One of Chou's men now had this device attached to the hangar door. He did not like what he was hearing.

Norton gave it a listen, and while the door was too thick to actually pick up conversation, he could hear the sound of metal clanging, and the faint crackling of electricity and electronics.

"What do you think they are up to over there?" Chou wondered aloud.

"I have a theory, but you ain't going to like it," Norton replied, giving the earpiece to Delaney. These sounds were very familiar to him. They were to Delaney as well.

Just then, they heard the unmistakable sound of one of the forward hangar's aircraft lifts.

"Whoever is over there is bringing something up top," Norton said. "Something big."

They ran to the rear passageway and started climbing.

After three ladders they finally reached the outer walk-way, which led up to the flight deck itself. They stole up to the top and peeked over.

The night was very dark. The wind and rain were so intense, they could just barely see the forward flight deck. It was still littered with bodies and the wreck of the ammo-bearing Kamov. Chopper Three was still hanging off the aft end of the ship, bleeding red hydraulic fluid from its massive engine wound.

Standing somewhere in between were two MiG-29 fighters, freshly rolled off the hangar elevator. Their en-gines were screaming, and it was obvious both planes were getting ready for takeoff.

"They're actually launching these guys?" Chou asked, astonished.

"Looks that way," Norton observed. "And both are loaded for bear."

It was true: The wings on both MiGs were nearly sagging, they were carrying so many bombs and rockets.

With their engines already hot-started, the MiGs did not have to wait very long to take off. Just seconds after the Americans arrived up top, there was an earsplitting scream as both warplanes began to rev up. Then the first plane popped its brakes and went careening down the deck. Its pilot nimbly avoided the wreckage of the ammo chopper—but then a strange thing happened. Just as the plane passed the chopper's debris, a fusillade of gunfire erupted from the Island. More than a dozen tracer streams followed the jet as it swept past the superstructure, gained the ski jump, and hurtled itself out into the stormy air.

An instant later, the second fighter went barreling down the deck. It too was able to dodge the chopper wreck; it too was met by a barrage of gunfire from the top of the Island. Though the Americans could clearly see bullets hitting the fighter's tail fins and undercarriage, the MiG was able to get airborne and turn swiftly away from the ship.

"Well, I'd say that confirms one thing," Norton said. "There *are* two factions still fighting each other aboard this ship."

"But maybe those guys are just defecting," Chou said.

"Not with ammo loads like that," Delaney told him. "Wherever they are going, they intend to drop all that ordnance on a target—and whatever that target is, it ain't that far away."

"There's only one IP I can think of that fits the bill," Norton said gloomily.

That was when it sank in for Smitz.

"The *Battev*?" the CIA man said.

"Where else?" Norton replied. "They probably think it's full of Spetsnaz instead of the supplies they were expecting to take on. Maybe they want to take it out because they think another assault is coming. Or they want absolutely no witnesses—to whatever the hell is happening on here."

"Little do they know," Delaney quipped.

They all watched the pair of MiGs sweep past the ship and disappear into the heavy overcast.

"Damn," Smitz whispered. "If they sink that ship, then we really *are* stranded out here. For good . . ."

11

Gillis was in the head when it happened.

He'd been washing his hands, over and over, for nearly an hour, trying to get Rooney's blood off them. But no matter how hard he tried, his fingers, nails, and calluses remained crimson-stained and dirty. Still, he kept scrubbing.

The first hint that something was wrong came when the lights in the filthy lavatory went out completely. This was followed by a huge bang, which Gillis had come to learn was the sound the *Battev*'s engines made when being asked to do something in a hurry, like speed up.

He waited for a long moment, hoping the lights would come back on, but it never happened. There was another loud bang; after that he knew the lights were out for good.

Next thing Gillis knew, he was running. He was sure

that something important aboard the *Battev* had blown up and that the ship was sinking. The last thing he wanted was to go down in an airless, pitch-black Russian coffin. His experience with the sea-insertion capsule had driven that stake of fear into him. Now he felt as if some cold, wet hand was gripping his heart and would not let go. He had to get out.

With much knee-banging and elbow-scraping, he somehow managed to reach a hatchway that led to the outside. He fought with the latch for a few breathless moments, but finally pried it open. There was a cacophony of horns, bells, and whistles going off all over the ship by now. These did nothing but confirm his fear that they were sinking. In the span of a heartbeat he tried to recall whether he'd ever seen any lifeboats anywhere on the Russian ship.

He could not.

He stepped out onto the gangway to find Ricco running up the stairs nearby. Cell phone in one hand, a disgustingly vile mouth rag in the other, he'd just spent the last two hours vomiting over the side of the railing, something he'd been doing ever since depositing Rooney's body in the ship refrigerator room.

"Jessuz, Marty, what's happening?" Gillis yelled to him. "Are we sinking?"

"Not yet," was Ricco's shouted reply.

They met at a ladderway that ran up to the top exterior deck. Below them the ship's crew was scrambling around furiously. The bells got louder and the alarms more shrill.

But what was happening?

Two crewmen went scurrying by them. Gillis grabbed one—he was only a kid.

"What gives?" he asked the scrawny recruit.

The sailor looked terrified. But it was obvious that he did not understand English. He paused only for a moment, then pulled himself away and resumed running down the gangway.

That was when Gillis realized that the sailor had been wearing a life jacket.

And they weren't.

Though it was as ugly and unimportant a vessel as ever made, the *Battev* was not unarmed. It boasted a pair of 57-mm guns on its bow. These were antiaircraft weapons. Gillis strained his eyes now and saw a dozen or so sailors buzzing around the forward gun turrets.

"Oh, shit," he said to Ricco. "I think these guys are expecting an air attack. . . ."

"Well, that's not good for us," Ricco replied.

They began searching the sky for something, anything, to confirm their worst fears.

And a few seconds later, they found it.

They appeared at first like two gray ghosts, way out on the dark, stormy horizon. They had come out of the north and were moving south.

"Out there!" Ricco cried. "See them?"

Gillis had been around military airplanes long enough to know these weren't airliners or cargo planes. These were fighter jets. Specifically MiG-29's.

And they were heading right for them.

They would never find out exactly how the captain of *Battev* knew the fighters were coming.

How he'd received the early warning, how he knew that two Russian Navy jets were about to attack a Russian Navy vessel. And how he knew that he should fight back. But he did somehow—and that was why the *Battev* was moving so fast right now. And that was why the crew had been called to battle stations.

And now Gillis and Ricco were running again—but where should they go?

They certainly did not want to be anywhere near the antiaircraft guns on the bow—that might be the first place the MiGs would fire at. But they didn't want to be on the stern either, where the helipad was located. That too was probably high on the MiG pilots' target list.

Of course, all of that was moot planning if the pilots' intention was to sink the *Battev* altogether. If that was the case, then there really was nowhere they could go to be safe.

Why they chose to climb up to the very top deck then, they would probably never know either. But at the time, in those insanely anxious moments before combat was about to begin, their combined instinct was to seek higher ground.

So that's what they did.

Scrambling up the aft ladderway, Gillis and Ricco found themselves next to one of the cargo crane towers, adjacent to the ship's smokestack. There was a low metal wall here, a protective ring around the stack, most likely used as a fire break. There was also a small boat tucked under the railing. No bigger than a rowboat, it offered the two National Guard pilots an option, though a tiny one, should the MiGs actually send the *Battev* to the bottom.

The jet fighters were now about a mile out. As they came in from the port side, twin trails of smoke were pouring from their rear ends. Gillis and Ricco could already hear their engines. Very high-pitched, screaming, typically Russian.

"Maybe they're just going to spook us," Gillis said to Ricco. "Make a few dry passes to scare us away from the *Kuznetsov* . . ."

"I don't think we're that lucky," Ricco replied grimly.

This notion was confirmed an instant later when their ears were suddenly assaulted by three massive explosions.

They immediately hit the deck, peeking up only to look for the telltale flashes of light indicating that the MiGs were firing. But neither Gillis or Ricco could see any.

That was when they looked forward and saw it was the *Battev's* 57-mm gun that had fired first. The earsplitting *boom! boom! boom!* shook the ship from stem to stern and back again. Gillis and Ricco followed the shell bursts, and saw the first MiG fly right into a cloud of AA fire. It took about a second before the pilot veered violently to his right. An instant later, they finally saw those incoming cannon flashes.

Gillis and Ricco dropped back down to the deck—the stream of searing cannon shells arrived a few seconds later. Then came the heart-stopping thumping as the cannon shells slammed into the *Battev*'s hull. Another second, and the two MiGs roared over the ship—so close Gillis could see both pilots inside their cockpits.

The jets went straight up, did a loop, then banked back and headed for the *Battev* once again.

And once again, the 57-mm guns opened up on them.

Gillis and Ricco scrambled to the other side of the stack.

"This thing is hollow," Ricco said, banging on the side of the smokestack. "Anything those guys are shooting will go right through it!"

Yet they had nowhere else to go. They were trapped, just like the ship.

An instant later they heard more firing, more cannon shells ripping into the *Battev*'s hull. The MiGs screamed over the ship once again.

"They playing with us!" Ricco yelled. "Testing the ship's defenses . . ."

"They're going to unload some of those bombs on the next pass, I'll bet!" Gillis yelled back.

They looked around. There was absolutely no cover they could seek if a huge bomb hit anywhere near them.

It was just about this time that they saw two sailors making their way past them and down the walkway toward the cargo crane. They were carrying a black canvas bag with them, long and tubular. As the MiGs turned for their third pass, the two men scrambled up the cargo crane, fifteen feet away from where Gillis and Ricco were hunkered down.

It was actually called the Solid Cargo Transfer rigging tower. It was about twenty feet higher than the highest deck. There was a crow nest-type assembly at its top, and it was into this that the two sailors climbed.

The MiGs came in again and as predicted, both dropped a single bomb right in the middle of the *Battev*'s cargo bay. The concussion from the resulting explosion was so intense, Gillis felt his ears go *pop!* Ricco's nose began to bleed. Their bones started rattling and would not stop.

A huge plume of orange flame erupted from the cargo bay—the National Guard pilots saw pieces of steel, wood, and possibly bodies go careening into the air. The ship immediately went over on its right side. Suddenly they were both looking straight down at the very stormy water below.

Jessuz!" Ricco yelled. "This tub can't take another hit like that!"

Somehow the ship righted itself though, even as the MiGs turned once again and came in for a fourth pass.

Ricco and Gillis looked up at the cargo tower again, at the two sailors who'd climbed up there. They were unsheathing something from the black bag they'd carried with them. The MiGs streaked by again. The leading one launched two rockets into the front part of the hull. Two huge yellow explosions rocked the ship. The wingman put two more rockets practically into the same spot. Once again the ship nearly went over. It appeared that the MiG pilots were aiming for the antiaircraft gun, which never stopped firing, but all four rockets missed their mark.

And that was what saved them all.

Because by this time the two men in the tower had completely unsheathed their weapon—and it turned out to be an SA-7 portable SAM launcher. With incredible coolness, they began tracking the lead MiG as it turned over and came right at them, cannons blazing, its wingman trailing close behind. Gillis and Ricco ducked as the hail of cannon shells went screaming by them.

Then they heard another sound. It was a *whoosh!* followed by the distinct crackling of a small rocket engine.

They looked up just in time to see the SA-7 missile get sucked up into the exhaust pipe of the lead MiG. There was a huge explosion—followed by a bright streak of light that seemed to appear from nearly straight up. Then there was a second explosion. From their perspective it appeared as if the two fighters had been flying so close together, the first plane's explosion had mortally crippled the second.

In any case, there was a third and even bigger explosion now—then a big puff of black smoke.

When it cleared, both MiGs were gone.

Somewhere in the Nevada desert

"God damn, that was close!"

"Those Russians are plucky bastards, we've got to give them that much."

"Plucky enough to live a few more hours. That will be all, though. . . ."

The seven men had watched the vicious nighttime battle between the *Battev* and the MiGs from several different angles. To a man, they were amazed at the courage and just plain luck the cargo ship's crew had displayed in managing to down both of the high-tech fighters.

Of course, *they'd* had something to do with it.

"The smartest thing they did was believe our radio call that something bad was coming," one voice now said as they watched a satellite shot of the *Battev*, smoking heavily from its midsection, yet still under way. "I didn't know my Russian was so rusty, though."

"It was the least we could do," another voice said. "Especially with everyone's cell phone on the blink. Can you imagine how infuriating it must be to hear a busy signal at a time like this?"

There came a long silence as the seven men watched two more replays of the incident. In both, they saw the mysterious white streak appear and just as quickly disappear at the climax of the battle.

"I don't even want to know what that was," one voice said.

Six more murmured in agreement.

"May I ask what the time line on the sub is at present?" someone finally said, changing the subject.

There came a rustling of papers as someone else checked their notes.

"They are about twenty-two hours away," came the somber reply. "Twenty-three at the most."

Another silence. The air inside the chamber was suddenly very heavy.

"And what of the *Battev*? Will it go up too when the carrier gets it?"

"No way to avoid it," was the grim response. "Even if it turned around right now, it probably wouldn't escape all of the effects of what is coming."

"Why *is* it staying?" someone wondered. "It really can't do much now, considering what has happened."

"Its captain is staying because the last order he received told him to," another voice said. "That Navy might be in tatters, but the old-school sailors still follow orders. This guy will be no different."

"I don't know whether that is high bravery, or just stupidity," someone observed.

"Since when are those two things different?" someone else replied.

12

**Aboard the *Kuznetsov*
December 24**

They'd watched the attack on the *Battev* from the *Kuznetsov* too.

From their vantage point, hanging off the outer railing just above the divided hangar bay, looking through the stormy black night, all that could be seen were brilliant flashes of light erupting below the southern horizon. These were followed by twin columns of dirty gray smoke, which quickly rose into the sky to mix with the wall of clouds within the still-impending storm.

And even though the MiGs never came back, the Americans were convinced that the *Battev* had been sunk, with all hands, taking with it their one last faint hope of being rescued.

• • •

A strange thing had happened, though, just after the MiGs took off and just before the attack on the *Battev* commenced.

Norton had been alternately speed-dialing both Krysoltev's and Gillis's cell phone numbers, and just as routinely, hearing busy signals in return.

But one time when he hit the button for the Spetsnaz officer, the response was not a busy signal. In fact, someone on the other end actually answered—only to hang up a few seconds later.

What did this mean? Was Krysoltev still alive and just unable to talk at that moment? If so, why had he answered the phone in the first place? Had his ringing phone somehow given him away to the enemy? If so, why hadn't Norton heard signs of a scuffle following the pickup? Or had Krysoltev's captors somehow discovered the phone beforehand and finally figured out how it worked?

Norton didn't know. But when he tried speed-dialing the number again, he did not get the busy signal, but rather endless ringing.

The incident only added to the creepiness and desperation of what would prove to be a very long night.

Certain the *Battev* was gone, the Americans knew they could not expect anyone else to come for them now.

The reason was simple: The mission to the *Kuznetsov* had been so damn secret, those handful of people both in Russia and the U.S. who knew of its existence couldn't possibly put together a rescue party in such a short time to do any good, especially with the worsening weather.

But being military men, the Americans knew they had to do something other than count down the hours until the embattled carrier crossed the Zero Red Line and was put out of its misery for good.

The question was, what could be done? For the answer, they turned to the only expert on hand: Captain Chou Koo. Despite Norton and Delaney technically outranking him, the Marine captain was the foremost military man among them. It was his expertise they would have to rely on for what seemed to be an impossible situation.

So when they all retreated back to the relative safety of the Fuzski after witnessing the attack on the *Battev*, Chou remained behind. Up in the cold, windy, rainy night air, all alone. This was where he'd said he would concentrate on the problem and develop their options. He'd then return with an answer in twenty minutes or so.

"Make it fifteen," was what Smitz had told him initially—with good reason. Everyone was very aware of the time now. Everyone had a watch and everyone was checking it at least several times a minute. The reason was part anxiety-driven, part psychological. Simply put: Barring a miracle, they probably had less than twenty-three hours to live. For them, time had just become a very valuable thing, every second suddenly very precious. There was no sense wasting any of it.

So Smitz had amended his earlier suggestion by telling Chou: "Better yet, make it ten."

But Chou fooled them all.

No sooner had they reached the Fuzski and hunkered down than the Marine officer slipped in. He'd been up top, alone and thinking, for less than five minutes.

And he had a plan, all right. An obvious one.

"We have a mission here we can do," he told them. "Our *original* mission: to prevent this ship from firing those RMB-1750's. Now finding the missiles might be impossible. But what we can do is locate to the RMB launchers and destroy *them*. Then, at the very least, we might prevent another missile shoot at the Pole, this time one with a real warhead attached."

They didn't even have to think it over; everyone knew Chou was right. Time might be ticking away for them, but they could at least accomplish *something* before the lights went out.

Plus, it sure beat sitting around, waiting for the end to come.

So they would attempt to destroy the RMB launchers.

"Yeah, but where are they?" Delaney asked immediately. "I mean, when I saw that first missile go off, it scared the shit outta me so much, I couldn't tell you exactly where its shooter was, other than it's somewhere at the front of the boat."

"Same here," Norton said. "I saw a lot of smoke, a lot of flame, but where it came out exactly, I don't have a clue."

Chou turned to Smitz. "You know this ship better than any of us. Any idea where the launchers are located?"

"Forward of the Island, on the sub-flight deck," Smitz replied with a bit of a shrug. "There's a lot of crap jammed up there. Radars, antennas, the antiship system. These missiles are launched through tubes recessed into the sub-deck, almost like the way our Navy launches cruise missiles, but much bigger, of course. But that's all I really know."

"That's not nearly enough," Chou told him. "We'll only get one chance at this, and that means we'll have to know exactly where those shooters are located, or at the very least, where their firing controls are, before we attempt to take them out. Even then, it's a long shot. If we even make it halfway down the flight deck, I'll be surprised. Not with the field of fire those guys on top of the Island have."

"We could try to move forward belowdecks," Norton suggested.

"True," Chou replied. "But with the lighting system going down, that would be like walking around with a blindfold on."

As if on cue, the faint lights inside the Fuzski dimmed a bit more. "There could be a dozen guns waiting in the dark for us every time we open a hatch," Chou added.

It was Delaney who then came up with the most interesting idea.

"What we really need is a prisoner," he said slyly. "Someone who knows what's going on aboard this boat— and knows the location of those launchers or maybe even the missiles themselves. If we could just snatch someone, we might learn a lot more about the wringer we've gotten our asses into."

"Not bad," Chou admitted. "But still the problem remains: For the most part the passageways in this ship appear to be completely dark. Our flashlights are getting weaker by the minute."

Delaney thought for a moment. Then he said: "Do you know how Indians knew the buffaloes were coming?"

The three others just stared back at him. Norton could tell the wheels in his partner's head were turning. The question was, in which direction?

"They used to put their ears to the ground," Smitz replied.

"Right," Delaney said. "And that's exactly what we should do."

It was decided that five of them would go.

Norton, Delaney, Chou, Sergeant Reaney, plus a Team 66 corporal named Mike Robinson. Each man would be carrying an AK-47 assault rifle with three banana clips full of ammunition. They had a pair of flashlights—one good, one failing—available to them, plus one cigarette lighter, which Smitz gave to Norton.

The plan was simple. They would utilize Team 66's combat stethoscope as a means of determining which passageways they could transit, and which ones they should avoid, by listening in on the other side of any closed hatch or doorway they came to. Going on the basis that not every inch of the ship was in enemy hands, they hoped to find a safe passage of sorts through which they could reach the forward part of the ship and possibly locate the RMB-1750 missile shooters, or at the very least, grab someone who could tell them where to look.

Smitz and three of Chou's guys would stay behind in the Fuzski. Norton would take his cell phone along; Smitz had one of his own. If anything stupendous happened—like an attack from the people on the other side of the hangar door or the 82nd Airborne landing—Smitz promised to give him a ring.

The patrol set off, flashlights up, walking quickly but carefully down two open passageways without incident.

These corridors were dark but uninhabited. They did not have any hatchways running off them, no cabins at all. This was not so unusual: They were at the bottom of the boat, on the very last deck level. The patrol did not expect to find anything of importance way down here.

In fact, the patrol moved for a distance of nearly two hundred feet before they reached a cabin door. Chou put the electronic ears on the hatch, but heard nothing. Reaney expertly picked the lock and slowly swung the door open. They found themselves looking into a compartment that had served as a food-storage locker. It had been looted. The only things left were broken bags of flour and salt. A squadron of mice scattered when Chou directed his flashlight through the door.

"Smitty said the crew was hungry when they left Murmansk," Norton said. "I guess they're still all hungry."

After coming upon a closed hatchway and determining through the stethoscope that no one was on the other side, they moved into the next passageway. Again it was dark and relatively featureless, except for the miles of wires and pipework running along the walls. The next cabin they came to had a white door with the Russian words *Mieditsinskii Kubrik* painted on it. Roughly, "medical room." Once again, Chou snapped on the electronic ears; once again, they detected no life inside.

They opened the door to find the cabin was actually a medical supply room. It too had been looted, but only partially. There was evidence of many yellow bottle caps on the floor of the cabin. Chou told them he'd observed in the *Battev*'s sick bay that yellow caps indicated pain-killers and narcotics. This presented the specter of at least some Russian sailors moving through the ship, armed and high on narcotics.

"Not a good sign," Norton observed.

They moved on.

Always moving as quickly as they could, they found and investigated several more supply rooms and storage lockers. Most had been ransacked in some way. A few had pools of blood on their floors. One appeared to be a place where ammunition might have been stored; the smell of cordite was thick inside. It had been picked clean.

Whenever they came to a closed hatchway, they would take up positions on either side of it and then let Chou do his thing. The Marine officer would listen through his electronic ears for a minute or so, and then confirm it safe to open. The only living beings they found were the small armies of mice that infested this part of the ship.

After twenty minutes of walking, the patrol came to a major intersection of passageways. At this junction, the passageways went off in four different directions, plus one ladderway straight up and another straight down. On closer inspection, though, they discovered that four of the six hatches had been welded shut. Even stranger, they had been sealed with two different types of welds. Two hatches had been spot-welded; the other two had weld lines pressed along the entire length of the door seals.

"Two different welds, two different camps," Chou said. It was further proof that there were two warring parties aboard the ship, and that their territories converged at this spot. Placing the electronic ears against the welded doors revealed nothing, however.

The only options left to them were a left-hand turn and a ladderway going straight up. Chou guessed that by going up one level they might reach the guts of the ship; meaning the cabins located forward of the hangar deck and almost under the Island itself.

Though it would be more dangerous to move through it would seem to be the perfect place to do recon and snatch their prisoner.

But just as they were all ready to move out in this direction, Norton froze. There were many sounds bouncing around the passageways. The deep groan of the carrier's power plants, still running somehow despite the chaos on the ship. The scraping sound of the carrier's propellers churning in the cold water below. Mysterious banging sounds. The low murmur of many voices talking far away. Gunfire, sporadic but always somewhere in the background.

But amidst all this, Norton heard something else.

Way off, deeper in the ship, possibly coming from the ventworks, a telephone was ringing.

It was strange, though. No matter how they tried, no one else could hear it, only Norton. But that didn't make any difference to him.

"Go get your mook," he told the others. "I'll meet you back at the Fuzski."

"Where the hell are you going?" Delaney asked him.

Norton pulled his cell phone from his pocket. He'd set it on automatic redial for Krysoltev's number after the hang-up incident about thirty minutes before. The tone he was hearing in the earpiece matched exactly the phone he heard ringing deep within the ship.

"Is it important that we find out if those Spets guys are alive or not?" he asked Chou.

The Marine officer thought for a few moments.

"It is," he finally replied.

"Then I'm going to look for them," Norton said. "They might be holed up in these vents, for all we know."

"You're going into the *vents*?" Delaney asked him.

"That's right," Norton said, yanking off a nearby grill and getting ready to push himself up into it.

"No fucking way, Jazz," Delaney told him. "Not the vents."

"Why not?" Chou wanted to know.

Delaney turned to the Marine captain.

"Haven't you ever seen a horror movie, dude? Anyone who goes into the vent system never comes back—not in one piece anyway."

Chou just shook his head. They all did. Sometimes Delaney was best taken in small doses.

Unfazed, Norton boosted himself up into the air shaft and before anyone could say anything more, started off in the direction of the ringing phone.

13

Midships
0200 hours

Aviation Specialist First Class Rudolv Seklovski hadn't slept in seventy-two hours.

He hadn't eaten either. Yet he was feeling better than he could ever recall in his twenty-five years of life.

He was smoking a cigarette, sitting in a small storage compartment known as the Midships Reserve Electrical Room, a place where electrical wire, batteries, lightbulbs, and so on were stored. There were no lightbulbs or batteries actually in here, of course—they had all been stolen by the crew and sent to their families throughout Russia long before the *Kuznetsov* ever left the Black Sea for Murmansk. All the electrical wire had been stolen too. Stripped of its insulation, the copper within had been sold on the docks of Sevastopol, again long before the carrier departed.

So the Midships Reserve Electrical Room was nearly

empty, and it was here that Seklovski had come to get away from the madness. As good as he felt, he needed time to clear his head and contemplate why he'd started seeing monsters roaming the decks of the *Kuznetsov*.

He'd seen the first one about an hour ago, right after he'd been hastily assigned to "guard duty" alone in a passageway near the ship's main medical room, a place that had been cleared out as well. He'd been issued a flare pistol, the only weapon available as all the rifles were being used in the battle up top, and a two-way radio should anything unforeseen happen in his little area. He was also given three amphetamine pills and a flask of oily water and then told to man his post for the next twelve hours.

He took one speed pill immediately, accelerating the shot of morphine he'd received earlier in the day, this on top of the three cups of homemade potato vodka he'd consumed shortly after the *Kuznetsov* left Murmansk.

The monster showed up shortly after Seklovski arrived at his station. The creature materialized at the far end of the passageway and in a odd way, started beckoning Seklovski to come to him. Seklovski fired his flare pistol at the monster instead, but the flare hit the ceiling and then the floor before it ever got close to the monster. When the smoke from the flare finally cleared, the creature was gone.

Seklovski was so shaken by the incident, he swallowed his second pill. This did little to settle him down; in fact his hands were trembling so much, he almost set off his second flare cartridge while reloading his gun.

Then he started wondering why he was seeing monsters all of a sudden. He recalled learning back in school that lack of food and sleep could cause hallucinations. But this thing he'd seen beckoning to him at the other end of the dark passageway, it had been real. He was sure of it.

He sat on duty for the next ten minutes trembling, yet feeling oddly euphoric. At least he was not up top, taking part in the never-ending gun battle, he remembered thinking. At least down here, he was relatively warm and dry—

and alive. He'd peeked into the main dining hall before reporting for duty earlier, and counted two dozen bodies laid out on the dinner tables. Blood and bodily fluids were nearly flooding the place. He was sure no one would ever eat in there again.

It was just before two in the morning when he saw the creature a second time. It appeared in roughly the same place where he'd seen it before, entering the passageway from a small storage area not far from the midships officers' berthing. Again the creature waved to him, but when Seklovski raised his flare gun again, the creature ducked back into the compartment, and vanished once more.

Then Seklovski took the third speed pill and walked back to where the other men were. He asked the man in charge to be relieved of his guard duty, and when this was hastily granted—they had so many other things to worry about besides him!—he took refuge here in the electrical equipment storage room.

He finally finished his cigarette, and saving the butt end for later, got down on one knee and said a prayer that his hands would stop shaking.

That's when the creature showed up again.

This time it came right out of a storage locker at him. It grabbed him around the throat and effectively shut off his cries for help. He lost consciousness in two seconds.

When he awoke again, the creature and its three friends, were dragging him through the dark passageways down on the sixth deck. They were bringing him someplace deeper within the ship, Seklovski was sure, in order to eat him alive. As horrible as this sounded, it was something that made crazy sense to him.

After all, maybe the monsters were as hungry as he. . . .

Norton's flashlight began fading about five minutes into his journey through the vents.

He stopped crawling, took out the batteries, and held them in his sweaty hands for a moment. Then he licked each end with his tongue, put them back in, and switched the light back on. The trick did no good. The flashlight was even dimmer than before.

He kept going, though. Putting away the flashlight and taking out the cigarette lighter given to him by Smitz before they'd left the Fuzski, he resumed crawling on his hands and belly in the pitch-black darkness. He had taken three left turns and two right turns since entering this maze of ductwork—he had to remember that route! But just before the flashlight became dull, the shafts had started becoming increasingly smaller. Now he was just barely able to squeeze through them. He wondered just how far he could go.

Clicking the lighter on, he saw beyond the flickering shadows that this particular vent traveled at least another fifty feet without a bend or a turn. This would put him right under the Island superstructure, he figured—and right in the heart of enemy territory. Or at least one of the enemies. He clicked off the lighter and resumed crawling in the darkness.

More than once he'd considered that the ringing he was hearing was actually in his head and not related to his cell phone at all. A wild figment of his imagination? What was that a symptom of? Stress? Insanity? Claustrophobia? He had to laugh at himself; at the moment he was suffering just a bit from all three.

It was not like him to do this, crawling through small places in the darkness. That might have been the most disturbing thing of all. Like most pilots, he hated closed-in areas, and the Russian ventwork looked like nothing more than a dirty, elongated sheet-metal coffin. Yet some things he just had to know, and if the ringing in his ears was real, then something was driving him to find its source. After all, there might be a pot of gold at the end of this rainbow. Maybe the Spetsnaz guys *were* alive, and they could link up and automatically double the size of their tiny force. Or maybe they knew where the RMB-

1750 shooters were. Or a way to get off the carrier before it was blown to radioactive smithereens. Yes, with the clock ticking down on his own mortality, there were some things he just *had* to know. This was one of them. Heroic? No. Stupid? Maybe.

He kept crawling anyway.

He reached another intersection and stopped. He tried to filter out all of the other sounds traveling up and down the vent tubes and concentrate on the persistent high-pitched ringing.

Was it real? *Was* it a telephone? He just couldn't tell. But whatever the sound was, it was now very close.

He crawled some more, and then saw a bit of light up ahead. Moving very quietly, he shimmied his way up to a small vent grate from which the bare light was coming, and looked through it. There was a large compartment on the other side. It appeared to be some kind of navigation station: desks, chairs, lots of ancient-looking radios, lots of charts, a number of old maps on the wall.

Bizarrely, though, the entire room had been painted red. Everything—the furniture, the walls, the ceiling and floor—had been splashed with red paint, or more accurately, red dye. He also saw many bedsheets that had been dyed red hanging just below him, apparently put up to dry. Several large buckets of red dye were sitting near the door to the station. And indeed there were many red footprints leading in and out of the place.

Why would someone want to dye a whole room red? Norton wondered.

Try as he might, he could not come up with a single reasonable explanation.

So he started crawling again.

He took a right turn into a very thin sub-tube, and then the smell hit him.

He'd experienced this odor before. A little like garbage,

a little like an unclean bathroom, a little like burnt metal. He kept on crawling. The ringing was now getting louder. In pulses of two, separated by three seconds exactly, just like the tone in his phone. He went along another ten feet or so. The ringing got louder, the smell got worse.

He was completely in the dark now; holding the lighter in reserve, using his fingertips as his eyes, feeling along a half foot in front of him, crawling ever deeper into the rapidly compressing duct.

Now the ringing seemed right in front of him. The smell was so bad, he had to cover his mouth and nose. He reached out in front of him, and for the first time did not feel emptiness.

This time he felt cloth, then a bit of metal, then a very cold piece of flesh.

He clicked the lighter on and found a face pressed up against his own. He slid backwards, but the body fell right on top of him. He kicked it away, but it seemed to fight with him for several frightening seconds. Finally he disentangled himself from the dead arms and legs.

Only then did he flick the lighter back on. He looked down at the corpse and found himself staring into the very dead eyes of Captain Krysoltev, the massive Spetsnaz CO. In his uniform pocket was his cell phone. It was ringing. . . .

Krysoltev's face was distorted into an expression of confusion and shock, one he would wear for eternity. All his gold teeth had been yanked from his mouth. His uniform pants had been stripped from his body. There were red hand prints all over his face and legs. There were bullet wounds up and down his torso. Behind him, their bodies also contorted into grotesque positions, were the other five men of his squad.

Norton pulled the phone from the dead man's pocket and finally shut it off. That was one question answered. The hope that the Spetsnaz guys were still alive was now gone. Judging by the condition of their bodies and the stink, Norton figured the Russian soldiers had been stuffed inside the ductwork at least several hours ago. This meant they'd all been killed shortly after coming aboard. Case closed.

He flicked out the lighter—but then another question hit him: If Krysoltev's body had been in the vents for some time, who had answered his phone less than an hour before?

Norton considered this for a long moment in the dark, then felt a wave of absolute panic wash over him. He began twisting himself madly in order to get his body going in the opposite direction. Once he did this, he began crawling back out very quickly.

There were some things he *didn't* want to know.

Delaney never really knew just how wary he was of the dark until the patrol started making its way back to the Fuzski.

Snatching their POW had been easier than they could have ever imagined. Too easy, in fact. The sailor they had taken seemed downright dopey, and was probably heavily drugged. Like a hungry animal coming for food, he had practically walked into their arms twice before they actually grabbed him. This did not bode well for the quality of the information they hoped to pump out of him.

But again, it was better than nothing.

Besides, these things weren't foremost in Delaney's mind at the moment—getting to see his hand in front of him again was.

They were moving back down a very long passageway Russian sailors sometimes called the *shpionits* or "spine." It more or less ran the length of the ship on the second sub-deck and was cluttered with electrical conduits and cables.

This was not the way they had traveled forward—it was decided it might be pressing their luck returning the same way they came. So this slightly higher route was selected.

But like before, it was pitch black inside the *shpionits*—none of the passageway lights were on, and neither were any of the emergency systems. The only illumination they had was the flashlight attached to the tip of Sergeant Reaney's Kalashnikov rifle, and to Delaney's dismay, its batteries seemed to be fading fast.

Now with each step they took—Reaney and Delaney in the lead, with Chou and Corporal Robinson dragging the goofy POW between them—it seemed as if things were getting darker and the walls were getting closer. Strange noises were echoing all around them. Thumps, bumps, maybe screams, plus the ever-present sound of gunfire, never-ending, far off yet close at the same time.

If I could just breath some fresh air, Delaney thought, *I'd feel a lot better. . . .*

But that seemed a very unlikely luxury at the moment.

They reached an intersection of sorts, and Reaney suddenly stopped in his tracks. Those behind him stopped immediately too, except Delaney, who was walking with his head down and nearly bowled Reaney over.

"What's up?" Delaney asked the Team 66 trooper.

Reaney did not reply. He simply directed his flashlight at the floor in front of him.

There was a pile of bodies not three feet away.

They had been shot, all at close range, many in the back of the skull, execution-style. Their blood had pooled at the intersection of passageways, and the patrol would have trooped right through it if it hadn't been for Reaney's sharp eyes and fading flashlight.

Sickening though it was, Delaney could not stop himself from examining the bodies. Chou was similarly enticed.

"Who are they? Officers or seamen?" Chou asked as they stared down at the pile.

"Hard to say," Delaney replied, suppressing a retch. Many of the bodies were not wearing clothes.

He counted at least fifteen corpses stacked atop another. In many cases the toes or fingers of one dead man had been stuffed into the mouth of another, giving the appearance of a Borsch painting, grotesque and disturbing.

Obviously that had been the intention of the killers.

"You see," the Russian POW said in thick, broken English. "There *are* monsters on this ship. . . ."

Reaney's flashlight died for good a second later.

The darkness that enveloped them now was so complete, Delaney thought he could see stars dancing before his eyes. There was absolutely no source of illumination anywhere around them. In one brief moment of terror, Delaney thought he heard one of the nearby bodies move. It was a very unnerving sound, as if one of the corpses had spat out the toes of another.

He took in a deep breath and tried to calm himself.

The next thing he knew, a flashbulb went off in his face.

In that one-twentieth of a second, Delaney saw many things. Off to his left, four people, in strangely colored clothes, weapons raised, ready to shoot. In front of him, two more gunmen, of short stature or possibly in a crouch, looking out of an open doorway. To their right, another figure holding the camera that had set off the blinding flash. And at his feet, indeed a corpse whose foot had been newly liberated from his partner's dead mouth.

All these things he saw in that brief moment—and in that time frame too he realized that he and the others had walked right into an ambush.

Whether it was their superior training, or just plain instinct, or both, or neither—all four Americans immediately hit the deck. Even before the last nanosecond of light from the flashbulb had disappeared, Reaney and Chou had their rifles up. When it went completely dark again, Delaney found himself cracking both knees and one elbow in his collapse to the cold steel floor. An instant later, a stream of tracer bullets went right over his head.

He rolled smartly away from the pile of bodies, and felt Sergeant Reaney rolling with him. He hit his shoulder hard on the left-side bulkhead, and when he realized he had no further to go, managed to bring his own rifle up to bear. The stream of tracers was going two ways now. Chou and Corporal Robinson were sending a deluge of fire down the hallway from which the flash had popped. The gunmen off to the left were firing against the bulkhead wall just above the pile of bodies, apparently hoping that a lucky ricochet might bring Chou or his corporal down.

Delaney had his gun up, but where was he to shoot exactly? The confluence of tracer rounds was not serving to light up the darkened passageway as much as it was blinding him and the others. The people shooting at them looked like fun-house ghosts, popping up and down, doing strange gyrations with their bodies as they fired their weapons. Like puppets caught in a strobe-light nightmare, some were laughing, others crying.

Delaney began firing anyway. He knew if he kept his rifle pointing in front of him, then he would only hit the enemy. All the while he was wondering—strange the thoughts that went through one's mind in the heat of combat—what they hell were these people taking his picture for?

The bizarre gun battle lasted but ten seconds—or at least the opening volleys did. Delaney heard three simultaneous grunts and knew that someone on the American side, possibly even himself, had found his targets and had blown away the three gunmen blocking the passageway in front of them. But they still had the four men in the hallway off to the left—the ricochet artists—to contend with.

And on this point they were stuck. There really was nothing else they could do but make a run for it.

He heard Chou whisper urgently: "On three . . . one . . . two . . . three . . . *go!*"

That was all Delaney needed. He jumped to his feet, collided with Reaney again, turned his rifle sideways, and began firing at the gunmen to his left. At that same instant, he saw Chou and Robinson rush by him, pushing the POW

out in front of them, and firing their weapons at the same
time.

It had been the quickness of the move that saved their
lives. Their bullet streams probably did not even hit any
of the enemy gunmen, but it did serve to startle them for
a moment, just long enough for the Americans to cross
over the intersection of the passageways and start running
toward the end of the ship.

As Delaney was rushing by, he could see down the passageway where the four gunmen were stationed. And by
the light of the tracer bullets he realized that this bad
dream was not over by a long shot. Because there were
more than four gunmen waiting for them around that corner; indeed the passageway was absolutely filled with the
enemy. Delaney could see them standing almost shoulder
to shoulder, hands painted red, eyes wide if small, as if
they were a horde of feeding animals waiting for some
more raw meat to be thrown their way.

It was a frightening snapshot of whatever was haunting
the *Kuznetsov*.

So they kept on running.

Heads down, full out, firing their weapons over their
shoulders, but concentrating more on trying not to stumble
in the darkness. Behind them, the horde was in pursuit.
Hooting and hollering, screaming and yelping. Like myth-
ical beasts from a feverish nightmare, they were literally
snapping at their heels.

The Americans and their prisoner ran for what seemed
like hours, but Delaney knew they could not keep it up.
There were just too many people chasing them—and as
fast as they were, he and the Team 66 guys were beginning
to trip over each other now. Added to this were the frightful howls of the Russian prisoner, who wanted to escape
this awful fate more than they.

It was when Delaney actually felt the warmth on his
neck of a pursuer's breath that he threw his rifle butt over

his shoulder and made contact with something that cracked. Still he felt hands reaching for him, grabbing at his shirt, his pants, his belt. The screaming went right through him. The image of the dead men with their toes and fingers jammed into gaping mouths was nearly overwhelming. They would need a miracle to get out of this one.

And then suddenly, a dark figure stepped right into his path. Somehow Delaney went around him, and a second later, this person opened fire on the frightful pursuers. Once again the passageway was lit with tracer fire. Once again the sickening sound of bullets tearing flesh echoed off the cold steel walls.

The one-man barrage lasted a long ten seconds, more than enough time to allow the entire patrol to get past him. When the gunfire finally stopped, there was no more howling, no more clomping of a million footsteps chasing them down. Instead, the stampede was running away. Delaney and the others scrambled down one more section to an open hatchway, where they finally pulled up and went into a one-knee stance, weapons up. The dark figure who had just saved their lives turned and quickly walked toward them.

A dying flashlight flickered on. The person held it up to his face, and at last the patrol saw who had just saved them from a very unpleasant end.

It was Jazz Norton.

"Everyone okay?" he asked.

There were four weary nods and one lusty, out-of-breath *"Da!"* from the Russian prisoner. Indeed it seemed as if he was the one most appreciative to be alive.

"Just in time, Jazz," Delaney said, not quite catching his breath yet.

"Just lucky, I guess," Norton replied. He looked back down the pitch-black passageway. "Anyone interested in going back down there to see who our enemy is?"

By unanimous vote it was quickly decided that was not the thing to do.

"We owe you one, Major Norton," Chou was saying. "Though I'm sure we can have a longer conversation about it someplace else."

But Norton wasn't really listening to him. He was shining his flashlight up and down the walls of the passageway they had just found themselves in.

To his astonishment, it was painted blue. Everywhere. On the walls, on the floor, on the ceiling. And there again were the long bedsheets recently dyed, hanging to dry, some still dripping into pools of dark blue.

"What the fuck is going on here?" Delaney exclaimed. "Why the hell is everything in here painted blue?"

"I don't know," Norton finally answered. "But there's another big room at midships that's just like this place, except it's all red."

Chou stood up and checked his weapon's ammo load.

"May I make a suggestion?" he asked them.

"You bet," Norton replied.

"Let's get the hell out of here?" Chou said.

Once again, the vote was unanimous.

14

Bridge level
Combat Room
Ten minutes later

They had agreed from the beginning not to use their given names. They thought this was the best thing to do security-wise. Besides, their given names were not their given real names anyway. So it had been an easy decision to make.

After the latest encounter in the spine, ten of them went to the carrier's Combat Room, the place where all the weapons on board were controlled. This was also where their leader could be found.

The photograph had been taken by the Russian version of a Polaroid camera, and thus was developed instantly. Now it was being passed around the Combat Room.

"We have another enemy on board," their leader explained to them after studying the photo. "These are Russian Marines—it is clear by the uniforms. They probably came aboard when the helicopters landed. Another army sent to stop us. Now we have the Sharkskis and these new people to worry about."

A silence came over the Combat Room. There was some sniffling, a few tears. Just about everyone in the room was exhausted.

"We must stay true to our word," the leader went on. "If we do not, then we are nothing. We won't be taken seriously. Our wishes will not be respected. And if we die out here before reaching our ultimate destination, then we will have died in vain. So, like the first time, we must act—only through actions will we be noticed, will we be given respect.

"Do we all agree?"

Everyone in the room agreed.

"Very well," the leader said. "Let us prepare another missile for launch."

Ten minutes later, the aircraft carrier *Kuznetsov* began to shake from stem to stern.

The sound of a huge explosion rocked every corner of the ship. Those lights still on dimmed dramatically. Fire and leak alarms went off unintentionally, their sensors disrupted by the shock wave permeating the hull of the giant carrier.

Seconds later, there came another sound, mechanical and muffled. Those on the flight deck and on the Island paused in their pitched gun battle to watch as a massive column of flame shot up from below the sub-deck just in front of the carrier's superstructure. The launch tube's cap had blown off and now smoke began pouring out in its wake.

An instant later the missile itself appeared.

It seemed to hover for a moment just a few feet above the launch tube opening. Then its primary motor kicked in. There was a great *whoosh!* and the red flames turned into a gigantic orange ball that nearly engulfed the missile itself.

The orange ball began to rise, slowly at first, but picking up more speed with each passing second. The noise was deafening; even the roar of the stormy sea bowed to its preeminence.

The gunfire stopped altogether as many eyes watched the missile rise into the clouds, disappearing in seconds into the low overcast, leaving only a white smoky trail as evidence of its launch.

A few seconds later, the scream of the wind returned, and so did the roar of the angry ocean.

No sooner had the missile's smoke trail blown away than gunfire erupted across the flight deck again.

NORAD headquarters
Cheyenne Mountain

Captain Richard Kennedy was sleeping fitfully when his aide came in and shook him awake.

"Sorry, sir," the man was saying. "But we have another weapons shoot on the Big Board."

It was strange because Kennedy had been dreaming that the Big Board was actually a gigantic TV screen and that he'd been watching some kind of huge sporting event on it, even as nuclear missiles were impacting all over the globe. That his aide would wake him up with this particular news was somewhat startling.

Kennedy was quickly up and dressed and into the main room of the NORAD headquarters.

The place was nearly empty. Many people had already left on their Christmas leaves. That was why Kennedy was here, doing double duty and catching a nap inside the break station during his dinner hour.

He hurried to his station now. His aides were already gathered around it.

"What's the read?" he asked one.

"That's the weird thing, sir," the man replied. "It's the same profile as the one a little while ago. Nearly the same part of the Atlantic. Same telemetry. Same track. Same impact area."

Kennedy looked at the Big Board and sure enough, saw that it was showing an almost identical indication as the missile shoot a few hours before.

"Any chance this is a glitch?" he asked his aides. "A replay of the one earlier?"

They all shook their heads. "No—this is a legitimate score, sir. A missile has been fired out there and it has come down in the higher Arctic—just like before."

This was getting crazy, Kennedy thought.

Still, he had his job to do. With slightly trembling fingers, he sat down at his station and pulled out the flash-message keyboard.

But before he could type out one letter, the red phone on the side of his desk rang.

This time, it didn't startle anybody.

Kennedy shoved the keyboard away and managed a weary smile.

"Thank God," he whispered.

Somewhere in Nevada

The TV projection on the big screen inside Level MQ said it all.

On display, via a heat-imaging videocast, was another real-time broadcast from the upper Arctic, showing another huge black scar soiling what was minutes before a pristine lake of snow and blue ice.

"So we got lucky again," one voice said worriedly. "But that can mean only one thing."

"That's right . . . the next one will be the real deal."

There was total silence for several minutes as the scene from the North Pole slowly began to fade away. Finally the big screen went blank altogether.

"Well, I hate to say it, but it's time we stopped screwing around," one Ghost announced. "The ship is now less than three hundred miles from the Zero Red line and it's even changed its course to due west. This means that by the time the sub gets into position, we'll have the authorization to pull the trigger."

More silence.

"It is the only option left," another voice said. "One way or another, the ship has to be sunk."

"If it fires another missile, we'll have to take it out with cruise missiles before it reaches the Zero Red demarcation."

"If it doesn't launch, the sub will get it with torpedoes. From this point on, it's not a matter of if . . . it's a matter of when."

A longer silence.

"Are we in agreement then?"

A murmur went around the room.

"With the lives of almost a thousand people on our hands, I guess we are. . . ."

Another long silence.

"Okay—let's send the full message to the sub."

15

Aboard the *Battev*
0335 hours

Jimmy Gillis was seasick.

At least he thought it was seasickness. His stomach was rumbling, his head was on fire. His joints felt weak and at times, he was having trouble catching his breath.

The *Battev* was rolling so much the conditions certainly qualified to cause the malady, but Gillis wasn't so sure. Maybe he was just dying—on the inside—a little piece at a time.

He was sitting in what was once Rooney's stateroom, going over the hundreds of notes the CIA man had left on his laptop. Ricco was sound asleep in the chair across from him, his finger poised over the automatic redial button of their cell phone. Even in repose, it was a futile gesture. They'd been trying to reach Norton or Krysoltev for hours. Yet all they were getting was endless ringing or busy signals.

Ever since the MiG attack on the *Battev*, Gillis and Ricco had been holed up in the stateroom, taking turns on Rooney's laptop, trying to decipher his very loose note-taking style. The CIA man had entered pages of random words, numbers, and sentence fragments throughout his files, few with any kind of reason to them.

It had taken them several hours and a very slow process of elimination just to find the entry that Rooney had spoken about in his dying breath, the message that those in control of the *Kuznetsov* had been broadcasting on a top-secret shortwave radio band almost since the takeover began.

But since finding it, and following Rooney's rudimentary translation, the mystery had only deepened. Neither Gillis or Ricco could figure it out. The message just didn't make any sense. "Bats . . . balls . . . fruit . . . pie . . . mother . . ."

Gillis stared at those words now, his stomach twisting inside out. What did they mean? And more importantly, how might they help them solve what was really going on aboard the Russian carrier?

He reluctantly opened Rooney's codebook again. It was thick with secret words and phrases, but the problem was the book had been prepared by the CIA, not as a specific guide to specific codes, but rather as a shopping list of code words that could be used in certain situations.

The book suggested using the word "senior," for instance, when indicating that supersecret aircraft or weaponry might be involved in a coded message. The words "ingress" or "egress" were usually used to indicate a rescue mission of sorts. A mention of weather conditions or tides was suggested as an indicator of the status of an evolving operation. If the tide was "high," that might mean the operation would begin as planned. If the day was "cloudy," that might mean something was holding up the works.

What's more, the codebook was the product of Roo-

ney's department at the CIA, a place Gillis knew only as
the Special Projects office. This meant that these code
words might not and probably *did* not apply to other sec-
tions of the CIA. This was not a universal bible he was
reading here.

Add to this the fact that these were Russians broadcasting the strange message from the carrier. Why would
they be using code words related only to Rooney's tiny
department within the vast CIA? Or using code words that
the CIA would understand in any case?

Still, the book did offer some intriguing possibilities.
"Fruit" turned out to be a term used often in the past by
Rooney's department. It suggested a tropical setting. The
word "bat" was suggested to indicate a nighttime operation
was in the offing—and in the long polar night that certainly applied here. There was no suggested word use for
"ball," but the words "ballroom dance" were in the book
several times and were to be used when one, two, or more
disparate forces were combining to do the operation. A
dance of forces.

There was no suggested use for the word "pie"—however, one of Rooney's notes indicated an idea he'd had.
Perhaps the sender meant "Pi" in mathematical terms. If
that was the case, then "Pi" was used in code to mean
some kind of telemetry or geometric equation was involved.

There was only one use for the word "mother" suggested. It was to indicate "homeland."

Put together in one possible sequence then, if judged by
Rooney's book, the message might read:

"Tropical . . . telemetry . . . at night . . . a gathering of
forces . . . homeland . . ."

It sounded like spy talk, but that only meant it was
almost impossible to understand.

Gillis picked up the wastebasket and threw up again.
All this heavy thinking was making him even more nau-

seous. He checked the time. It was almost 0400 hours. He felt his forehead. It was hot.

He needed some air. Tapping Ricco awake, he listened in on the cell phone, and again, heard only a busy signal. Dropping the laptop into his partner's hands, he somehow struggled into his foul-weather gear and staggered out onto the deck. The sight of the rolling waves—they were nearing twenty feet high by now—did nothing to improve his condition.

He walked to the far railing and looked out across the helipad. The ship stank something awful of cordite and burned steel from the MiG attack. The crew was working around the clock to repair the damage, but it was obvious that every last person on the *Battev* was pissing their pants, waiting for the next attack to occur.

Gillis included.

He was physically ill now. The weight on his shoulders was nearly unbearable. He was sure that save for Ricco, all his colleagues were dead. He was also sure that the people on the carrier were intent on creating a catastrophic nuclear disaster. He was sure he'd never see his home or family again. He was sure he would somehow die out here alone on a strange ship—and for what?

That was the worst thing of all . . . he would die for nothing.

He stared out at the stormy water and the huge bank of clouds that by now seemed to have been hanging perpetually over the northeast horizon. Somewhere out there was the *Kuznetsov* too—out of sight, just over the horizon. His few minutes spent down on the carrier had been more intense, more nightmarish than anything he'd done during the ArcLight mission. Or at least at the moment, it seemed that way.

He looked at his hands, and could still see Rooney's blood on them. He shivered to think that the CIA officer, alive and bouncy that morning, was now lying in the ship's food freezer, next to the cans of bad soup, the old meat, and the bodies of the sailors killed in the air attack. How many corpses could that place hold? Gillis wondered grimly. Was there room for two more?

He shook away these morbid thoughts, made his way down the ladder, and staggered past the helipad. He was soon leaning on the aft railing, a tailwind of sorts blowing madly in his face.

He looked down at the water. It was absolutely black, with huge chunks of blue-white ice floating on it.

Gillis just shook his head. How he wished that he was back in his van, with Ryan, driving home from Christmas shopping. It seemed as though all that had happened a million years ago. In reality, it had not even been forty-eight hours.

His eyes were now mesmerized by the freezing black water. How simple it would be for him to just step over the railing and go down into that cold dark abyss. If he did that, at least he would have the feeling that his life ended on his terms, not someone else's.

He surprised himself by lifting his left leg up to the middle rung of the rear railing.

It would be so easy . . . just one more step . . . and the nightmare would be over . . .

It was at that moment that he felt a hand on his left shoulder.

He froze. Who could this be? Certainly not one of the crew. They had been told to stay away from all Americans and they had obeyed that order to the letter. And it was not Ricco—Gillis would have heard him coming a mile away.

Who was it then?

He turned, slowly—and found a man dressed in a bright white flight suit and a huge white crash helmet standing beside him.

"Hi, Jimmy. Remember me?"

Gillis almost went over the railing anyway; the man had startled him so. He regained his footing and stared at the figure in white. He seemed like a ghost, standing in his sparkling ivory clothes against the backdrop of dark clouds and black water.

And then it began to sink in.

Yes, Gillis *did* remember this guy. . . .

Back during ArcLight. In the middle of the mission, when all seemed lost, this guy—this man in his white flight suit—had come out of nowhere, literally, to give them a potent piece of information that resulted in their completing the mission with no lives lost.

Who was he again? A CIA man? Gillis didn't know. How did he get here? Gillis didn't know that either. But he'd obviously had access to some kind of high-performance, highly secret aircraft back during ArcLight. The same must be true now.

And what was his name?

As if to answer him, the man took off his helmet; he had a baseball cap on underneath it, its bill turned backwards.

He turned the cap around and Gillis saw the inscription. "Not All Angels Are Good Angels."

Yes, that was it. This guy's code name was Angel.

But Gillis was still almost too shaken to speak.

"Jessuz . . . how? How did you get here?" he finally stammered.

Angel just smiled. "You must know by now that's classified information."

Gillis just stared back at him. How strange was this?

"Well, have you come to take us out of here, I hope?" he asked him.

Angel just shrugged. "Sorry, I'd like to, Jimmy. But that's impossible."

Gillis wasn't surprised to hear that.

"Would you go, though, if I could take you?" Angel asked.

Gillis thought about that for a moment, but then shook his head.

"No, I guess not," he murmured. "Not with so many . . . well, loose ends . . ."

Angel nodded slowly.

"I've been following this little adventure of yours," he said. "It's really not going very well, is it?"

Gillis almost laughed in his face. "That's an understatement."

"Well I hate to tell you this, but it's going to get a lot worse real quick. . . ."

Gillis looked at him closely. "How can it possibly get any worse?"

Angel looked worried—not a good sign.

"I can't tell you everything," he began slowly. "But I can tell you this: That carrier—or more specifically its long-range weapons—will soon be within range of the American coastline. My bosses have drawn a line in the ocean. The Zero Red Line. If nothing changes, and that ship crosses that line, well . . ."

"Well . . . what?"

"Well, they're going to sink it."

Gillis felt a chill go through his bones.

"Sink it?" The words just spilled out of his mouth.

"Is that so much a surprise?" Angel asked him. "The situation is totally out of control. What makes you think the powers that be will let that ship get within missile range of the East Coast?"

"But we still have men on that ship," Gillis said. "And a lot of innocent Russians."

Angel just stared back at him. "So?"

They let a long moment pass between them. The wind was howling madly again.

"Look," Angel began again. "That ship had four missiles capable of throwing warheads. The crew—or whoever else is in control—has already launched two of those missiles at the North Pole. Luckily both were duds. But that just means the remaining two will definitely work. Not to mention its belly being stuffed with deactivated—but still dangerous—nukes of all shapes and sizes. That ship could be in sight of New York Harbor in less than three days. What would you do?"

Gillis became angry. "I'd try to save the people on board . . . both Russians and Americans."

"Well, that ain't going to happen, unless . . ."

"Unless what?" Gillis asked.

"Unless you do it yourself," Angel told him starkly.

"Me?"

"You and your partner—there's no one else," Angel said. "This thing is so secret the President has been briefed on it exactly once. There is no rescue force that can be assembled before the carrier passes that line in the sea. *You guys* were supposed to be the rescue force, remember? There's just not enough time to assemble another one. And even if it there was, what would they do? Try to land a thousand paratroopers on the carrier? In this weather? Or try another chopper landing—and walk into another meatgrinder?"

Angel just shook his head. "I've been in this business for a very long time," he said. "I've never seen anything so screwed up—or so dangerous as what this has become."

"But what can *we* do?" Gillis asked him. "It's just me and Marty and a chopper that's shot full of holes."

Angel just shook his head. "That's just it," he said. "I don't know. There are no ships within eighty miles of here. The closest U.S. ship is more than one hundred miles away. The nearest Russian ship is twice that far. Time is the enemy here."

He looked up at the monstrous storm, still frozen on the northern horizon. "That, and the weather," he added.

He paused another moment.

"All I can suggest is that you dream up a miracle," he said finally. "Use whatever assets you can muster."

"Even a miracle wouldn't work now," Gillis said somberly.

"Well, let me just say this," Angel concluded. "There

is a Navy submarine en route as we speak. As soon as they are in range, and if nothing has happened, well . . . it won't be a pleasant Christmas for anyone within a hundred miles of that ship. So think, pray, or do whatever. Because there really isn't much time left."

He put his huge helmet back on.

"Now what I usually tell people at this point is to close their eyes," he said. "You don't want to see what's going to happen next."

Gillis took this to mean that whatever Angel was flying, it was extremely top secret.

But before he closed his eyes, he grabbed the pilot by the arm.

"Where are you off to now?" he asked him. "Is that top secret too?"

Angel just nodded. "You bet it is."

Gillis persisted, though. "Are you going back to your base? Is it in the United States? Can you tell me that at least?"

Angel shoved up the reflective visor on his helmet.

"It is," he said. "And that's all I can tell you."

But Gillis would not let go of his arm.

"This thing you fly around in," he started. "It can go anywhere—right?"

"Again . . . classified," Angel replied firmly.

But Gillis was gripping his arm very tightly now.

"Okay then, look, pal, you've got to do me a favor," Gillis told him. "You've got to let my family know I'm still okay. And that . . . that I love them."

Angel just shook his head. "That would break every rule in the book."

"I think you're no stranger to that," Gillis told him.

Angel just shook his head.

"Look, I feel for you, Jimmy. But if I spoke one word about this mission, or any aspect of it, or even a message from you, to anybody, not only could they shoot me, they *would* shoot me!"

"But there must be a way," Gillis thought desperately. Suddenly this was the most important thing on his mind.

Then he reached into his pocket and came out with a small shiny object.

He pressed it into Angel's glove.

"I'm sure you know where I live," Gillis told him. "Go there and give this to my son. If you do, he'll know I'm okay."

Angel did not argue. The weather was getting worse and he had to leave.

He indicated that Gillis should turn away, and then took a device from his pocket that was about the size of a TV remote control.

He pushed a series of buttons and looked straight up.

Several seconds later, there was a sharp flash of blue light.

When Gillis opened his eyes a few seconds later, Angel was gone.

16

"Well, if we are still alive, then the second missile must
have been a dud too," Gene Smitz was saying. "If not,
we'd be fish food by now."

It was close to dawn. Outside the carrier, the sea was
still whipped up, the storm still hanging over the *Kuznetsov* like a giant, just waiting to pounce.

The patrol sent out to capture the prisoner had returned
to the Fuzski nearly two hours before. By that time, everyone knew that another RMB-1750 had been launched. The
ensuing 120 minutes had been an exercise in excruciating
anxiety. Everyone just sitting on the floor of the Fuzski,
very quiet, alone with their thoughts, waiting for the fatal
blow. Their reasoning was simple: If the second RMB-
1750 was not a dud, then the U.S. would certainly launch
cruise missiles at the carrier, whether it had crossed over
the Zero Red Line or not.

But now after more than two hours, the ship was still afloat, still heading west, and still in one piece. That was enough for Smitz. He declared that the second missile must have been defused too.

And that started everyone's heart beating again—at least for a while.

"Next time we hear the sound of one of those babies going off, though," Delaney said, "we might as well just jump overboard and start swimming."

"We'll cross that bridge when we come to it," Smitz told him. "Until then, let's go talk to the prisoner."

They had left him inside the nuclear weapons bay.

He was sitting in a chair, his feet wired together. They had given him a small cup of precious water to drink. He'd gulped it greedily.

Now when they reappeared, the prisoner looked not at all frightened. Actually, he was very puzzled.

He asked them in his thick broken English: "Why are you Americans on this ship?"

"Now that's a good question," Delaney cracked.

While Norton undid his binds, Smitz took full measure of the prisoner. He checked his arms and spotted needle tracks.

"Damn," he cursed. "Did you have to snatch a junkie?"

Chou took immediate offense.

"We didn't have much of a choice," he told the CIA man. "If you want a choirboy, I suggest you go crawling through those passageways yourself."

Delaney checked the guy's arms.

"He might not be a junkie," he said—somehow this was another thing Delaney was an expert in. "He only has a few punctures."

"Plus he's the only thing we got," Norton said.

Smitz had to agree with that. He began the interrogation by asking the man his name and rank. The Russian seaman gave it without a second's hesitation, using very bad but understandable English.

Smitz's next question was the most important: What happened on the ship after it left Murmansk?

Seklovski started talking—and did not stop. Like everyone else on the ship, he said, he did not want to be sailing with so many nuclear weapons, deactivated or not. And he especially did not want to make such a treacherous voyage with an undermanned crew and with so many inexperienced kids on board. Yet he did not have the guts to jump ship the way nearly three hundred men had done back in Sevastopol. So he was stuck on board.

He'd helped load the deactivated weapons onto the carrier, always working at night. Considering the condition of the nukes, the job went well. Only three people were exposed to deadly radiation, and only because, he had heard, they'd been moving warheads while drunk.

The real trouble started after the ship sailed from Murmansk. The first blood was drawn with a stabbing in the mess hall after just one hour at sea: An officer had his throat slashed and was left to bleed to death. This man, as it turned out, was the first casualty in the "mutiny" that had to be staged in order to get rid of Kartoonov and any other innocent officers.

Once word of the man's death flashed through the ship, more fighting occurred. Sailors against sailors, officers against officers. Within an hour, it was open warfare, those in on the arms deal battling against those unaware of it.

"In the first two hours, many low-level officers and several pilots were murdered by a gang known as Sharkskis," Seklovski said. "Anyone who stood in their way was killed."

"Shark-skis?" Delaney said mouthing the word. "What's that mean in Russian?"

"Just what it says," Smitz told him. "The Sharks. The bunch of lowlifes and drug addicts who stayed on board when everyone else took off in Sevastopol. These are the enlisted guys who were supposed to do the heavy lifting during the weapons exchange."

He prodded the prisoner. "Go on."

Seklovski's involvement started when he showed up for mess late and was herded along with many others into a midship berthing by the Sharkskis. They heard nothing but shooting for the next twelve hours. At first the word was that Kartoonov's staff officers were being executed by the Sharks, but Seklovski doubted this because the Sharks appeared to be too scared, too disorganized to be in control during the first day at sea.

In that time he saw dozens of Sharks who had been shot and brought back to the berthing to die. Some Sharks went away and never returned at all. Soon enough the Sharks began asking for "volunteers" to "guard" the ship. Seklovski was selected, given a flare gun, a walkie-talkie, a shot of morphine, and the pep pills, then sent to watch over a deep passageway midships. He was snatched soon thereafter.

"But what was in it for you?" Smitz asked him.

Money, was the sailor's reply. Lots of it.

He had been told that anyone working with the Sharks would be rich, as the Sharks had made a deal to sell some of the nuclear weapons on board to black marketeers. Plus Seklovski knew that refusing the Sharks would mean he'd die anyway, so he joined up. But obviously things had gone wrong early in the "mutiny."

"If these Sharks were getting their asses kicked," Delaney asked, "who were they fighting for control of the ship?"

"Is not officer staff," Seklovski said. "They were all dead. Is other set of sailors who have made deal with the black marketeers—that's my theory."

By this time, though, Chou was doing a slow burn. He checked his watch. Everyone was checking their watches now.

"This is all very fascinating," he said. "But we've got

less than eighteen hours to do something here. And this guy isn't really helping us."

"Relax," Smitz told the Marine captain. "We're just getting to the good part."

The CIA man turned back to the prisoner.

"What do you know about the submarine that was to pick up the nuclear weapons?" Smitz pressed Seklovski.

The Russian sailor just shrugged. "I know only that we are supposed to meet in mid-sea any time now. They have money. We have weapons. We do business. That's it. Byebye."

"If the guys in that sub have any sense, they're putting as much distance between us and them as possible," Delaney said. "I mean, if you're buying a stick of dynamite, it does put a crimp in the deal if the dynamite's fuse is already lit."

"These mystery men," Smitz went on. "The ones fighting the Sharks. Are they the ones who wired all the nukes in here too?"

"*Da,*" was the reply. "The wires stretch all the way to the Island—to the bridge. They did this work at the same time they took live missiles out of storage. They know that if we make a move down here—they flip switch. We all go up."

He eyed the wired-up weapons magazine again.

"I cannot believe crazy American soldiers would want to be down here," he said with a shiver. "Personally I do not want to see the bomb that blows me up."

"Can't argue with that philosophy," Delaney said.

That was when Chou picked the Russian sailor up off the chair and pushed him to the grimy floor.

"Draw us a map," he said. "Tell us who controls what."

The man began tracing lines on the oily floor. It took him about a minute, but by then he had made a passable outline of the *Kuznetsov*.

He pointed first to the lower decks that ran the length of the ship.

"No-man's-land," he said. "Most doors welded shut."

Then to the mid-level decks running from the hangar bay forward to right under the Island.

"Sharkskis," he said. "All doors welded shut."

Then he pointed to the area around the Island, and the so-called Combat Rooms.

"This is where the Drugiye are," he said.

They all turned to Smitz for a translation.

" 'The Drugiye means the Others," the CIA man explained. "The mystery men."

"Right," the prisoner agreed. "The Drugiye are in charge of the most important places on ship. They control the Island. The weapons rooms. Everything else—welded shut. We shoot at them from flight deck, they shoot back. This battle up top, been going on three days. Many friends of mine go up there to fight, they don't come back. The Drugiye. Crazy. Very bloody."

He turned to the men who had snatched him, and who had shared the terror in the spine.

"You saw them," he said. "*They* are the monsters. Sharkskis are bad. The Drugiye—much worse."

"But where are the officers who were in on the original arms deal?" Smitz asked Seklovski. "Do you know?"

The Russian sailor took his finger and drew an imaginary line across his throat.

"The captain, his boyfriends, and Kartoonov," he said. "From what I hear, all of them—boom! Off with their heads and into the drink. Some by rope, others . . . well, they hit the water sooner."

Smitz was confused. They all were.

"Are you saying the Sharkskis turned on their officers?"

The man shook his head no.

"The corrupt officers were killed by the Drugiye as well," he said. "We don't know who they are, or where they came from. But after the first night of killing on the ship, it was the Drugiye who took over."

Norton stepped forward now.

"What about these missiles?" he said, drawing a crude picture of an RMB-1750 on the dirty floor. "Two have been launched already. Who fired them?"

Seklovski shrugged and smiled grimly. "The Drugiye control the buttons," he said. "The Sharkskis want to, but cannot get to the main Combat Room. That's what the gunfight up top is all about. They know they have to get into the bridge and get control of the ship if their deal is to be made. But across the deck is the only way to go."

"Just what the Spetsnaz guys were trying to do," Norton said. "And look what happened to them."

"Do you know where the missile launchers are?" Smitz asked him.

Seklovski pointed to a section just forward of the Island.

"There," he said. "One deck down. You see them only from a height. At level deck, they are invisible."

Silence came over the weapons bay.

Capturing a prisoner had been a sound military judgment. But how were they to know that his information would just put them deeper in the hole?

The problem for the Americans was maddeningly simple though: If the Spetsnaz and the Sharkskis, well-armed and ruthless as both were, could not stop the Drugiye, how could *they*?

Norton was constantly checking the time now. It was close to dawn, December 24th. By their calculations, the carrier would be approaching the Zero Red Line within eighteen hours. After that, anything could happen.

"It's going to be tough just to sit back and watch them launch another missile—whoever *they* are," Delaney was saying.

Chou turned back to the captured sailor.

"Are you sure that every passageway is sealed from the Island forward? Every last one of them?"

The sailor just nodded his head wearily.

"Sealed tight," he said in thick English. "Welded shut.

Welds upon welds. When we try to blow doors off hinges, we see nothing but bullets from other side. . . ."

"Whoever the hell these Others are, they're damn good," Smitz observed. "They must know the ship like the back of their hand. They knew where to defend, where to block, where to place their weapons. Not to mention how to wire up the bay full of nukes—*and* shoot the RMB-1750's."

"The question is, what the hell do they want? Do you really think they've made a separate deal—with someone else?"

Seklovski just shrugged. "Big mystery," he replied.

Smitz said, "I was in Russia for a month before I got put aboard the *Kuznetsov*. In that time I never saw more intrigue, double-dealing, double-triple-dealing in my entire life—and I'm just talking about in the butcher shop. A separate deal? Made by another bunch of sailors? Sure. No problem."

He paused for a moment.

"At this point, I'd believe just about anything about these Others."

Another long silence. Some gunfire from up above.

"Well, let's face facts. We can't get to those launchers belowdecks, and we certainly can't get to them across the flight deck either," Smitz was saying. "I think that leaves us up the creek."

"Unless . . ." Norton said.

Everyone in the small room turned to him, even the captured sailor.

"Unless what?" Smitz asked.

Norton turned to Delaney. "Just how fucked up is the Kamov?"

Delaney shrugged. "Its main hydraulic line is shot out," he replied. "How much more fucked up could it be?"

"Could it be repaired?" Norton asked him.

Delaney laughed. They all did.

"Sure," Delaney answered. "By a bunch of mechanics,

with the right tools and a few gallons of hydraulic fluid."

Norton thought a moment. "Well, you don't really need hydraulic fluid, do you?"

"What do you mean?" Delaney asked.

"I mean, if we could somehow fix the severed line, does it really make a difference what we fill it with?" Norton asked.

"It makes a difference to the helicopter, I'm sure," Delaney said. "What are you proposing, that we put water in the lines?"

"No, not water," Norton said. "But there are barrels of plain old oil upstairs in our half of the hangar. Would that do in a pinch?"

"For a little while, *da*," came the answer. But it was not from Delaney. It was from the captured sailor.

Norton crouched down beside him. "You sure of that, Igor?"

The man just shrugged. "I am aviation mechanic," he said. "I work MiGs. I work Flankers. I work Kamovs. If you ask can you put oil into hydraulic line, I say yes. If you ask, will hydraulic line then work, I say yes. If you ask, can you go very far in helicopter with oil in hydraulic lines—I say no."

"Why not?" Chou asked.

"Because oil is more slippery," the sailor replied. "No muscles for hydraulics. It will seep out, pass through things that hydraulic fluid might not. The pressure will not last long."

"How long?"

The man shrugged. "Five minutes. Ten maybe."

Norton thought a long moment. "Maybe that's enough."

"For what?" Smitz asked. "Certainly not to fly back to the *Battev*? It's probably at the bottom of the sea by now."

"No, not that," Norton said. "I'm still on the page where we try to blow up the missile shooters."

"Now even I'm confused, Jazz," Delaney admitted.

"Well, dare I say, it's simple," Norton told them. "We

can't get to the shooters belowdecks. We can't get to them across the flight deck, right?"

There was a chorus of nods.

"Well, then," Norton said. "Maybe we *fly* over to them. . . ."

17

Lieutenant Commander Andy Rogers was asleep when the call came in. He was wanted in the captain's quarters immediately.

By instinct the first thing Rogers did was check the *Skyfire*'s position on his berth's computer screen. They were more than 1000 miles out from Norfolk now and still heading east, very quickly. Their brief GPS shakeout cruise was a thing of the past now. A ghost.

They were under new orders. Possibly the last ones they would ever follow.

These instructions had come in earlier by secure fax. They were as mystifying as the letter secretly delivered to Captain Bruynell just before the submarine left Norfolk. The new orders had them proceeding at engines full to a coordinate approximately one hundred miles south of

Greenland. Because of the *Skyfire*'s high speed, they were now less than a day away from that goal.

Yet still they did not know what they were supposed to do once they arrived there. Not exactly anyway. But the secret inquiry they'd received before leaving Norfolk had left a chilling possibility up for grabs: sinking a ship filled with nuclear weapons from a "can't miss" range of twenty thousand yards. Rogers had had a frightening vision at chow about just such a scenario. The *Skyfire* fires a spread of the new MK-86 torpedoes at a ship stuffed with nuclear weapons and it blows up with such force, the *Skyfire* is thrown all the way back to the American East Coast, where boat and crew, pulverized and irradiated, wash up in front of friends and family. This image had come to him in the officers' mess as he was staring into a cup of coffee. It had not left him yet.

He'd been avoiding sleep since then. At full out, the *Skyfire* could go faster than any submarine ever built, but it wasn't just a case of putting the pedal to the metal. It took a series of precise, choreographed movements, which, if performed properly, would allow the reactor to do its job and provide robust quantities of steam to the turbines, which, in turn, would spin the sub's huge propeller, which would push them through the Atlantic at an unheard of, and a highly classified, speed.

Rogers had worked hard at keeping this dance going—so hard in fact, that it got to the point where he looked so tired, the ship's doctor ordered him to get some rest. Only if he didn't dream, Rogers had told the doctor. This resulted in a sleeping pill being prescribed. Rogers downed it and went to sleep in less than two minutes.

But only an hour had gone by since then.

And now the captain was summoning him.

That was why he knew it must be something important.

He stumbled out of his berth and up to the captain's

quarters. He walked in to find the *Skyfire*'s CO—Captain Chip Bruynell—hunched over his desk once again.

"What's up, Skipper?" Rogers asked.

Bruynell was not a man given to exaggeration or fantasy. Or panic. But right now, he looked dreadful.

"Read this," Bruynell said, handing a yellow sheet of paper to Rogers. "It just came in."

Rogers read the communiqué. By the time he came to the last sentence, he could barely hold it in his hands.

"Does this mean what I think it means?"

Bruynell wiped his forehead with his hand. He was sweating.

"That our worst fears have come true?" Bruynell asked. "Yes, I'm afraid it does."

He took the message from Rogers and read it again.

"They want us to proceed to the Zero Red Line and sink a Russian carrier. That's pretty straightforward, don't you think?"

Rogers was numb. The message ordered the *Skyfire* to use as many torpedoes as it would take to sink the Russian carrier *Kuznetsov*, at the "can't miss" distance of twenty thousand yards, even though there was an extremely good chance that if the thousands of megatons of nuclear weapons on board the carrier were detonated by this act, the *Skyfire* would go up too.

"Whatever is going on out there," Bruynell was saying, "they want us to make sure we kill it the first time."

"Or they don't want any witnesses," Rogers said angrily. "Not us, and apparently not any Russians either. They'd nail this thing with cruise missiles if that wasn't the case."

He bit his lip so hard, it began to bleed.

"This is a suicide mission," Rogers said finally. "Plain and simple."

Bruynell was staring at a picture of his wife, his four daughters, and his grandkids. Thirteen people in all.

"When I first went to sea," he began sadly, "every time

we put out, I expected it to be the last. Early sixties—we were always one blink away from getting it. We usually knew where the Russians were, and they usually knew where we were. Like two gunfighters on the street; we both pull the trigger at the same time. We both get it between the eyes. Now *that* was suicidal."

He turned away from the photograph. His expression looked even worse than before.

"So, I've always been prepared," he said, his voice fading a bit. "But never did I think it would come like this."

Rogers studied the message again.

"Could this be a drill, Skipper?" he asked. "A security check? Or even a loyalty test of some kind?"

Bruynell considered this for a few seconds, then just shook his head no.

"I've been in the service almost forty years," he replied. "I've never been involved in a loyalty test. Even when we were ass-to-eyeball with the Russians—nothing even remotely like that. Why would it start now?"

They both sat in silence for a long moment.

"Sinking a Russian carrier, though," Rogers murmured. "I mean, never mind what might happen to us. That's an act of war. Has this message been rechecked?"

Bruynell pointed to a row of numbers at the top of the message. These were the decoded transmission time codes, a gobbledygook of phrases that, if interpreted correctly, revealed the time zone from which the message originated, among other things.

"Look at this," he pointed out. "The message is from the President, there is no doubt about that—all the proper code contexts match. But according to the time code, the point of origin is definitely not from Washington. It was sent from the Pacific Time Zone."

"Pacific Time Zone?" Rogers repeated the words. "Is the President skiing in Tahoe?"

"That's just it," Bruynell said. "He's in Washington. I checked. At Camp David for the holidays."

Rogers thought for a moment. "Then what the hell is in the Pacific Time Zone that could issue such an order in his name?"

Bruynell just shrugged.

"Maybe Area 51?" Rogers said in morbid jest. "Or some wacky secret base out that way? I mean, I've heard rumors. . . ."

"Don't even kid about that," Bruynell said, cutting him off. "This message is so weird, I might be inclined to believe you."

Rogers checked the new sailing headings and then looked at the time.

"And if it wasn't bad enough, they want us to do this on Christmas Eve," he groaned.

Bruynell put the message in his ashtray, flicked a cigarette lighter, and then lit it.

"They gave this to us because we could get real close, real fast, and do it without any questions," he said. "And that's exactly what we're going to do. You'll have to really lay on the coals now. This thing might break apart if we are to reach that coordinate in time."

Rogers cleared his throat. "And what shall I tell the crew, sir?"

Bruynell stopped for a moment and watched the last of the embers die in the ashtray.

Then he said: "Tell them they won't be home for Christmas after all."

18

Aboard the *Kuznetsov*
0730 hours

The deck of the *Kuznetsov* was awash in tracer fire.

Like some kind of living, breathing piece of modern art, the red streaks were going every which way, carving through the stormy darkness, ricocheting off the deck, off the Island, off the wreckage of the Kamov ammo chopper. And as always, the racket of all this gunfire rivaled the screeching of the wind.

The strange thing was, who was shooting at who, from where, and whether the constant stream of gunfire was actually hitting anything or anybody was impossible to determine. Much of the firing was coming from the top levels of the Island, undoubtedly from the Drugiye. But there were also fusillades coming from both sides of the sub-deck, the recessed railing that stretched completely around the outside of the flight deck, as well as from the flight deck itself. These were the positions held by the

Sharkskis. But in the confusion and the darkness and the wind, sleet, snow, and rain, from the aft end of the carrier, it seemed as if the gunfight was an entity in itself. Bolts of static electricity, lighting up the night, with no human involvement at all.

Except for the occasional cry of pain when a bullet finally found its mark.

It was into this confused state of affairs that Norton, Delaney, Chou, and Sergeant Reaney climbed.

"This has got to be the craziest thing you've ever talked me into," Delaney was saying to Norton as they peeked over the flight deck from their position on the aft exterior ladderway.

It was a bit like looking out of a trench across some murderous fields of fire from a war long ago.

"When the fuck are these guys going to run out of ammunition?" Norton replied. "That's what I want to know."

The only positive aspect of this very dangerous mission was that most of the gunfire was concentrated around the Island and along the decks on either side of it and across from it. The nearest flashes of fire Norton could see were diagonally across the deck from them, maybe two hundred feet away from their position.

The Kamov, on the other hand, was actually behind them, its tail nearly hanging off the back of the carrier itself. That was their immediate goal.

Norton was the first to crawl up onto the flight deck. Staying as low as he could, he went on elbows and knees across the bullet-scarred surface, his chin sinking into an inch or so of ice, oil, jet fuel, metal fragments—and maybe a little blood.

After a half minute of sloshing, he reached the front wheels of the chopper with no problem; he knew he was getting close when he detected the telltale odor of hydraulic fluid. Delaney was right on his heels, with Chou behind him. Reaney was left on the walkway to cover their backs.

The three Americans stopped crawling once they were under the body of the Kamov itself. A massive pool of blood-red hydraulic fluid awaited them here. It had run out of the rotors, through the right engine exhaust, down the side of the aircraft's body, down the extended landing gear to the deck below. There were at least ten gallons of it spilled about.

"I hope we've got enough oil downstairs to fill this thing," Delaney commented.

Now came the hard part.

The Kamov's nose was pointing straight down the deck. To check the main hydraulic lines, someone would have to climb up to the rotors and inspect the main hose, exposing himself to gunfire. Delaney had volunteered for this mission down below. But now, up top, with the fierce wind blowing, and the gunfight in full fire, climbing the eighteen feet or so up to the chopper's engine mounts seemed like climbing the Empire State Building.

"Go ahead," Norton urged him. "You've got to have something to brag about once this is over."

"Wise-ass," Delaney replied.

He unstrapped his AK-47, wiped the grease and oil as best he could from his puffy uniform, and then set out. He shimmied up the side of the left rear landing strut, which actually gave him a foothold to the top of the rear cabin door. Then it was over to the exhaust pipe to the rotor mount. This was where the hydraulic leak was so severe, it looked like the Kamov was bleeding human blood.

As Norton and Chou hunkered down to wait below, they were suddenly aware of Sergeant Reaney crawling across the flight deck towards them. He'd been told to hold his position unless there was a change in the situation.

And there was.

He reached their spot under the chopper.

"Take a look straight down the ramp, sir," he told Chou.

Chou did so, and let out a long whistle.

"This isn't good," he said.

Norton took a look for himself.

Although the ambient light was very low, it was enough for him to see what Reaney and Chou were talking about. There were at least a dozen men moving very slowly across the flight deck toward the bottom of the Island—all while their confederates along the deck railing were pouring tracer fire into the top half of the superstructure itself.

The crawling men were being very stealthy; obviously they were trying to get into position to storm the Island.

"Which side are we on for this little fight?" Norton wondered aloud.

"Neither," Chou said. "But my money sure ain't on the Sharkskis. What they're doing is like trying to attack a fortress—and they're about to get what they came looking for."

No sooner were the words out of his mouth when there was a tremendous flash of fire from the top of the Island. It was so bright it nearly blinded them. By the time Norton was able to refocus his eyes, he could see shadows belonging to the Drugiye moving on the upper levels of the Island and sending a stream of ignited flammable liquid onto those down below. It was horrible. The Sharkskis who just seconds earlier had been creeping up on the superstructure were now engulfed in an ocean of flame. Norton saw at least a half-dozen men totally engulfed running in panic back across the flight deck, only to be cut down by the never-ending stream of gunfire coming from the top of the Island.

It was sickening, unnerving.

Medieval . . .

Then the fires all went out, and those Sharkskis that had somehow survived the immolation began crawling back to the far deck railing from which they'd come. Then the gunfire began again.

The next thing Norton knew, Delaney was beside him.

"Wow, did you see that?" he asked excitedly. "These freaking Russians. They really are Vikings with guns, aren't they?"

Norton quickly changed the subject. "How's things up top?"

"The main line is fucked up but fixable," Delaney reported, his arms and chest now soaked with red hydraulic fluid. "If we're only talking about a Band-Aid approach."

"That's all we have in mind," Norton said. "Now, if those knuckleheads down below can just do their part . . ."

While it was true that there were two main factions fighting for control of the *Kuznetsov,* their numbers did not account for everyone aboard the ship.

Throughout the carrier there were isolated pockets of crew members who had little knowledge of what was going on, or into whose hands their fate would eventually fall.

One of these solitary groups had been holed up in the forward part of the carrier's hangar bay. Originally this group was made up of four pilots and ten aircraft mechanics. Now it consisted of exactly two people. Both pilots, both majors in Russian Naval Aviation. Their names were Yevgeny Sotnikov and Gennadi Balandin.

Before the troubles began on board the *Kuznetsov,* there was a total of twelve fighter pilots on board. Eight were killed when the Sharkskis staged their mutiny. Along with the ten aircraft mechanics, the four remaining pilots, including Sotnikov and Balandin, sealed themselves into the forward part of the hangar bay, even going so far as to point one of the MiG-29 fighters toward the main forward hatchway—the most likely place from which an attack would come—its massive nose cannon powered up and ready to fire.

Living on rations found within survival packets inside the dozen jet fighters on their side of the hangar, the tiny group hoped to stay alive long enough to weather whatever storm was tearing up the carrier from within.

All this had changed the previous morning when an intermediary from the Sharkskis called into the hangar bay via the ship's inter-phone system. He had a deal to offer. Fearing that more Spetsnaz soldiers were riding aboard the *Battev* supply vessel, the Sharkskis were willing to pay two pilots a huge share of their black arms money if they agreed to bomb the replenishment ship.

Though Sotnikov and Balandin warned their colleagues that this was a huge mistake, the pilots accepted the offer. They took off from the carrier the night before—and never returned. At the same time, the ten mechanics agreed to join the Sharkskis, again the lure of money made once the nuclear weapons were exchanged proving too much for them. They never returned either.

This left Sotnikov and Balandin alone inside the forward hangar bay, eating stale chocolate bars, listening to the nonstop gunfire up on the flight deck, and wondering just how long it would be before the nightmare engulfing the ship came through the front door.

As it turned out, for them destiny would be coming from the opposite direction.

"Open up, comrades! The war is over!"

The banging had started right after Sotnikov and Balandin had finished their morning meal of hard biscuits.

They had heard some commotion from the other side of the hangar fire door earlier that morning, but compared to the gunfire raging up on the deck, it had seemed like a minor thing.

But now someone was pounding loudly on the fire door, claiming that peace had returned to the *Kuznetsov* and that all those in hiding should come out.

This created a real dilemma for the Russian pilots. There was no way they could turn the nose of the MiG around to face the rear sliding wall—not just the two of them. Besides, what if the message was true?

"If there is peace, why do we hear gunfire still?" Sotnikov yelled back to those on the other side of the wall.

"We are liberating the ship one compartment at a time," came the reply. "It is now your turn."

Both pilots were crouched up against the fire door, trying to see through the slightest crack in its seal.

"Why should we believe you?" Balandin yelled.

"Because it is a friend who is telling you this," came the answer.

"What is our friend's name?"

"Aviation Specialist First Class Rudolv Seklovski . . ."

The pilots looked at each other. Indeed, Rudy was a friend of theirs, a man assigned to fix their planes. And they were relieved to hear his voice again. He'd left for mess call the night the trouble began, and had not been seen since.

"In you, Rodolv Seklovski, we trust!" Sotnikov yelled.

With that, they pushed the door open.

The next thing they knew, the pilots were looking down the barrels of five AK-47 rifles. Four of the men behind the guns were Russian Marines. Or so it seemed.

"You have tricked us, Seklovski?" Balandin roared at him.

"I have helped you," Seklovski said, standing a few paces behind the men with the raised weapons.

"By arranging for our executions?" Sotnikov asked bitterly.

"Calm down, pal," Smitz finally said, breaking through the wall of Team 66 men. "We're not here to shoot you. We're here to make you a proposition."

Norton heard the sound about ten minutes later.

It was a combination of gears grinding, chains rolling, and motors squeaking.

He, Delaney, Chou, and Reaney had been lying under the bleeding Kamov, waiting for just such an earsplitting squeal. Looking up through the rain now, they saw the hangar elevator, which had been locked in a halfway position above the forward part of the aircraft bay, rising fully to the top of the deck.

The knuckleheads had come through.

"Well? Now what?" Delaney asked Norton.

Norton inspected the chopper's undercarriage. It too had taken some bullet hits, but at least all the wheels were still inflated.

"The question now is," he said finally, "how hard is it going to be to push this thing?"

Suddenly the thirty feet or so to the rear aircraft elevator looked like a mile.

"Only one way to find out," Delaney said.

With that he got in back of the right front tire and, leaning his shoulder into it, started to push.

Norton, Chou, and Reaney soon joined him on the other three wheels and slowly but surely, the Kamov started to roll.

But no sooner had they moved it a few feet than the storm of tracers started again—and many of them were pointed right at them.

"Shit!" Delaney yelled as the sickeningly familiar sound of bullets pinging returned. "Don't these guys ever get tired?"

"Keep pushing!" Norton was yelling.

And push they did. The gunfire was all around them, but the four men kept the Kamov rolling and after much effort, somehow made it to the middle of the aircraft lift.

"Take us down!" Norton was now yelling to those below.

Delaney crouched beside him and almost started laughing.

"Those assholes in the Island must be wondering who the fuck we are and what the fuck we are doing," he said.

Norton turned to reply. That was when he saw the bright flash of a tracer bullet go right by him and hit Delaney in the chest.

His friend was thrown over on his back, hitting his head hard on the icy flight deck.

Legs bent awkwardly, arms collapsed at his side, Delaney let out one great gasp of air—and then stopped moving.

Gene Smitz was pushing the big red button with all his might—but nothing was happening.

The button was supposed to activate the mechanism that lowered the aircraft elevator. But for some reason, the lift just did not want to work.

He could hear Norton and Chou yelling from up top that they needed the elevator taken down—and fast!

Smitz could also hear them screaming that someone had been shot.

Growing furious, Smitz balled his fist, wound up, and with all his might, punched the red button. He succeeded in breaking a knuckle on his right index finger—but apparently that was what it took to make the mechanism work.

A second later came the sound of gears grinding and chains meshing, and finally the elevator started coming down.

It seemed to take a very long time, but the lift was actually at the bottom of the hangar bay inside of ten seconds. The Kamov helicopter was dripping water in some places, frozen in ice in others. Under the chopper he saw Delaney stretched out, both Chou and Norton cradling his head.

The Team 66 men rushed forward, as did Smitz. The center of Delaney's uniform had been blown away. There was blood all over him; his arms and face were covered with it. Or at least it looked like blood.

"Jessuz . . . Delaney?" was all Smitz could say.

But then he saw something that bordered on both the grotesque and the miraculous.

Though it appeared that Delaney's chest cavity had been

torn away, the pilot groaned, rolled over, and somehow got to his feet. He began staggering towards Smitz. Arms outstretched, he looked like something from a horror movie.

"Jessuz! Get him back down!" Smitz yelled to the Team 66 guys.

But the joke was on them.

The red liquid all over Delaney's uniform was hydraulic fluid. The hole in his chest had been caused by a bullet—but the round had only burned his clothing and had not penetrated his skin, even though he felt as if a sledgehammer had hit him in the rib cage. How had he survived such a direct shot?

He reached inside his suit and came out with a hand full of broken plastic, seared wires, and busted circuit boards.

It was his cell phone. The bullet had hit it instead of his heart.

19

Seaman First Class Sergei Konstannonskyi couldn't remember the last time he'd slept.

It was at least four days ago. Probably more.

He had gone without sleep for so long, in fact, something inside was telling him he would never be able to go to sleep again—ever. That didn't bother him too much. He'd been popping amphetamine pills for the past four days, and sometimes they made him feel so good, he didn't want to sleep again—ever.

Konstannonskyi was one of the original Sharkskis. He had been in on the nukes-for-money scheme nearly from the beginning. As one of several supply specialists on the *Kuznetsov*, it had been his role to smuggle aboard the five dozen AK-47 assault rifles and literally a half ton of ammunition with which the Sharkskis would secure the ship during the arms transfer if necessary. He was also one of several men responsible for putting the nukes into crates and getting them ready for transfer to the black marketeers' submarine.

When first learning of his dual role, Konstannonskyi had been ecstatic. His cut of the loot was almost a quarter of a million dollars, essentially for doing what he did aboard the ship anyway. Dreams of fine cars, a nice house, and the best whores in St. Petersburg had spun around his head for weeks.

But now, he was earning that quarter million—the hard way.

He'd been out on the flight deck of the *Kuznetsov* in the thick of the never-ending gun battle for the past forty-eight hours. He and sixteen fellow Sharkskis held a narrow railing directly across the flight deck from the center of the Island. As far as front lines went in this strange little war, they were it.

For the past two days and nights, they had been shooting at the ghosts who inhabited the Island—shooting but not sure if they were hitting anyone, shooting because the people who had so suddenly taken over the Island and the bridge in the midst of the staged mutiny, the people who had thrown a monkey wrench into the nukes-for-money deal, were shooting back. Shooting, because at the moment, there was nothing else anyone on either side could do. The people in the Island weren't going anywhere—though holding precarious positions, the Sharkskis virtually had them surrounded. But then again, the Sharkskis were finding it impossible to dislodge the Drugiye from even the smallest compartments they held down below, never mind from the massive Island itself.

The difference was, of course, the Drugiye were controlling the ship—and that was something the Sharkskis had to wrestle from them if there was any hope that the arms deal could still be salvaged.

So this was a war for war's sake across the flight deck. And in the two days of nonstop fighting, the only things that Konstannonskyi had for his efforts were skin so wet and cold it had shriveled him up like a dead man, and the habit his eyes had taken up lately of playing tricks on him when he least expected it.

Sleep? No, sleep was out of the question. At least not until this little war was finally settled.

And maybe not even then.

Konstannonskyi emptied his rifle's last few bullets into a window on the carrier bridge and then ducked down beneath the railing to reload.

If his brain was still working right, the Sharkskis currently had thirty-four men up on deck, besieging the Island. Their main force was here, with Konstannonskyi, arrayed along the port-side deck railing. But they also had a dozen gunmen on the starboard side, holding a position about one hundred feet forward of the Island. Another six men were in a gun nest off to his left, up where the carrier's deck veered inward at an angle.

The Sharkskis battle plan—if one could call it that—was to keep the pressure on the Drugiye up top in the Island while below decks the leaders tried to somehow undermine the mysterious men from within. Neither strategy was working too well. The fact that the Drugiye had nearly as many weapons as the Sharkskis was bad enough; the fact that they seemed infallible in their knowledge of the carrier and the best means to defend it bordered on the spooky. Whoever these enigmatic Drugiye were—and no one in the Sharkskis had the faintest idea who any of them could be—the tenacity and sheer bravery with which they were holding their positions were almost admirable.

Konstannonskyi's eyes had started playing tricks on him the night before. He'd been looking up at the impending storm when he thought he saw a corps of angels flying high above him. Earlier that day, he'd thought the tracer bullets coming out of his rifle had turned green, yellow, purple, and orange—every color but red, which, of course, was their true color.

He knew these were hallucinations caused by his lack of sleep and food—but he was not really prepared for the vision that materialized at the far end of the deck during a rare lull in the gun battle just before noon.

It was odd, but Konstannonskyi had not noticed that the helicopter that had been abandoned at the far end of the carrier during the bizarre assault the day before was not there anymore. One of his men had pointed this out to him, but in the rain and screaming wind, Konstannonskyi theorized it had fallen off, not knowing that some Shark-skis in another position further down the railing had actually fired on the people who had moved the Kamov off the deck about five hours earlier.

So it was with great surprise that Konstannonskyi heard the ungodly roar of a helicopter's engines starting up. The noise was so loud, it got everyone's attention on both sides of the pitched gun battle.

This racket continued unabated for nearly five minutes. Then suddenly from the rear of the carrier, they saw the aft aircraft elevator rising to the top. It was carrying the Kamov helicopter on it.

But something was very wrong here. The chopper looked to be in such bad shape, it seemed impossible that it could actually fly. Its exhaust pipes were belching large clouds of thick black smoke. Its engines sounded perfectly horrible. Konstannonskyi swore he could see bolts of flame shooting out of the rear of the engine mounts, some-times igniting gas vapors in the exhaust flow and causing a sharp quick *boom!*

Perhaps even stranger, there were huge holes cut out of the chopper's left hand side, and now a gaggle of gun barrels was protruding from those openings.

Seemingly defying all laws of aerodynamics, the heli-copter began to rise very unsteadily over the aircraft lift. The winds began blowing it crazily in several directions at once. The flames shooting out of the back of the aircraft became more intense. Indeed, to Konstannonskyi's eyes, this looked like a helicopter that had been shot down and was suddenly rising from the dead, coming back to life before their eyes.

That was when Konstannonskyi thought to himself: *I really got to get some sleep.*

Now came some scattered firing at the aircraft from both the Sharkskis' positions and those of the Drugiye on the Island. Everyone just assumed that the helicopter had been commandeered by some crew members caught in the middle of the little war and was now being used to escape—though just how far an aircraft that was just barely flying could go in this weather was debatable.

But the people inside the chopper had a surprise for those on deck.

Instead of turning east and leaving the aircraft carrier behind, the chopper actually began moving along the flight deck towards the Island.

Whether it was surprise or shock, all firing stopped as the chopper bore down on the superstructure. With a great puff of smoke, it jigged to the right and went by the Island on the seaward side, leaving Konstannonskyi's view momentarily.

When it reemerged in front of the Island, he could see that the guns poking out of its fuselage were now blazing away. There were at least six of the them and the combined aerial fuselage was ripping into the Island's bridge, doing more damage in a few seconds than Konstannonskyi and his men had been able to do in more than two days.

The suddenness, the totally unexpected aspect of the attack had even made the Drugiye's guns fall silent. The chopper swept right around the Island, passing again over the deck, its guns still firing nonstop. Konstannonskyi could see a shower of glass and metal explode out from the bridge level as the chopper's gunmen tore up the windscreens, the radar dishes, and antenna poking out of the Island's lower roof.

Like fools, Konstannonskyi's men began cheering at this. Whoever was flying the Kamov had obviously come to their aid, so they thought. Taking cover, maybe even panicking, the Drugiye inside the Island were suddenly getting the worst of the two-day battle. And the Sharkskis had the people in the helicopter to thank for this grand turn of events.

But Konstannonskyi was smarter than that. He knew that they were not worthy of such a miracle—and he was right. For as soon as the chopper completed its slow, deadly pass by the Island, its pilots gunned their balky engine, went into a slight hover, put the aircraft into a 180-degree turn, and then started forward again.

That was when the Sharkskis stopped cheering.

Now those aerial guns were pointing at them.

"Get down!" Konstannonskyi yelled to his men, but the helicopter was moving way too fast for all of them to comply. The barrage from the half-dozen AK-47's came a second later. Four of his men were caught in it immediately—all four were blown right off the boat. The noise was tremendous, sparks were flying all around Konstannonskyi. Though common sense defied it, he dared to take a peek over the railing. For his trouble he found the chopper hovering so close to him, he could actually see the faces of the men behind the guns.

They were wearing the battle dress of Russian Marines.

The Kamov made two more passes by the Island, and then two more passes by the Sharkskis' positions.

At one point a Sharkski gunner positioned near the flight-deck angle opened up on the Kamov—and paid the price. The chopper immediately turned on its tail and bore down on the small gunner's nest, its combined rifle assault throwing up a spray of sparks that lasted more than ten seconds, killing three of the six men stationed there.

Only then did Konstannonskyi scream to his men not to fire at the Kamov.

Message received, he thought. *We don't shoot at you, you won't shoot at us.*

Then all firing on both sides of the flight deck ceased. The Kamov, its engine still smoking mightily, stopped firing as well. Its pilots jerked the aircraft back around the Island again, and then slowed into a hover over a spot just forward of the superstructure.

Konstannonskyi watched this strange maneuver, and knew immediately what the people in the copter were up to. They were hovering over the recessed launching platform for the RMB-1750 missiles, two of which the Drugiye had already fired off.

Just as he had guessed, the copter tipped a bit to the side, and then the combined rifle barrage began again— this time right into the missile-launching area itself.

"They don't want us," Konstannonskyi said aloud. "They want those missiles."

With some fascination, he and his men watched as the people in the chopper poured rifle fire down into the launch tubes. Small packets that appeared to be filled with gasoline were dropping from the copter as well.

As they were doing this, no one was firing at them—it was almost as if no one dared, especially from the Shark-skis' positions.

The Drugiye were also curiously silent.

They found out why a few seconds later.

It would never really be clear whether it was the combined gunfire from the rifles aboard the shaky Kamov or someone inside the carrier's Combat Room pushing a button— but about fifteen seconds after the Kamov took up its position over the launch tubes, the carrier's hull began shaking violently.

Then came a huge burst of smoke from right below the hovering helicopter. At first Konstannonskyi thought that the men on the copter had hit something vital and that the innards of the launching platforms were blowing up.

But then a dual stream of flame shot out of the launch tube. These plumes were so powerful and had come so suddenly, they pushed the Kamov at least thirty feet straight up into the air.

The missile emerged two seconds later.

The glare from its engine flare was so bright, it blinded Konstannonskyi and his men. Holding his hand over his eyes, Konstannonskyi was astonished to see the RMB-1750 rise out of its launching tube, its primary motors holding it stationary for just a second. Then, the missile's much more powerful secondary motor kicked in and it began to shoot away.

But simultaneously, the Kamov was falling back towards the deck. By a coincidence of angles and gravity, the tail of the copter collided with the rapidly ascending missile about twenty feet above the deck. There was a huge explosion. Half the Kamov simply disintegrated in the air. The forward half began falling very quickly. The missile, meanwhile, continued its ascent. But the collision had thrown off its guidance system, and it began to wobble out of control.

Konstannonskyi felt his heart begin beating madly. He watched the RMB-1750 turn over to the horizontal and start flying crazily, like an out-of-control bottle rocket. This was a missile with a 150-kiloton warhead in its nose and it was flying in loops, circles, figure eights above the water, sometimes heading right at the carrier itself.

Finally, though, it started going straight up. But it quickly lost power and turned over. It hit the water an instant later, smashing into the waves about a half mile from the carrier and blowing up with a concussion so severe, it made Konstannonskyi's ears bleed.

But the warhead did not detonate. It sank quickly to the bottom along with the rest of the missile.

No sooner had this happened than Konstannonskyi

turned back to see the Kamov, on fire, gyrating wildly, yet still airborne even though its tail section was missing.

He knew right away this was a battle that gravity would win, and sure enough, a moment later the big copter began plummeting to the deck.

Konstannonskyi screamed to his men to get below, and with him scrambling right behind them, they all managed to get through the nearest hatchway and get the door closed and locked before the copter plunged into the flight deck not twenty feet from their former position.

The resulting explosion was so powerful and the flash of fire so bright, it actually leaked through the sealed hatchway. Konstannonskyi and his men hugged the walls as the vibration from the copter crash reverberated throughout the ship.

Then it became quiet again. All they could hear now was the crackle of flames and the roar of the ocean.

It was clear to them that no one could have survived such a crash.

"Crazy, but brave men," Konstannonskyi muttered. "Whoever they were."

The first thing Norton recalled after coming to was a strange ringing in his ears.

He tried to open his eyes, but this slight movement caused him such excruciating pain he had to stop halfway. For some reason, his lips seemed very dry and when he licked them, he tasted blood. He spat—and one of his teeth came flying out.

"Jazz? Jazz!"

Norton shook his head. The odd ringing was even louder now.

"Jazz? You still with us, dude?"

Norton finally opened his eyes and found himself looking up into the weary, burned face of Gene Smitz.

"I'm here," he heard himself blurt out. "Wherever 'here' is."

He felt two hands yank him up by his collar, and sit him up. Then he realized that he was leaning against the back of the carrier's sub-deck railing.

It started coming back to him slowly. The Kamov, firing at the Island, firing at the Sharkskis, trying to destroy the missile tubes . . .

"Jessuz, what happened?" he asked Smitz finally.

"Let's just put it this way," Smitz said, also speaking through bleeding teeth. "Santa Claus is safe . . . at least for the time being."

Then the rest of it came flooding back. The RMB-1750 had hit the Kamov and the Kamov had come down hard. Norton remembered flames, breathing in a lot of smoke, being soaked with some kind of fluid—from the smell of it, aviation fuel.

After that, it was all a blank.

He suddenly sat up. He could see a handful of men crouched beside him. He started picking out faces. Everyone was there—except Delaney.

His friend had been flying the Kamov during the desperate mission, and Norton's last image of him was battling the chopper's controls as the aircraft was falling out of the sky.

Just as Norton was about to ask Delaney's whereabouts, the man himself came flying out of nowhere, leaping down onto the railing, nearly flattening Smitz and Norton in the process.

He was carrying three AK-47's under both arms.

"Took these off of those dead Sharks over there," he said, indicating the gun position formerly held by the Russian sailors before the Kamov had strafed it. Then Norton realized for the first time exactly where they were. They were huddled under the *Kuznetsov*'s flight deck's angled edge.

This put them about two hundred feet diagonally across from the Island. Between them and the Island was the burning wreckage of the Kamov, which coincidentally had come down nearly on top of the ammo chopper that had crashed during the abortive chopper assault the day before.

Delaney squeezed into a small area between Smitz and Norton.

"Hey, Jazz, enjoy your nap?" Delaney asked him.

"How . . . how long have I been out?"

Both men shrugged.

"Half hour maybe?" Smitz finally replied.

Norton shook his head again. Some of the cobwebs were brushed away, all except the persistent ringing in his ears.

"What's our situation?"

Smitz and Delaney just laughed.

"In two words," Delaney replied, "we're fucked."

He pulled Norton up to his knees and put one of the Russian Marine scoop helmets on his head.

This allowed Norton to take a look across the flight deck. There was still gunfire coming from the Island, most of it being directed at Shark positions further down the railing and directly in front of the superstructure. But he also became aware of bullets pinging around their position as well, and the Team 66 men were returning it with gusto.

"Now instead of two sides shooting at each other," Smitz explained, "there are three of us down here. . . ."

Though he was still woozy, it was beginning to sink in for Norton. They had crashed onto the deck and scrambled to the nearest safe position, but by doing so had come down right in the middle of the gunfight between the Sharkskis and the Drugiye, thus creating . . .

". . . a three-sided war," Smitz said for him. "We're shooting at two groups, and two groups are shooting at us, even while they are still shooting at each other. Complicated enough for you?"

Norton took a glance at their ammo supply. They barely had two clips per man. There were Sharkskis to their right, and directly across the deck from them. They were now exposed to the elements, with no way to go on the railing itself.

"And the hatchway here," Smitz was telling him, pointing to the nearest door, "is double-welded shut."

Norton just looked back at Delaney.

"Just like I said," Delaney told him with a grim smile. " 'We're fucked.' "

"A very astute military analysis," Norton replied.

Norton knew this was not good. While they might have succeeded in destroying the third RMB-1750 missile, they had most likely done so at the expense of their own lives. They were trapped out on the flight deck, with little ammunition, little protection, nowhere to go, no one to call, pinned down from all sides by two well-armed groups—all while the clock was ticking away and the ship was getting closer every minute to the fatal Zero Red Line.

How could it get any worse than this?

"Jessuz Christ!" he heard Delaney bellow, almost in reply to his unspoken question.

Delaney had a look of absolute horror on his face. He was pointing numbly, not to anything on the flight deck, but in the opposite direction, out to sea.

Both Norton and Smitz twisted around to see what had frightened Delaney so—in an instant they had their answer.

The huge black storm that had been hanging in the background for the past day and a half was suddenly right beside them. Not a mile off the bow, the gigantic swirling clouds were bearing down on them just like an anticipated wave coming crashing toward a shore. In front of it was a sheet of rain so thick, it made the constant downpour they'd experienced since coming aboard the *Kuznetsov* seem like a spring shower. The waves below the tempest were rising up to thirty feet or more. The winds, now eerily calm, would soon be blowing at seventy knots.

And it was all heading right for them.

Norton was speechless—he'd never seen anything quite

as large, quite as frightening as this. At that moment the storm seemed big enough to swamp even the massive aircraft carrier.

"We're double-fucked now," he heard Delaney say. "Make that triple-fucked."

But strangely, in this calm before disaster hit, Norton became aware of yet another oddly familiar sound. The ringing in his ears. It wasn't bells exactly, it sounded more electronic. And this time, it wasn't his imagination.

He reached deep down into his torn and oil-stained combat suit, into a utility pocket down near his waist, and came up with his cell phone.

It was ringing.

"You've got to be shitting me," Smitz said, realizing what was going on. "*Now* someone calls us?"

Norton calmly hit the receive button and listened.

"Jazz? Jazz! *Are you there?*" a voice asked anxiously.

It was Jimmy Gillis.

20

Marty Ricco was downing his sixth cup of coffee of the morning when Gillis finally got through to Norton's cell phone.

They had spent the last twelve hours inside the *Battev*'s boardroom, redialing both Norton and Delaney's phone numbers, getting busy signals and endless ringing for replies.

Ricco was simply amazed that they had actually gotten through. This meant that Norton, at least, was still alive and the mission, such as it was, still had a life too.

But from the look of the hasty scribbling Gillis was doing, that also might be a temporary thing.

"All Americans alive . . ." was the first note Gillis had scribbled down. This was followed by, "All Russians dead."

These were followed by a series of phrases like "pinned

down," "low on ammo," "storm has arrived."

Gillis was having a very hard time talking to Norton, which made it even more difficult for Ricco to follow along. But clearly their colleagues were in dire straits.

The connection broke off about thirty seconds into the call. Gillis tried redialing again, but it was no use. This time there was no busy signal, no endless ringing. Nothing.

Gillis finally gave up and then looked at the words he'd scratched out.

"They are in a very bad way," he told Gillis. "They've got themselves stuck out on the flight deck of that floating pig with Russians all around them, shooting at them."

He tried to decipher some further scribbling.

"They nailed one of the RMB-1750's," he said. "Or it nailed them. Either way, there's only one of those SOBs left."

"Yeah, but one's enough," Ricco said.

They were both silent for a long moment. Finally Ricco broke the spell.

"Well, now that we've finally got through to them . . . what can we do to help them? It doesn't look like we've got a lot of options."

Gillis just shook his head. "Even if our Kamov was in top shape, if we tried to pull them of off that deck in this weather—well, we might as well shoot ourselves now for all the good that would do."

Ricco bit his lip.

"We've got to do something," he said. "I mean, despite all the bullshit we've gone through with those guys, you and I both know if it was us out there, they'd come for us somehow."

Gillis nodded grimly.

"I have to agree with you," he replied.

Ricco looked at the last line Gillis had scribbled on the sheet of paper. Try as he might, he could not translate it.

"What's this?" he asked, pointing to the scribbled last line.

Gillis studied it and then just shook his head.

"The last thing Norton said was: 'We'd need a tank to get us out of this one.' "

Ricco laughed grimly.

"Just like Norton to ask for the impossible when the world is coming down around him," he said. "I mean, where the hell would we find a tank?"

At that moment, Gillis's cell phone rang again. It startled them for a moment. He hit the receive button, expecting it to be Norton sounding very far away, updating them on their very hopeless situation.

But it wasn't Norton. Instead it was a deep voice, with a slightly Western twang to it. Its owner sounded elderly, but clear and strong.

And very eerie indeed.

"Listen up, Jimmy," the voice told Gillis. "I'm only going to tell you this one time. . . ."

21

Somewhere in the North Atlantic
1330 hours

The SS *Ashmont* was not a military ship per se.

It was a heavy cargo hauler, under contract to the U.S. military as part of the prepositioned war materials program. Basically a container ship, the *Ashmont* had spent the last two years shuttling heavy equipment—APCs, missile batteries, tanks—to points near the Middle East, most notably Diego Garcia, the small Indian Ocean island that supported a huge American supply base. The thinking was this: Because the Pentagon assumed that a military confrontation in the Middle East was always a good bet, it was smart to preposition a lot of the war materiel that would be needed by the troops when the call came.

The *Ashmont* had made the trip from the U.S. to Diego Garcia no less than sixteen times in the past twenty-four months. The usual run consisted of hauling the heavy equipment plus spare parts to the Indian Ocean base and then returning to the U.S. with any broken-down or obsolete equipment, or workable weapons that for one reason or another were being sent home.

That was what it was doing this day—after having left the Med twenty-four hours before, it was steaming west, towards Charleston, South Carolina. On board was a menagerie of heavy assault weapons: an Abrams M1-A1 tank that needed a thorough engine job; an ancient M110A2 self-propelled gun that the Army was selling to the National Park Service for starting controlled avalanches; a half-dozen M198 howitzers whose barrels needed realigning; and a truck/tractor portion of an MLRS rocket launcher that had wound up on Diego Garcia without its connecting weapons pack.

Also on board was a battered U.S. Marine Corps LAV—or Light Armored Vehicle. The LAV was a combination light tank and armored personnel carrier. It was about twenty feet long, almost nine feet high, and eight feet wide. It rolled on six heavy-duty tires, not tank tracks, but it did carry a 25-mm cannon on a turret, an M240 7.62-mm coaxial machine gun, and a .5 Browning M2HB heavy machine gun. It could accommodate up to six people, could go sixty miles per hour on a hard surface or six miles per hour in the water.

The important thing about the LAV, though, was its weight. As its name indicated, it was "lightweight"—if one could consider fourteen tons lightweight. This meant it could be airlifted by a cargo plane very easily—and even a helicopter, if the chopper had the balls.

It would be this question of weight, and just how ballsy a Kamov-27 helicopter really was, that would bring the SS *Ashmont* into the drama happening about 150 miles to its north.

The first indication that this would not be a uneventful trip for the cargo ship came when a strange message was received in its communications hut shortly after 1330 hours on December 24th.

The communications officer had just poured himself a cup of coffee when his board came alive and began transmitting a message to the *Ashmont* on a little-used military-band radio frequency.

The radioman double-checked his comm set—this wave band was utilized so infrequently he thought something was askew with his equipment. But a quick check told him that was not so. All his gauges lined up, all his switches were in their right positions.

The radioman then pushed the receive button and responded to the call. The teletype began printing out.

"This is a high-priority emergency message, security level six," the first line of the message read.

The radioman was more baffled than anything else. Why would a high-security message be coming into the *Ashmont*?

The only possible explanation was that the ship was being ordered to reverse course and head back to the Middle East, perhaps because some kind of conflict was about to flare up.

But the next part of the message dispelled that notion.

"Please confirm that you are carrying a Marine Corps LAV serial number 6172827397."

The radioman grabbed the ship's manifest and quickly turned to the list of equipment belowdecks. He confirmed that such a vehicle was on board and hastily typed out that reply.

"You are to lighten the vehicle by at least two tons and have it unpacked and topside by 1430 hours," the message went on.

The radio man just stared at the teletype. What the hell was this?

He hastily typed in the code asking for the message to be confirmed as it was "garbled in transmission."

But the same message clacked out several seconds later,

followed by a dire coda: "This order comes from the highest authority, code of the day: Vivid Emerald."

The radioman grabbed his military codebook, looked up the code words, and saw that the message was coming directly from the White House.

To this the radio man had no choice but to reply: "Message received. We'll try our best."

The captain of the SS *Ashmont*, having been alerted to the strange message, was now on his bridge, electronic binoculars in hand.

A series of subsequent messages from the same mysterious source had instructed him to turn to a course due north at full speed. This was a troubling order to fulfill. The huge storm was racing southward, and if the *Ashmont* had not been drawn into this new situation, they would have skirted the tempest with a few hours to spare.

Now they were being asked to sail right into it—at top speed.

The LAV was up on deck as instructed by 1400. After reading and reconfirming the original message, the captain had instructed four of the ship's engineers to start stripping the LAV of all nonessentials: repair treads, extra batteries, towing chains, and so on. They had no way to weigh the LAV, of course, other than a guesstimate when the deck crane was pulling it out of the ship's hold. So they also took out the radio set, all the external flare dispensers, and the spare tires.

The engineers test-fired all the guns—each one was functioning. They also got the engine warmed up and oiled.

By 1415 hours, the LAV was as light as it was ever going to be.

Fifteen minutes later, the Russian chopper showed up.

One of the secure messages to the *Ashmont* told the captain that an unmarked Naval helicopter would be coming to retrieve the LAV and that he and his men should assist this aircraft crew in getting the LAV off the deck.

The captain knew that when in use, LAVs were usually airlifted by the Marines' CH-53 Sea Stallion, huge choppers that doubled as heavy lifters and troop carriers.

But when his radar man reported that a helicopter had been spotted inbound from the north, the captain did not expect to see a relatively small antisubmarine chopper. Nor did he expect it to be Russian in design.

It was, of course, the Kamov-27 from the *Battev*. Like the LAV, the chopper had been stripped of all unnecessary equipment to lighten its load. Like all Russian choppers, the Kamov was known to be overpowered, if not overpowering. But the LAV weighed now about twelve tons—carrying one at full weight was a task even for a behemoth like a CH-53. Would the Kamov be able to pull it off?

That certainly was the number-one question on the minds of the Russian chopper's pilots, Jimmy Gillis and Marty Ricco.

They'd flown the aircraft from the *Battev* thirty-five minutes before, and made a beeline to where they hoped the *Ashmont* would be.

That they were able to find it on the first try was a small miracle in itself. Had they strayed from their course by just a few degrees, they might have spent hours trying to locate the cargo ship. But for once in this long adventure, the stars had aligned for them. They found the cargo ship quickly and with a minimum use of fuel.

Now came the hard part.

They did not want to land on the *Ashmont* and get into a conversation on how best to pick up the LAV. There was no time for that, plus the fuel they would use on such an exercise would only serve to further drain their tanks. As it was, if this all worked out, they would make it back to the *Battev* on just fumes—if they made it back at all.

So they circled the cargo ship once, and watched as the captain slowed his vessel considerably. Then they lowered the Kamov's cargo-lift assembly from the automatic mine-laying winch in the back. The assembly was really no more than a heavy-duty chain about twenty-five feet long that held five lighter chains at its end, like five fingers on a hand. The hooks would be attached to strong points on the LAV and secured by the *Ashmont's* crew.

The moment of truth would come when they gave the chopper the gas.

If the LAV moved at all, then they knew there was a good chance the Kamov could lift it. If the small tank didn't budge on the first try, then this would all be an exercise in frustration—and wasted time and fuel.

Gillis was behind the main controls of the Kamov. He went into a ragged hover while the *Ashmont*'s crew attached the LAV to the lift chain. This took about two minutes. Coordinating the operation from the cargo bay, Ricco was checking his watch like a madman throughout.

Finally, an indication came from the deck crew. The small tank was hooked up. Now it was the chopper's turn. Gillis gave the Kamov the gas and heard the big engines roar in reply. If anything, the chopper's coaxial rotors became even noisier. Gillis lifted the control column and gave the LAV a jerk.

The engines screamed, the rotors roared—but the LAV did not budge.

Gillis tried again. More gas. More noise. More black smoke from the engines.

Again, the LAV did not move.

This was not good. The wind was picking up, the waves growing, the ship was starting to pitch—and it was all Gillis could do to keep the Kamov in a reasonable hover.

He gave it another go. He pushed the fuel levers as far north as they would go and jerked on the stick with all his might.

Nothing . . .

Gillis's mind started racing. He was burning fuel, time. The LAV was too heavy—but maybe not by much. Yet

the small tank had been stripped of just about everything
extra but its guns and ammo.

He craned his neck and looked out the open window
down at the armored vehicle. What was on it that it
wouldn't need in the next life?

That was when a strong wind came up and nearly
knocked the Kamov out of the sky. The chain tightened
and the LAV started rolling dangerously on the deck.

All this went through Gillis's brain in a microsecond.
The chopper bucking, the chain close to snapping, the
LAV rolling, scattering the *Ashmont*'s crew.

That thing has too many wheels. . . .

And that was when he got one last good idea.

He gave the crew a signal telling them to wait. Then he
pulled out a pen and paper and started scribbling madly.
He gave the note to Ricco, who wrapped it in a cockpit
wrench and threw it out the open window.

It got caught in the stiff wind, but finally clanged down
onto the *Ashmont*'s deck.

The note was retrieved—and the *Ashmont*'s crew went
right to work. They came up with a simple lug wrench
and a couple of hammers. Two minutes later, two of the
LAV's tires and wheels had been removed. Ricco got a
signal from the deck crew; he yelled for Gillis to try again.
More gas, more stick, a mighty jerk—and the damn thing
finally moved.

Gillis thought he heard a cheer from the *Ashmont*'s
crew—or maybe it had come from Ricco, or even his own
throat. But he had no time to savor the moment.

He started moving the Kamov sideways, slowly but
surely. Clearing the edge of the deck, he felt the LAV sag
a bit.

"More throttle!" Ricco yelled forward to him.

Gillis complied, but there really wasn't any more to
give. The Kamov started dipping precariously. The water
started coming up at them very fast . . . but Gillis kept his

cool. He simply pushed his stick forward and changed the direction that all that energy was moving in.

The Kamov kicked a few times, but then grudgingly obeyed. The chopper started moving forward, the LAV dragging a bit behind.

Gillis let out a long whistle, and then turned the chopper north again.

He checked his watch. It was now 1435 hours.

They would have to hurry.

22

"Well, can this get anymore fucked up?"

Norton could barely hear Delaney even though his partner was screaming directly into his ear.

The cacophony of noise around them was incredible. Norton wasn't sure what was assaulting his eardrums more. The wind, howling like a thousand banshees. The roar of the ocean, deafening and frightening. Or the sound of thunder, going off like a string of howitzers. No doubt, the gigantic storm was in full blow.

Then there was the sound of gunfire.

It too was all around them. They were still hopelessly pinned down on the sub-deck railing, just forward of the angled deck. And the gunfight had indeed intensified into the most bizarre situation Norton could imagine in combat—a three-way firefight. The Sharkskis had set up a barricade about fifty feet from the angled deck. Using the two burned-out Kamovs for cover, they had the perfect firing point to shoot at both the American position as well as those on the Island. Meanwhile, the Americans continued taking gunfire from the Drugiye, even as the mysterious gunmen poured fire onto the Sharkskis' positions as well.

So there was a three-way stream of bullets crisscrossing the carrier deck, a crazy quilt of tracer fire, mixed in with the occasional heart-thumping report of a self-propelled hand grenade going off.

Norton and Delaney were trying hard to conserve their ammunition, but there was a basic human instinct to shoot back at the people who were shooting at you. The problem was, no matter how many bullets were pinging off the deck and ricocheting all around them, there was no way to tell from which side the gunfire was coming—the Sharkskis across the deck or down the railing from them, or the weapons of the Drugiye on the Island.

So against their better judgment, both men were popping up every once and a while and firing off a stream of bullets towards the Island and then the Sharkskis' positions. Their comrades along the rail were doing the same thing.

It had been going along like this for what seemed like three hours now.

With no end in sight.

Chou was now making his way up to where Norton and Delaney were positioned.

"Does anyone have any idea as to what the fuck is going on here?" the Team 66 leader asked them, trying to scream above the roar.

"We were hoping you knew," Delaney yelled back, firing off a burst at the Island.

"Well, whatever it is, it can't last much longer," Chou shouted. "We are running out of ammunition, and in these conditions, my guys will start dropping off from hypothermia any minute now!"

Their conversation was interrupted by a murderous three-way barrage of tracers, from their position to the Island to the battered helicopters and back again.

"This is fucking nuts!" Delaney yelled. "Maybe we should try to pal up with one of these groups—and work together to get the other."

An RPG round went off dangerously close to their position. All three men ducked quickly as a small storm of shrapnel went over the heads.

"Good idea, pard," Norton yelled as he checked his gun clip. "You want to be the one who goes out there waving a white flag?"

Another chilling three-way exchange of gunfire replied for Delaney.

"I think I'd rather freeze to death," he said.

"Be careful what you wish for," Chou cautioned him. "It might come true sooner than you think."

As if to emphasize that point, they all looked up and realized that it was beginning to snow very hard.

"Great!" Delaney spat. "*Now* we get a white Christmas!"

Norton checked his watch. They only had a few hours to go before they reached the Zero Red Line—and as far as they knew, the one last RMB-1750 launcher was still intact. All this would really go for naught if the Drugiye launched the last nuclear missile anyway.

"Hey, Joe," he yelled over to Chou. "Isn't there any way we can get across to that launcher?"

Chou stuck his head up over the lip of the deck. A storm of gunfire immediately came his way.

"Not that I can see," he replied, yelling over the gale. "I can't imagine crawling across, here or even up on the ski-jump tip. Plus we'd still have to make our way back down the other side and you can see those guys got the railing blocked."

He paused for a second.

"And with all the doors on this side welded shut," he

concluded, "I'd say we're stuck out here, to freeze our asses off—or get them shot out from underneath us. . . ."

"We just need one advantage," Norton said to himself. Yet there were none to be found.

Then they got some more bad news. It came from one of Chou's men. He scrambled up beside them, face frozen with snow, and pointed an icy finger towards the middle of the deck.

"Here they come!" he was yelling.

All three officers looked out and sure enough, they could see about a dozen armed men moving out from behind the wrecked chopper and climbing down onto the railing next to them. By moving along the outer railing, they would be upon the American position in less than a minute.

"Shit, this is not a place for a knife fight," Norton said. The railing was barely three feet wide. Any close combat here would be brutal and very bloody.

Chou sent the man back with orders to bring up the other Team 66 guys. They would have to make their stand here, at the elbow on the railing forward of the angled deck, simply because there was no place else to go.

Then even more bad news arrived.

Just as the first six Sharkskis appeared along the railing on the far side of the angled deck, Chou began pounding on Norton's back.

The pilot turned and followed the Team 66 CO's snow-covered glove towards the tip of the ski-jump. In the light of the tracer fire, they could see *another* dozen Sharkskis moving across the lip and down onto the railing walkway right in front of them.

"Jessuz! They're coming at us from both sides!" Norton yelled.

At that moment a burst of gunfire exploded over his head. Then there was an explosion—an RPG had gone off not ten feet away from them. It was only the angle of the deck that had deflected the blast away from them. By all rights they should have all been killed.

Norton raised his M-16 just as Delaney began firing. There was a crazy stream of tracers—it was blinding in intensity, and Norton found himself firing wildly in the general direction of the oncoming enemy.

Another grenade went off—this one launched by the other gang of Sharkskis moving in from the ski-jump tip. Norton and Chou twisted around and fired in that direction. Another storm of tracers came at them in reply.

Norton turned and again fired at the Sharkskis coming at them from across the angled deck. He emptied his rifle into a man not twenty-five feet from him, and quickly jammed in another clip—his second-to-last.

It doesn't matter. The crazy thought went through his head. *You'll be dead before you make it through this clip. . . .*

He started firing anyway. His stream of tracers combined with Delaney and two Team 66 troopers put up a wall of bullets in front of the advancing enemy. An RPG round exploded right above them—again, it was only the lip of the deck that saved them from getting their heads blown off.

Still Norton hit the metal deck hard. A burst of gunfire ripped up the walkway not two feet in front of him. He felt the steel splinters hit his face, and he immediately began bleeding from a hundred little cuts on his forehead and cheek. He managed to jam in his last clip and fire off a stream of bullets that nailed the Shark who had just shot at him. The man was no more than fifteen feet away when Norton's fusillade caught him in mid-chest with enough impact to hurl him over the railing to the raging sea below. Norton heard his screams all the way down.

Delaney was trying to help Norton up now, and fire his AK-47 at the same time. Norton could hear explosions going off behind him—the second gang of Sharkskis were over the tip and now on the very same railing way as the Americans were.

Norton somehow got to his knees and wiped the blood from his eyes. When he could see again, he noticed, of all things, how oddly beautiful the snow looked coming down in the glare of the tracer fire. It looked like a perverse Christmas display—tracers of yellow, red, and white flashing through the waves of snow.

So this is how it will end? he began thinking with startling clarity. *On a ship. In the middle of nowhere. In a storm. Fighting people he didn't know. On Christmas Eve?*

And he'd always thought he was destined to die in a plane crash. . . .

Another explosion. This one ten feet away. Another storm of shrapnel in his face. Norton wiped more blood from his eyes. Three Sharks were coming right at him along the railing. He fired off a three-round burst, but the men kept coming. He fired again. Still to no effect. The men were so close he could see their faces. He raised his gun to fire again—and that was when his clip ran out.

The men were looking down at him. One had a fire ax. He raised it over his head. . . .

A long burst of tracer fire came from over Norton's shoulder. It hit the man with the ax in the throat, shattering his head and taking off his shoulders in bloody clumps. His two companions were both gut-shot. They all went over the side. Norton looked up and saw Delaney's hand come down, grab him by the collar, and drag him further along the railing.

They wound up on a small platform built to hold one of the carrier's radar systems. The big radar dish and the equipment block gave them cover, but this was only a temporary solution. The American unit was now trapped here, with Sharkskis approaching from both directions on the railing and gunfire still coming from the Island itself.

One of Chou's guys appeared, wiped Norton's face clean, then smeared some kind of ointment on his forehead. It stung like crazy, but stopped the blood from running into his eyes.

Then the man took out a hypodermic needle and discharged it into Norton's right arm.

Norton's pain began fading away.

"Jazz? You okay?" Delaney was screaming in his ear. "You still with us?"

"Looks worse than it is," he was able to sputter.

Which was the truth. But now he could see his life coming to an end right in front of him. They were trapped. The enemy was advancing on both sides. Tracer fire filled the air. The wind was at full howl. The sea was crashing against the side of the carrier with such force, it was actually moving the huge ship sideways.

"We need a miracle now," he heard Delaney yell.

Yet in the utter earsplitting racket—above the screams of everything—Norton thought he heard another odd noise.

He wiped his eyes again—he wondered if it was the drugs. But there was a very mechanical buzz in his ears. Getting stronger. Getting closer. Was this what Death sounded like?

Or was it something else?

Like a helicopter . . .

What happened next would be told in several different ways by those who witnessed it.

Some things are certain. All agree that at the very moment the small American unit was about to get annihilated, a helicopter appeared out of the middle of the storm.

Its sudden arrival alone was enough to stop gunfire on all three sides. It tore through the blizzard, with a large object hanging from its cargo chain.

Some say the chopper made several passes, weaving in and out of the snow gusts, just missing the forest of antennas atop the Island at one point, at another nearly getting tangled up in the wreckage of the burned-out Kamovs further down the deck.

Others say the chopper strafed the carrier's bridge, silencing the gunfire there at least temporarily. But this might have been an optical illusion. The chopper did pass by close to the Island, so close it drew some sporadic gunfire—shooting by startled Drugiye gunmen—and many tracers bounced off the chopper's rotors. But these ricocheted back at the Island, giving the appearance that the chopper was firing on it, not the other way around.

In any case, the chopper finally came in low and dropped the object onto the carrier deck—it was only then that everyone on hand saw that the object was actually a small tank called an LAV.

It came down hard—this was no precision hover-and-drop operation here. The cargo chain let go while the LAV was still about twenty feet above the deck. It hit, bounced once, came down again, bounced again, and then finally came down for good.

There are those who say the tank rolled back and forth on the deck quite a few times before coming to a stop. Others say it came down and after it stopped bouncing, eventually rolled over to the side of the deck closest to where the Americans were trapped.

Then the gunfire broke out again. But it was the Americans who made it to the LAV first—that was another strange thing. Later on, when Gillis would be asked how he knew where to drop the LAV, flying as he was with no lights below him except the eccentric streaking tracer bullets, through heavy snow, in high winds, his answer was: He didn't know. He wouldn't even remember pulling the cargo-chain release lever, but the chain did not break, so he must have.

In any case, the LAV came down on the wildly pitching deck exactly where it should have.

In doing so, it saved the lives of the American team.

• • •

From Norton's point of view, heavily drugged and
wounded slightly as he was, the chopper's arrival came as
a screeching above everything else and then a gigantic
bang! as the LAV slammed down onto the deck.

How long it actually took for the armored vehicle to roll
over to them, he didn't know. In his mind, he heard the
chopper's approach, heard the LAV come down, and the
next thing he knew, he was running. Up over the lip of
the railing, onto the deck, through a stream of renewed
three-way tracer fire, and to the LAV itself.

He didn't remember actually leaping up onto the LAV,
though later on, others told him he did. His next conscious
thought was jamming himself down through the turret
hatch and into the cabin of the small tank—and then
having Delaney fall right on top of him. And Chou right
on top of him.

There was a near-farcical tangle of arms and legs as the
three tried to orient themselves. Already the sound of bullets pinging off the side of the LAV was reverberating
inside the tank. With no small amount of stretching and
kicking they finally found themselves settled. Delaney
wound up in the driver's seat, Norton was in the turret
behind the massive cannon, and Chou was beside him,
manning the coaxial machine-gun.

But immediately, there was a problem.

"I can't drive this thing!" Delaney yelled up at them. "I
don't know where to begin!"

"Just start pushing buttons and turning things!" Norton
yelled back down to him, trying as well to figure out the
cannon's firing mechanism.

"Look for a key or a start button!" Chou advised.

It was pitch black inside the LAV—that was the problem. And there was no way to turn on any interior lighting
until the engine was running.

High as a kite, Norton was also fully aware that the
shock of the sudden appearance of the LAV was beginning
to wear off both the gunmen inside the Island and those

creeping along the deck's outer railings. Both sides had turned their guns on the small tank and were firing wildly at it.

"Jessuz, pard!" Norton yelled down at Delaney. "Hurry!"

No sooner were the words out of his mouth than Delaney finally succeeded in pushing a button. The engine did not start—however, four high-explosive smoke canisters were shot out of the rear of the LAV, causing the gunmen on the forward railing to hit the deck and covering Smitz and the remaining Team 66 guys in a welcome blanket of thick smoke.

The next button Delaney pushed was the start button—at the same time he found the LAV's throttle. He pushed and pulled and poked and twisted and, inside of five seconds, the vehicle's mighty 325-horsepower engine roared to life.

Now came the matter of steering and going forward or in reverse. This took Delaney some practice. To those watching from the outside, the LAV began lurching madly. At the same time both Norton and Chou figured out how to fire their weapons. The result was a firestorm of chaotic fire that seemed to cover just about every square foot of the carrier deck and the port side of the Island.

This caused another cessation of gunfire from these points—and the billowing smoke aided in this. But Norton and Chou did not stop firing. As long as they were facing away from the Americans' hiding place, then they were firing at an enemy of one kind or another.

The LAV's cannon was huge, and it packed a punch so powerful that when Delaney's crazy driving turned the vehicle directly at the Island, a string of shells from the cannon had no problem puncturing the heavy steel of the carrier's superstructure.

But staying straight and level was a rarity. In fact, Delaney's wild steering had nearly driven them off the side twice in a fifteen-second span.

"Jessuz, Bobby!" Norton yelled. "How hard can it be?!"

At that moment, things finally clicked in for Delaney, and he was able to begin controlling the bucking LAV. The first thing he did was reduce the throttle. Then he was able to grab the steering controls and start coordinating his feet between the gas and brake.

The LAV settled down. Delaney backed it up ten feet and then pointed the front of the LAV so it was facing aft.

Then the makeshift tank crew got down to business.

Norton estimated there were as many as two dozen Sharkskis hiding behind the wreckage of the burnt-out choppers, now about fifty feet away from the LAV. Many more were stretched out on the deck itself, firing from a prone position.

Norton swung the turret aft. Then he pulled the firing mechanism.

A long steady stream of fire suddenly erupted from the cannon's huge muzzle. The wreck of both Kamovs began lighting up, not unlike a Christmas display. It was as if someone had suddenly turned on hundreds of tiny light-bulbs up and down the pair of twisted hulks. Soon these bits of lights began throwing off hundreds of angry sparks. Then small fires began to mushroom from the wreckage. Then puffs of smoke. Then came men on fire running in panic away from the fusillade.

Norton never let up on the trigger. After a long, punishing barrage, what was left of the two chopper wrecks and those hiding behind them went up in a huge ball of flame. The carrier shuddered from the explosion. When the smoke cleared, there was nothing left. The choppers were now just a pile of smoldering, white-hot metal. The men who had hidden behind them had been incinerated or like the choppers, blown apart.

Finally, Norton stopped firing. Silence fell upon the carrier. The snow still came down, sizzling as it landed in those few fires remaining where the wreckage had once been. The wind began howling once again.

Then the LAV turret turned around to the port side.

Gene Smitz saw the LAV's big gun swiveling over towards the smoky radar platform, and simply yelled out two words: "Get down!"

The Team 66 members alongside him needed no further prompting. All of them collapsed to the slippery deck and covered their heads. Chou opened up with the LAV's co-axial gun an instant later. Like ducks in a shooting gallery, he picked off more than a dozen Sharkskis advancing around the outside of the angled deck. Six of those unfortunates were immediately blown off the carrier. Three more were first cut in two, and then thrown over. It was a brutal, yet perversely clean disposal of the enemy gunmen.

After two more passes, the turret swung around toward the front of the ship. The Sharkskis there were already in full retreat, running in a panic up the slippery slope of the carrier's ski jump. But the high angle was death to them as both Norton and Chou opened up. Those hit by machine-gun bullets were simply stopped in their tracks. Those caught in the gunsight of the cannon were blown apart. This was brutal, efficient—and very unclean.

And suddenly, it got quiet again.

There was no more gunfire coming from anywhere. Only the sound of the wind blowing and the seas crashing could be heard. That and the soft sound of the snow hitting the bloody deck.

Then the LAV turned once again and leveled its weapons on the Island itself.

Seaman First Class Sergei Konstannonskyi considered himself a brilliant man.

Had he and his men not escaped belowdecks when the Kamov helicopter slammed into the deck, they would have all been killed, either in the crash or the fierce fighting that followed.

As it was, he and his dozen compatriots had been huddled below the flight deck since the chopper went down, listening to the battle going on just a few feet above their heads and agreeing that they wanted no part of it.

One of his men had stuck his head up briefly, and reported back to Konstannonskyi that the Russian Marines had somehow managed to drop a small tank onto the deck of the carrier, and that they were now in the process of ripping up the last of the unfortunate Sharkskis stuck up top.

This news gave Konstannonskyi pause—and it was not out of sympathy for his fallen brethren up on the bloody flight deck. No, he was doing calculations in his head. He knew that with each Sharkski that was killed, his take of the nukes-for-money deal increased by that much more—if the exchange could still be made, that is.

And that was a very large "if." But Konstannonskyi not only thought of himself as a brilliant man, he also was an opportunistic one. He had no idea who these "Russian Marines" were, or even if they were Russian or not. It made no difference to him. Whoever they were, there was a chance that their sudden infusion of firepower could turn things around to his advantage.

But like all great leaders and brilliant men, he would have to hurry to exploit the situation.

He gathered his men around him, and they began moving very quietly across the first level, directly under the flight deck. Their destination: the area known on the carrier as the Combat Rooms.

That they faced no opposition while crossing from one side of the ship to the other did not come as a surprise to Konstannonskyi.

Those mysterious Marines were doing battle against the Drugiye too, and that meant the people controlling the bridge, the Island, and the Combat Rooms would be soon fighting for their lives just as the Sharkskis were. Konstannonskyi expected some lapses in the previous invulnerable defenses as a result. And he was right.

He and his men walked right up to the main Combat Room itself unchallenged. This was the place where all the ship's weapons were controlled. Yet no welded doors blocked their way; no sentries were guarding any of the main hatchways. Just as Konstannonskyi had predicted, all of the Drugiye soldiers had been rushed to the front line, which in this case meant up into the Island itself.

Konstannonskyi himself was the first one to look through the thick glass of the window surrounding the main Combat Room. He saw two figures huddled up against the far hatchway, obviously listening to the chaos one level above them on the flight deck.

Konstannonskyi smiled. Just two individuals left behind to guard the rear?

The Drugiye weren't that smart after all. And for that, they were about to pay.

He called up his best marksman and silently worked out a plan. The two figures across the room were little more than shadows because of the low light in the combat center. Seaman Konstannonskyi wanted to eliminate them quickly but quietly.

On his count, he raised the butt of his rifle and smashed a hole in the window large enough for his shooter to push his rifle through. The man raised his AK-47 and took two shots. Both Drugiye soldiers went down without so much as a squeal, each dead from one shot to the head.

Konstannonskyi and his men flooded into the Combat Room. Not even bothering to look at the bodies, they were awestruck by the prize they'd just so easily garnered. Not only had they discovered the end of the miles of yellow electrical wire that ran all the way down to the nuclear weapons bay, they had also found the control panel for the RMB-1750 launcher, with several blinking lights indicating that the fourth and final missile was still functional and ready to go.

It was almost too good to be true—but that did not bother Konstannonskyi either. After all, he was a brilliant man.

He sat down in what would be the commander's chair and smiled at his men.

"*Vstrechayte novogo nachal'nika,*" he said. "Meet the new boss . . ."

Throughout all this, Gillis and Ricco were still in the air over the carrier, battling the high winds and snow, trying their best to see what was happening on the deck below.

It was clear to them that after dropping the LAV, there had come a storm of gunfire crisscrossing the ship. And after a few minutes, most of that gunfire had died down. Now they could see little or nothing at all. What did this mean exactly?

Had the LAV reached the people for which it had been intended? Or had they just caused a catastrophe by putting the heavy weapon into the hands of the very people trying to annihilate the American unit?

There really was only one way to make sure—by flying over the deck as low as possible, and trying to catch a glimpse of something, *anything*, that would answer these questions.

So Gillis put the Kamov into a tight spin, lowered their airspeed, and came down to an altitude of twenty-five feet off the deck. They ran the entire length of the ship this way, starting at the stern and moving forward. They overflew the wreck of both Kamovs, now just a pair of black smudges on the deck where they had been blown away by the LAV's cannon. They saw many oily, bloody spots along the sub-deck railing where the fierce battle had been the worst. Then Gillis flew through the cloud of smoke still rising from the point just forward of the angled deck—and that was when they saw a very beautiful sight:

One of Chou's guys was standing atop the radar dome waving a small American flag up at them. Gillis felt his heart lighten by a couple tons. Ricco slapped him a high five.

Their guys were still alive down there.

For the moment, at least . . .

They had agreed to stay over the carrier for as long as possible. The wind was doing an awful job on the Kamov's steering ability, and the mix of rain and snow was causing the chopper's engines to sputter. But they were determined to remain.

They went past the Island again, and that was when Ricco spotted a half-dozen Team 66 guys lining up behind the LAV. By the looks of it, they were preparing to attack the superstructure, using the small tank for cover and fire support.

And at that moment, Gillis had a strange thought. Maybe this bad dream was almost over. Maybe the American team could finally get inside the Island, oust its occupants, take control of the bridge, and put an end to it, once and for all.

"This might be wrapped up in ten minutes!" Ricco declared, bolstering his hopes. "Damn, maybe we *will* make it home by Christmas after all. . . ."

Gillis felt a strange warmth go through him. Was that really possible? *Home by Christmas?*

"Maybe . . ." he replied in a murmur.

They swept past the deck, pulled up, and turned around again. Now they could see scattered muzzle flashes erupt from below. Several fires had broken out around the Island as well. Obviously there was still some fighting left to be done. So it was odd that at this moment Gillis's mind started to wander.

He recalled reading once how the pilots of the famous Blue Angels jet demonstration team had become so used to flying their perfect formations, their minds would sometimes go to the most unlikely places even while they were in the midst of the most hair-raising supersonic maneuvers.

That was what happened to Gillis now.

His train of thought was triggered by the falling snow. Even out here, in the most hostile of environments, the thought of Christmas was impossible to get out of his mind. And that led to thoughts of his family, and of his home, and the tree, and the roaring fire. And of his wife and Kristin. And Ryan.

These thoughts went to the last time he'd been called away by the CIA. And when he'd returned home that time, he'd found Ryan at the playground, trying to play baseball all by himself. So they'd played together. Then he'd raced him home. Then his wife had fed him. A huge meal. And for dessert . . .

Apple pie . . .

And that was when it hit him.

The message. The one that kept repeating from this ship: Bats . . . balls . . . fruit . . . pie . . . mother.

Could it be as simple as that?

Suddenly Gillis was spinning the Kamov around again and looking frantically for a place to land.

"What the hell are you doing?" Ricco asked him, startled.

"We've got to get down there!" Gillis told him. "And I mean *right now*. . . ."

Norton pointed the LAV's cannon at the Island's main hatchway and opened up from twenty-five feet out.

Only with the tracers could he keep the stream of cannon shells concentrated on the sealed door. It took only about twenty seconds to disintegrate the hatch. It went in an explosion of deadly sparks and a cloud of smoke, which was blown away instantly by the gale. The middle part of the carrier shook from top to bottom. The LAV began moving forward again.

At ten feet out, Chou fired a long fusillade into the

newly opened doorway. Again, there was a storm of ricocheting bullets as the barrage tore away what was left of
the hatchway and the bulkhead beyond.

This done, the LAV backed up a little, allowing Smitz
and the Team 66 troopers to fight the high winds and
stream through the opening. Norton and Chou jumped
from the LAV and went in on their tails, leaving Delaney
and Sergeant Reaney to work the small tank. Already they
were elevating the cannon's muzzle to fire directly up into
the bridge.

In a scary piece of irony, the Americans began advancing through the same dark passageways and up the same
bloody ladders as Krysoltev on his ill-fated dash to the
carrier's bridge. They came upon the same burned bodies,
the same blind corners, the same blown hatches. It was
pitch black in some places, and the smell of death and
cordite was everywhere.

One small piece of Hell, Norton thought.

Using their dimming flashlights, he and Chou led the
way up to the second level. The signs of Spetsnaz battle—
and several other battles—were much in evidence here.
There were scorch marks and bullet holes everywhere.
Norton was trying to move quickly, but he was increasingly cautious of what—or who—he was stepping on.
He'd told Delaney to hold fire on the LAV until they broke
out onto the open bridge deck—that is, if they didn't draw
any fire first. If they could reach the bridge without any
fighting, that would leave them all with much more ammunition to use for the final assault.

They reached the second level, and that was where they
found the first welded-shut hatch. It was atop a vertical
ladderway; the weld marks were still warm.

A more careful operation might have suggested recon
at this point to seek out an alternative way to get up to
the next level. But they had no time for that.

Chou called up one of his men, who hastily ringed the
hatch with plastic explosives and with only a cursory

warning to the rest of the force, blew it to smithereens. Chou himself went up first, firing his weapon over his head in a 360-degree arc.

When they received no return fire, they pressed on.

By this time, Gillis had set the Kamov down just shy of the carrier's angled deck. Leaving Ricco to stay with the aircraft, he sprinted through the blowing snow, heading towards the LAV. The small tank was waiting, like a cat, poised to strike, right next to the Island.

Gillis was soaked by the time he reached the armored vehicle. Scrambling to the top, slipping and sliding the whole way, he saw a head just below the main turret. He reached in, grabbed its owner by the collar, and yanked him up through the hatch.

"Jessuz! *What the fuck!*"

It was Delaney.

He came out swinging, connecting a hard right to Gillis's jaw. The National Guard pilot went tumbling back over the rear of the LAV and falling hard to the icy deck below.

He did not miss a beat. He jumped right back up on the small tank, and cursing all the way, grabbed Delaney by the shoulders again and screamed at him: "Do not shoot this gun at that bridge. . . ."

Delaney looked back at Gillis, absolutely dumbfounded. "What the fuck? *Gillis? What the fuck are you doing?*"

Gillis was right in his face.

"I said: Do not shoot this gun . . . at the bridge."

Delaney was finally getting over the fact that Gillis was here, seething in front of him.

"What are you talking about? Don't shoot the gun?" he began yelling over the screaming wind. "You *dropped* the gun to us. Jazz and the rest of them are climbing that hill and when they get to the top, they'll need firepower and I'm giving it to them, full boot—kapeesh?"

"You can't!" Gillis yelled back. "It will be a huge mistake! And I don't have time to explain it to you—of all people."

He fell off the LAV again, and battled the high winds to the blown-open hatchway. Talking to Delaney was useless.

He had to catch up with Norton and Chou.

"Okay, get back . . . again!"

Norton, Smitz, and the Team 66 guys all hugged the bulkhead wall and blocked their ears.

Two seconds later, there was another huge explosion, another flash of fire, and then the inevitable cloud of smoke. They all started coughing. Chou went up the ladder, fired off ten rounds in all directions, and got no response. They pressed on.

This was the sixth hatch they'd blown in two minutes, and it was getting to be an earsplitting routine. They had encountered no resistance yet—but that was nothing to cheer about. Before the LAV was dropped on the carrier, the gunfire coming from the bridge level had been as intense as from the Sharkski gunmen, if not more so. This told Norton that what was waiting for them once they reached the top would not be pretty.

Whoever was up there was heavily armed, ruthless in their means of attack, and apparently feeding off an endless supply of ammunition. They would be holding not only the bridge, but a patchwork of cabins and passageways behind the main navigation room, places reinforced with enough steel to withstand all but a direct nuclear hit. It could be a bloody fight, trying to dislodge a fanatical force from such a strong point—if in fact the Americans even made it that far.

They finally reached the top hatch; beyond lay the outside railing and then the bridge. To their surprise, the hatch was not welded shut. Chou gave the quiet sign to all involved. There was a soft clicking of rifles as ammo loads were checked. Chou took out two magnesium grenades.

With admirable deftness, he raised the hatchway, threw the two grenades in two different directions, and then slammed the hatch back down again. There were two loud thumps—and then silence.

Chou looked at Norton, who just shrugged.

"Nowhere to go but up," Norton said.

Chou poked the hatch up with the butt of his rifle, ever wary that someone up top might be waiting with a grenade of their own to push back down at them.

But there was no such telltale ping of a grenade pin being pulled, no sounds of footsteps scurrying away. Chou looked up and over the lip and saw nothing but the heavy snow, blowing down.

He crawled up through the hole, the wind nearly sucking him out on its own. Norton and Smitz went up right behind him. Suddenly they were outside again—and it was at that moment that the storm seemed to reach its peak. The snow was blinding. The ship was pitching madly. The gale-force winds made it impossible to hear, impossible to speak. They were forced to crawl along the deck until they reached the outer railing. That was when they looked over the edge and peered down at Delaney below.

They'd expected him to be inside the LAV turret, cannon ready to open fire. Instead he was standing on the top of the LAV itself, waving his arms wildly and yelling something up to them.

But in the wild conditions, they could not hear him, so they had no idea what he was trying to say. And they didn't have the time to find out.

There was a dim light coming out of the multi-window bridge—they could see its reflection in the blowing snow. There was no evidence of any gunmen on the deck outside the bridge or in the mast full of antennas and radar dishes above.

That they had to assault the bridge quickly was a given. But how to do it against a hidden mysterious enemy, one that could be very well moving down into the ship, even as the American team was moving up, was somewhat of a dilemma. The Americans were clustered around a wide gangway that led to a narrow railing and the main door to the bridge itself. There was blood on the bridge entrance hatchway—Krysoltev's among others'—and hundreds of spent shell casings, many now hidden in the accumulating snow. This was silent testimony that any battle that began by rushing that door in force would be bloody and costly. There had to be a better way.

Chou crawled up to the bridge door itself and took out his trusty electronic combat stethoscope. He attached the business end to the door near the hinge and turned the device on. He listened intently for thirty seconds, then disconnected and crawled back to their position.

"They're still inside," he reported to Norton and Smitz. "Lots of Russian voices, whispering. Lots of sniffling. They might be snorting drugs for all we know. But they are still sailing the ship—I'm pretty sure I heard some navigational commands in there."

"Okay, now what?" Smitz asked, as the wind blew up again and the snow began whipping fiercely through the walkways at the top of the ship.

"Well, if they're so dumb to stay holed up in there long enough, I suggest we burn 'em out," Chou said. "There'll be no survivors—but we really can't worry about that at this point."

Norton and Smitz did not disagree.

Chou gave a signal, and two of his men crawled up to his position. He whispered a few instructions to them, and then the two men crept forward dragging a satchel of plastic explosives behind them.

Now came five minutes of excruciating tension as the troopers attached plastic explosives around the main doorway, the air vents, the electrical conduits, and anything that ran to the inside of the bridge. Their work was hampered greatly by the wind and blowing snow. The rest of the American team kept their weapons trained on the main bridge door, knowing that at any second a gunfight could break out, one that would be brutal in such extremely close quarters.

Finally, the explosives were laid in. The two troopers retreated, unfurling a long electronic fuse behind them.

"There's enough bang there to take off the top of the ship," Chou told Norton and Smitz. "We'd better get back down the hatch or we'll all go up with it. . . ."

No one needed any convincing. They all scrambled back down the hatchway, pulling the electronic fuse with them.

Once down below, they took a quick head count. Everyone was accounted for. Chou gave the trooper with the detonator the signal.

"Count it down," Chou said.

The trooper connected the leads and started counting backwards:

"Ten . . . nine . . . eight . . ."

That was when they heard a disturbance coming from below.

"Seven . . . six . . ."

Then came a running sound. Seven guns pointed down the blown-up hole.

"Five . . . four . . ."

"Wait! Stop!"

Norton looked down the ladderway to see the terrified face of Jimmy Gillis looking up at him.

"Three . . . two . . . one . . ."

"Don't do it!"

"Okay, hold it a second," Chou said.

The trooper with the detonator had about a half inch to go before he would have blown most of the bridge right off the ship, incinerating anyone inside.

"Jessuzz, Gillis," Norton yelled down at him. "What the fuck are you doing here?"

Gillis climbed up to their level.

"Look, you've got to listen to me for a second." The

pilot was speaking so rapidly he was tripping over his own words.

Chou turned to the trooper with the detonator.

"Stand down for a minute," he said.

The trooper disconnected the leads. The tension eased a bit.

Gillis opened his mouth to speak—but then he spotted Smitz. They hadn't seen each other since the climax of ArcLight.

"Smitty?" Gillis whispered, as if he was seeing a ghost. "What are *you* doing here?"

"It's a long story," the CIA man told him.

"Yeah, you two can have tea together," Norton said sharply. "But for now, spill it, Gillis—and it better be good."

Gillis caught his breath and gathered his thoughts.

"Did you guys hear the message that's been coming out of this ship since it was taken over?"

Norton and Chou just looked at each other and shrugged. Smitz nodded.

"The thing about the fruit bats?" he asked.

"No," Gillis corrected him. "It said: Bats . . . balls . . . fruit . . . pie . . . mother . . ."

"Yeah, so?" Norton said. "It's some kind of wacky code."

"Is it?" Gillis challenged him. "Well, maybe it's not so complicated."

Norton just stared back at the National Guard pilot. While he was grateful that Gillis had come through by dropping the LAV to them at just the right moment—and showing a vast amount of courage in doing so—he was in no mood for this shit. They were about to end this nightmare with the pressing of two leads to a detonator— why was Gillis taking this moment to play games?

But Gillis was dead serious—as always.

"Look, maybe everyone was reading that message all wrong," he began. "Maybe it's been a message for *us*—

or someone other than the arms dealers they were supposed to meet."

"What difference does it make?" Norton roared back at him.

Gillis turned to Smitz.

"Smitty, listen. Fruit pie—that could be apple pie. Bats and ball, that could be baseball. Mother, that could mean, well . . . mother."

Smitz thought a moment, but then shrugged. "So?"

"Baseball . . . apple pie . . . mother?"

The three of them just stood there thinking.

"Equals?" Gillis asked desperately.

"America?" Chou answered.

"Exactly!" Gillis roared. "Don't you see? If you had someone who couldn't speak the language but wanted to, how would they best define America? From a cliche they heard? Mom . . . baseball apple pie . . ."

"This is nonsense," Norton said. "That's a Chevrolet commercial, for God's sake."

But Gillis was gaining an unlikely convert in Chou Koo.

"But if you had just one opportunity to make a statement about America," the Marine officer said, "that might be the one a foreigner who can't speak English would make. . . ."

Norton was just shaking his head. "This is crazy," he said. "At best you might get a kid to send such a message, but . . ."

He stopped in mid-sentence.

"Jessuzz . . ." Norton murmured. "A kid?"

Now came a dreadful silence among them. They were all thinking the same horrible thing.

"No, that would be too crazy," Norton finally blurted out.

"Has anything that's happened in the past two days *not* seemed crazy to you?" Gillis asked him. "After what we've been through, would anything surprise you at this point?"

Norton turned to Chou. He was the true military man.
Norton and Gillis were just misplaced jet pilots and Smitz
was a Company man.

"What do you say, Joe?" Norton asked the jarhead.

Chou just shrugged. "I could give the word and that
bridge is nothing but little specks of dust in two seconds,"
he said. "But I'm worried about whether I could ever sleep
again, if we didn't . . ."

His voice trailed off.

"If we didn't find out first?" Gillis filled in the words
for him.

Chou just nodded, eyes down. "Yeah . . ."

Finally Norton had to agree.

"Okay," he said. "Let's go find out for sure. . . ."

Less than a minute later, they were all topside again. Guns
raised, Norton, Smitz, Chou, and Gillis crawled through
the blowing snow up to the bridge doorway, the rest of
Team 66 close behind.

Chou indicated to his demolition men that should anything unforeseen happen and the four officers got iced on
this fool's mission, they should blow the bridge immediately.

Then he reattached his listening device.

"I hear lots of voices," Chou reported to them in an
urgent whisper. "But who—or what—they belong to, it's
impossible to say."

Norton felt his fingers going numb. He wanted closure—
now.

"Fuck it—let's just take the direct approach," he suggested.

He motioned Smitz forward.

"How's your Russian?"

The CIA man shrugged. "Too good."

"Bang on the door," Norton told him. "Tell them we're
Americans. That we want to come in. That we are
friendly."

Smitz seemed confused.

"Really?" he asked. "Just like that?"

Norton looked at Chou, who looked at his five troopers. They were all in place, with free fields of fire should anything go wrong.

Smitz just shrugged. "Okay, here goes. . . ."

He banged mightily on the door and screamed out a long mouthful of Russian, emphasizing, "Amerikanskis . . ."

And to everyone's astonishment, after a few seconds, the door to the bridge slowly opened. . . .

The Americans froze in place. One wrong move on either side and a bloodbath would result.

Norton stood up, Gillis beside him, and toed the door open farther.

He pointed his flashlight inside.

What he saw were dozens of terrified faces looking back out at him.

"Son of a bitch . . ." Norton whispered.

They were all kids.

None of them were over the age of twelve. Most of them crying.

They were all holding AK-47's, yet some weren't as tall as their weapons. The bridge was awash in empty shell casings, bloody bandages, and spent ammunitions belts. A huge welding torch stood in one corner. Several bloody axes occupied another. The only things relatively clean on the entire bridge were the steering controls and the main systems panel. Next to the steering comm was an ancient reel-to-reel tape recorder, playing a single piece of tape in one continuous loop.

"Bitka . . . miachik . . . frukt . . . pinozhak . . . mats . . ."

Gillis held up his hand in a gesture of peace. "Who speaks English?" he asked.

A very dirty, very weary boy of eleven walked out of the crowd and raised his hand.

"I do," he said weakly. "Little bit . . ."

Gillis was beside him in a flash. He was Ryan's age.

"What do you want kid?" he asked the boy. "Why did you do all this?"

The kid started crying again.

"After all the bad things we had to go through, after seeing what the Sharkskis did, we only wanted one thing."

He paused, sniffed, and wiped his eyes.

"We just wanted . . . to go to America."

Norton took off his helmet and ran his fingers across his very tired head. He knew the faces of the thirty or so young boys staring back at him would haunt him forever.

"Kids?" he mumbled.

"Kids . . ." Gillis told him. "The sea scouts. Orphans . . ."

Norton just couldn't believe it. But it was impossible to deny: The mysterious Others who had commandeered the bridge soon after the Sharkskis made their move, were actually the Nahimoutsi, the sea scouts put aboard the carrier in Murmansk to fill out the depleted crew.

But could this happen? Really?

"I've seen nine-year-old soldiers in Africa," Chou said, answering Norton's question before he could ask it. "Middle East and Asia too. Give a kid a gun, teach him to point it—you've got an instant soldier. It's the latest rage."

"But how could a bunch of kids run an aircraft carrier?" Norton asked, as the Team 66 troopers began patiently relieving the boys of their weapons.

"Did you have any help, kid?" Gillis asked the English-speaking boy.

The boy was sniffling, but finally wiped his eyes, nose, and mouth and nodded.

"Yes," he said, pointing across the bridge to another darkened corner. "He told us what to do."

Norton directed his flashlight that way and sure enough, there was an old man huddled in the corner. He was dressed as the kids were, in a dirty T-shirt and baggy black pants. He too was crying.

"And who *the fuck* are you?" Norton yelled across the room to him.

The man did not reply.

That was when Smitz pointed his flashlight at the old man—and recognized him right away.

"Oh, man, how can this be?" the CIA man gasped. He looked as if he was seeing a ghost. And in a way, he was.

The old man was Admiral Kartoonov.

He wanted to go to America too.

In the Combat Room
Level 2

Seaman First Class Sergei Konstannonskyi had it all figured out.

The control panel to the left of the commander's chair operated the RMB-1750 launch systems. It consisted of six buttons and four panel lights, three of which were currently showing red, the fourth blinking bright green.

To the right of the commander's station, there was a very rudimentary setup of several connected batteries and the termination of the massive spaghetti tangle of yellow electrical cord that led all the way down to the nuclear weapons bay.

It was simple, at least to Konstannonskyi. Push the green flashing panel on his left and the RMB-1750 is launched, towards the North Pole to cause all kinds of environmental havoc, according to rumors that swept the ship months before the carrier ever went to Murmansk. On his right, just make the connection of the two wire leads to the core of batteries and the one-thousand-megaton arsenal at the bottom of the ship goes up, along with everything within a couple-hundred-mile radius. If he chose this route, at the very least he would be responsible for the largest explosion in history.

So he could blow up the ship or blow up the world. Quite a choice. And seeing as it was in his hands, in his drug-induced, sleep-deprived state, Konstannonskyi was suddenly infused with a massive dose of megalomania.

"I have become the most powerful man in the world," he declared to his men. "Simple as that."

But his men weren't listening. They were gathered in the corner, examining the bodies of the two people they'd shot in order to take over this place. Far from celebrating, the twelve sailors looked like they were at a wake. Their faces were ashen, their eyes watering. The madness of the past few days had come crashing down on them at that very moment. All of them felt as if they'd just awakened from a bad dream.

The bodies lying before them were two kids; neither one was more than eleven years old. Each had a bullet in his head.

The sailors dropped their guns to the deck. Then they began to slowly walk out of the room.

Konstannonskyi watched them with a mixture of amusement and confusion.

"Where . . . are you going?" he asked them.

"Back to work," one sailor replied.

"But what has happened?" Konstannonskyi asked, a bit more desperately. "We are about to reap all of the riches in the world."

One man came close to him, pointed his head toward the two bodies, and said: "Nahimoutsi. The kids. That's who we've been shooting at."

Konstannonskyi's face drained of color. It took a few moments for it to sink in. Then it started to make some crazy sense to him. No wonder the Sharkskis never knew who made up the Drugiye. It was the kids. . . .

"But . . . but we hold all the power here," Konstannonskyi was saying as his men continued to file out. "Everyone else is dead. That means we can still be very, very rich!"

"On the lives of children?" one sailor called over his shoulder. "It's not for us any longer."

The last man to go turned for a moment and looked Konstannonskyi right in the eye.

"Get some sleep, Sergei," the man said. "You need it. . . ."

Delaney was getting tired of wondering what the hell was going on at the top of the Island.

He had not heard any gunshots, though with the storm raging at full blow, he wasn't sure he could hear much of anything. Still, he had to wonder: Had the battle ended peacefully? Was that possible? And what message had Gillis brought to the top of the Island? Things had certainly seemed to calm down after that.

What's that all about? he wondered.

As the minutes ticked by, he grew more antsy.

He stuck his head out of the top of the LAV and tried to see through the blowing snow if there was any activity at all going on up on the bridge. But while he could see shadows moving back and forth in front of a very dull light, he could not tell if there was fighting going on, or whether the Americans had retaken the place.

He looked behind him—the Kamov that Gillis and Ricco had flown aboard was still waiting by the angled deck, rotors turning, Ricco presumably behind the controls, ready for another quick getaway. Delaney really couldn't blame them for that. Just like in Operation ArcLight, the two tankers pilots had really come through in the pinch.

He looked aft and saw that a MiG-29 fighter had been brought up to the deck. It was sitting about twenty feet from the ass-end of the carrier, its engines turning and giving off vast amounts of smoke and steam in the freezing hurricane-like conditions.

Delaney knew the two Russian pilots, Balandin and Sotnikov, were sitting inside the two-seat warplane, cashing in on their half of the deal offered to them earlier in this long, surreal day. In return for letting the Americans use the aircraft elevator to get the busted Kamov off the deck, Smitz had agreed to let the two Russian pilots leave the ship whenever they wanted. Delaney theorized the Russian fliers were now waiting for just the slightest break in the weather to allow them to take off. They would have to display much skill to negotiate the clutter now littering the carrier's deck.

And if they did make it off the ship, where 'the hell would they go? Delaney wondered. Back to Russia?

He doubted that.

Finally Delaney's impatience got the best of him.

Leaving the LAV in care of Sergeant Reaney, he bounded across the flight deck, through the blizzard conditions, and into the hatchway.

Using Norton's cigarette lighter as his guide, he started up through the Island. Like Norton and the others before him, he retraced the steps of Krysoltev and his Spetsnaz guys, passing by the burned-up bodies and blown-up hatches. He could hear no noise at all inside the Island, no noise anywhere within the carrier. That was very strange. With all the gunfire and explosions and other weird things going on aboard the ship, to hear nothing at all was a bit disconcerting.

Reaching the third level, he heard footsteps coming his way. It sounded like a group of people, and he crossed his fingers that it was Norton and the American team. But as soon as he pulled himself up the ladder, he came face to face with the twelve sailors who had just left the Combat Room. Delaney was carrying his rifle, but it had no bullets in the clip. He raised it in a provocative manner anyway.

But the sailors had no intention of harming him. They were sick of fighting, sick of killing, sickened by the deaths of the Nahimoutsi.

Plus, they assumed he was a pilot for Russian Naval Aviation.

They stopped just before the ladderway leading down

to the third level. One man started talking very slowly, yet passionately in Russian to him. Not knowing quite what to do, Delaney just nodded as if he understood.

This fooled eleven of the sailors. They moved past him and went down the ladderway. But the twelfth man somehow saw through his ruse.

"You are not Russian?" he asked in very thick English.

Delaney just shrugged. "Guilty," he said.

The man smiled wearily. "Are you a ghost then?" he asked.

Delaney just shook his head. "Not yet," he replied.

The sailor smiled again. His eyes looked as if they hadn't closed in days, which was close to the truth.

"If you have come to save us then," he said slowly, "in the Combat Room, God is planning to blow us all up. You might be stopping him."

With that, the sailor brushed past Delaney and went down the ladderway.

Seaman First Class Sergei Konstannonskyi was still deciding which control he should push when he felt the sting of cold steel touch the back of his neck.

He froze, one hand hovering over the RMB-1750 launch button, the other over the control that would send a jolt of electricity down to the wired-up nuclear weapons bay. He was so out of it at this point, he had convinced himself of three things: First, that it was his destiny to be here in this place at this time with the power that lay beneath his hands. Second, if he launched the RMB-1750 and it hit its mark at the North Pole, the world would actually come to fear him so much, he could extract any price from those who survived the catastrophic effects of massive tides, millions of dead sea creatures, and radioactive rainfall.

Third, he believed that if he decided to ignite the megatonnage inside the ship's nuclear weapons bay, he alone would survive such a detonation, be blown free of the blast, and by his very survival force people around the world to take an accounting of him.

So he had some very big decisions to make now, and any interruptions would just be a waste of time.

So who then dared hold a gun to his neck?

He turned his head slowly to see a man in a Russian Naval Aviation uniform standing behind him.

This was not good. None of the pilots on board had been directly in league with the Sharkskis, so he had no reason to believe this man would be sympathetic to him. But what could he want?

"Just take a deep breath and sit back," Delaney said to him slowly, in English. "If you move a muscle, I will be forced to blow your brains out."

Konstannonskyi paused a moment. "You are not Russian?"

"That's what everyone keeps telling me," Delaney replied.

There was a long silence.

"Well, whatever you are, you are standing in the way of great things here," Konstannonskyi finally told him. "I have much to do and you are just delaying me."

Delaney was eyeing the control panel. It didn't take a rocket scientist to figure out that the RMB-1750 control sat ready to be activated under the man's left hand, and the switch to light up the nukes down below was under his right.

If he slugged the man, his body actions alone could depress one or even both controls—that option was out of the question. But he couldn't shoot him outright, because his rifle was empty.

So he was left to the only option remaining: a bluff.

And at the moment, he didn't have much faith in it.

"Okay, pal, this is how it's going to be," he said slowly. "If you don't raise your hands above your head in five seconds, I pull the trigger. You understand what I'm saying?"

Konstannonskyi just laughed. "How could I not? You are practically screaming in my ear."

"Okay then," Delaney said, trying to keep his voice steady, "Now that we understand each other, let's start counting."

He made a cocking motion with his rifle.

"One . . ."

Konstannonskyi's hands remained frozen above both controls.

"Two . . ."

The Russian lowered his right hand, inching it closer to the weapons bay switch.

"Three . . ."

His right hand dropped a bit further—it was now just two inches away from detonating the nukes down below.

"Four . . ."

Delaney was sweating. He knew this wasn't going to work.

"And five . . . okay . . . raise them."

Konstannonskyi laughed. "No, you shoot me instead."

Delaney nudged him with his rifle barrel. "I said up, now!"

But the sailor just laughed again. He sounded like a madman.

"You cannot pull the trigger!" he yelled. "I knew it!"

A second later, Delaney did pull the trigger. The click from the empty chamber echoed throughout the room.

Konstannonskyi laughed again, louder, more maniacally.

"See? I am supposed to be here!" he roared.

Delaney pulled the trigger again and again. But he got nothing but clicks.

"Thank you for deciding for me," Konstannonskyi said.

His hand went for the nuclear bay detonation switch. Totally on reflex, Delaney pulled his trigger again—and suddenly, part of Konstannonskyi's skull exploded.

Everything just stopped for a moment. Delaney froze,

looking at his gun and seeing no smoke coming from it. Konstannonskyi sat absolutely still, with blood running out of a wound just above his left ear and another just below his right.

Then Delaney looked up and saw Sergeant Reaney standing in the doorway, his rifle raised. He'd put a bullet right through Konstannonskyi's head.

"Jessuzz Christ . . ." Delaney breathed.

"I got tired of waiting too," the Team 66 man said.

Then Konstannonskyi's body began to fall, heading right for the nuclear detonation switch. Delaney tried to grab the man by the collar, but succeeded only in pushing him away from the electrical wire device. But in that movement, the body's dead weight drooped and Konstannonskyi's face hit the RMB-1750 control panel instead. His nose landed squarely on the green launch button.

A second later, the whole carrier began to shake. . . .

23

On the bridge

No one on the bridge knew what the flashing lights on the main system control panel meant at first.

One moment everything was quiet—all except for the weeping of the relieved Nahimoutsi; the next, it seemed like every bell and whistle on the bridge was going off.

Then they felt the whole ship begin to shake. Then Delaney and Sergeant Reaney rushed into the bridge—and were stopped dead in their tracks at the sight of the ragged, bloodied young kids.

But their astonishment lasted only a split second.

"We've got big trouble," Delaney told Norton.

By this time the Americans had figured out that the last RMB-1750 was about to launch—and that the vibrations they were feeling were coming from the missile's initial rocket motor getting ready to fire.

"Jessuz, we've got to do something!" Smitz cried. "We just won this thing. . . ."

Chou looked to his men, and as one they ran outside and around to the front of the bridge, Norton, Delaney, and Smitz right behind them. Down below was the recessed launching platforms for the RMB-1750 missiles.

The Team 66 troopers began pouring gunfire down onto the launching platform. The fusillade created a small storm of sparks as their tracer bullets ricocheted in every direction. The distinctive sound of bullets hitting steel could be heard above the cry of the wind and the dull scream of the MiG-29, still waiting poised at the end of the runway.

Like before, they were trying to hit something—a control panel, a junction box, a critical cable assembly—anything, to prevent the missile from launching. For good measure, someone dropped a magnesium grenade into the hole. It blew up with a blinding silver light.

Then everything got quiet again.

Just the wind and the MiG's engines. For the first time in a long time, there was no gunfire, no explosions, no screaming.

"God damn," Delaney breathed. "Did we do it? Is it really over?"

It was . . . for about three seconds.

Then the carrier began shuddering again. Then a klaxon began wailing. There was a huge explosion of fire and smoke blowing up from the launch pit.

Two seconds later, the RMB-1750 began rising through the cloud.

They watched with a mixture of shock and bewilderment as the missile shot up right in front of them, going straight up into the sky, leaving a long plume of flame and white smoke behind it.

Everyone hit the deck.

Delaney yelled: "You've got to be shitting me!"

"It ain't over till it's over!" Norton cried.

"We've *got* to do something!" Delaney yelled back to him. "We *know* that one ain't a dud."

The next thing he knew, Norton was up and running

again. Down the nearest ladderway, along the lower bridge railing, to the stairs that went down to the flight deck itself. He was dragging Delaney behind him.

"Jessuz, man," Delaney kept yelling. "What are we going to do?"

Norton wasn't sure himself.

"We're going to stop that missile," he finally yelled back at his partner. "Or kill ourselves trying."

Norton would never really know why, but all six members of Team 66 were soon on their heels.

Rifles up, heads down, they were all running through the blowing snow towards the aft end of the carrier. To where the MiG-29 was still poised, engines warming, waiting for a break in the weather to take off and leave the hellish ship behind.

It was a matter of youth and leg strength that caused the Team 66 troopers to reach the Russian fighter before Norton and Delaney. And again, Norton would never really know how the Team 66 guys knew what he wanted to do, especially since he wasn't sure himself. But they jumped up onto the MiG's wings and began scrambling up towards the canopy. The stunned faces of the pilots inside said it all. Still in shock from the missile launch, now they were suddenly being invaded by these crazy armed men from nowhere.

Balandin was in the front seat; Sotnikov was sitting in back. Balandin began revving the MiG's engines, as if the noise alone could shake off the American soldiers—but they were having none of that. The first trooper to reach the canopy stuck the barrel of his AK-47 right up against the cockpit glass, its barrel pointing at Balandin's head.

With the other hand he began counting down with his fingers.

Five . . . four . . . three . . .

His intention was clear: Open the canopy or I'll blow your head off.

Balandin opened the canopy.

"Comrade! Comrade!" both pilots began saying at once.

But the Team 66 guys were not there to make friends. They were all up near the cockpit now, and working as one, they reached in, took both pilots by the scruff of their necks, and yanked them out of the jet fighter, dropping them to the icy deck below.

Both Russians landed in a heap next to the airplane's front tire. They began screaming: "We had a deal!" along with some choice Russian curse words. But the wave of a few weapons from the Team 66 guys above gave them the good sense to crawl away.

By this time Norton and Delaney were up on the fighter's wing too. The Team 66 guys were urging them forward.

"I guess they want us to fly this crate?" Delaney asked Norton.

"That looks to be the plan," Norton yelled back.

Norton jumped into the front seat, Delaney into the back. The engines were still screaming; the RMB-1750's smoke plume was still fresh in the air.

Norton scanned the fighter's control panel. Everything was written out in Cyrillic writing. The same was true in the backseat.

"Christ, can you really drive this thing, Jazz!" Delaney yelled up to him.

"Beats me," Norton yelled back. "But I guess we better try."

He waved off the Team 66 guys, who began dropping from the airplane now. He closed the canopy and started pressurizing the cockpit. Both of them found their oxygen masks and hastily strapped them on, as well as their safety harnesses.

Norton located the throttles, put his feet where they had to go, and switched on the cockpit intercom.

Then he stopped for a moment. The storm was still blowing full force, the carrier pitching like never before. He really didn't know how to fly the Russian warplane or the correct procedure for taking off from a carrier.

In fact, he'd never performed a carrier jump before, ever.

So, it led to a question.

"Are we really going to do this?" he asked Delaney.

"Shit, yes!" was Delaney's reply.

That was all Norton needed to hear.

He pushed the throttles up full, and pressed as hard as he could on the brakes. The carrier's ski jump suddenly looked very close to them—as if it was just off the MiG's nose. Could he generate enough speed before reaching the twelve-degree incline to get airborne? If not, then they would simply be flinging themselves out into space for a few long seconds before crashing into the very wild sea.

It was strange because Norton didn't really remember popping the brakes on the MiG. It was as if some unseen hand had reached in and lifted his feet from them, for the next thing he knew, they were racing down the wreckage-strewn flight deck, heading straight for the ski jump.

His ears were filled with the sound of Delaney alternately cursing and screaming. He was forced to perform a bit of a jig around the tail section of the long-ago-destroyed Kamov ammo chopper, and then suddenly, they went up the ski jump . . . and out into space.

There was a very long, very surreal moment when the MiG just sort of hung there . . . suspended in air . . . not moving . . . not flying. Norton could see the water below them, how rough it was, and the dark clouds all around, and even individual ice floes heading towards the carrier.

It was almost peaceful.

But then Norton's hands instinctively punched the throttles, which automatically kicked in the afterburner. Suddenly it felt as if some gigantic boot had reared up and kicked the MiG in the ass. The jet fighter shot forward with an acceleration that Norton had never experienced before in all his years of flying.

They were on their way. . . .

But now the g's suddenly pressing down on Norton's chest were almost unbearable. He could barely catch his breath. He had yanked back on the control stick all the way so they were going almost straight up. But just the torque alone was causing the big fighter to spin. In effect they were corkscrewing their way straight up into the very thick clouds.

"Muthafucker!" Delaney was screaming. "Someone must have filled this baby with high-test!"

Up they went. Twisting around and around, the afterburners at full thrust, Norton trying to wrestle the controls to regain command of the MiG. But it was no use. The laws of aerodynamics had taken over. They were going up as high and as fast as the MiG wanted to take them. They were just along for the ride.

Somehow Norton managed to keep his eyes on the panel altimeter, and in his mind he was clicking off the miles as the hands spun around like a kitchen clock gone crazy.

One mile up. Two. Then three. Four . . . five . . .

The clouds around them were thick and black, and they were taking so much sleet and rain on the canopy, it was like driving through a car wash.

Then, suddenly, they broke through.

The airplane stopped spinning; the force of the afterburners pushing them towards outer space eased off.

The first thing Norton realized was that for the first time in a long time, the sky above him was absolutely clear. The moon was full and shining—it almost felt warm. The stars were brilliant. A very odd sensation washed over him—it really *was* as if they had just broken through to another world, one where it wasn't cloudy and black and stormy all the time.

"Motherfucker," Norton heard himself whispering. "Where the hell have we just been. . . ."

He put two hands on the control stick and managed to pull the beast of an airplane to the left, folding it over and not stopping until he'd leveled it out. The plane responded somewhat reluctantly, but cleanly. In a matter of seconds they were level at 27,550 feet.

And there, about twenty miles north of them, they could see the flare and smoke trail of the RMB-1750 missile going straight up toward the stars.

"Whew, Jessuz!" Delaney was yelling now. "I think I left my nuts back on the deck."

"Do you see what I see?" Norton called back to him.

Delaney caught on right away. "That's affirmative," he answered. "Leave it to the Russians to make the smokiest missile around."

It was true. The RMB-1750 was leaving a very distinct inky gray smoke trail behind it. Norton could see it ascending to at least forty-angels, where it became less distinct, but obviously kept on going.

"Well, now that we are up here, what the hell are we going to do?" Norton called back to Delaney.

"Only one thing we can do," was Delaney's reply. "We've got to follow that smoke trail and hope we can catch it when it starts on its way down."

Right away, Norton knew this was just about an impossible task. First of all the missile had had at least a four- or five-minute head start on them. Secondly, its arc would carry it much higher than the MiG could ever hope to fly. Thirdly, it could go much faster than they could. And fourth—what would happen if they did find it? What were they going to do?

"We're going to shoot the mother down!" came Delaney's voice in his headphones, as if he had read Norton's mind.

Yes, that was what they were going to do, Norton decided suddenly. But they were not going to chase the missile all the way to the moon and back in order to catch it.

Rather, they were going to head it off at the pass.

Or at least, try to . . .

•   •   •

The top speed of a MiG-29 was around 1500 miles per hour.

This at an altitude of twenty thousand feet or above, where the air is thinner, offering less resistance.

Under certain conditions, like a monstrous tailwind, such an airplane might be able to go faster.

But within five minutes of taking off on their wild pursuit, the MiG that Norton and Delaney were riding in was moving at a speed in excess of 1800 mph.

This was, of course, close to impossible.

And both Norton and Delaney knew it.

In fact they were going so fast, neither of them could speak without maximum effort and no little pain.

But that never stopped Delaney.

"These . . . fucking . . . Russians must . . . have been . . . lying their asses off . . . about the top speed of this son of a bitch," he said through a series of grunts and groans.

Neither man had real flight suits on—they did not have the luxury of inflating air bladders that would force the blood to stay in their brains instead of pooling in their legs, as it was wont to do at supersonic speeds.

That was why the whole incident had taken on a dreamy, surreal aura.

For whatever reason, the airplane was going so fast, Norton knew that to find the missile again, they only had to follow one direction: north.

And this was where he was pointing the nose of the airplane—all the while looking up with a mighty effort in the chance he might spot the missile's very smoky trail again.

How they happened to see it again was nothing short of miraculous.

But see it they did. After about twenty minutes of absolutely bone-crushing near-Mach 3 flight, Norton saw the faint wisp of a smoke trail way up through the cockpit glass.

Delaney saw it too. It looked like a very faint airplane contrail. But way, way up there.

"Hey, pard, you got a good eye for these things," Norton called back to him. "How high do you think that SOB is?"

Delaney could still hardly speak.

"It's got to be at least at seventy-angels," he grunted. "Probably more."

"Any idea what the service ceiling is for this airplane?"

"Nope," Delaney replied. "But I got a feeling we're soon going to find out."

He was right. With all his strength Norton was able to pull the steering column back. The MiG began a forty-five-degree climb that only added to their already monumental discomfort.

Norton was soon seeing stars—not just real stars—but stars like in cartoons when the character gets hit over the head. That was approximately how he felt at the moment. They were going so fast and climbing so quickly, his blood-deprived brain began playing tricks on him.

But again Norton was faced with a big question: What would they do if they got a chance to get close to the missile?

"Can you see any kind of launch systems back there, pard?" he called to Delaney.

"All I see is a million buttons," was the reply. "I think it's because my vision has gone triple."

"Do a crash course on how to launch some ordnance, will you?" Norton asked him. "We might be needing some."

He heard another series of grunts and groans from the backseat.

"Only if you promise not to use the word 'crash' again," was Delaney's eventual reply.

They flew like this for five minutes, Norton straining his eyes trying to keep the contrail in sight, while Delaney tried to make some sense out of the backseater's weapons array.

The earth beneath them was clearing of clouds now. They had at least gotten beyond the reach of the gigantic Atlantic storm; everything below them was snow-covered and white. They were certainly over the Arctic. Even the air felt different.

"I think I can make some sense of this," Delaney finally radioed ahead to him. "What's our fuel load looking like?"

"I'm afraid to look," Norton replied.

And he was. Because if they ran out of fuel up here— well, there weren't many things worse than crashing in the Arctic.

They were now passing through 55,000 feet. The MiG might have been solid, but as a test pilot Norton knew it couldn't take much more of this abuse; exceeding its normal velocity and its service ceiling could only result in a catastrophic breakup. In fact, it could happen at any second.

Just when he thought neither they or the fighter could take any more, Norton glanced up at the missile and saw its smoke trail had changed direction.

It was starting to come down.

This was where it started to get very weird.

Norton could see the missile turn over and start its descent. He eyed a place in the sky where he thought they might be able to get a chance at intercepting it. But right away that seemed doomed to failure. The missile was moving way too fast for them to reach that particular point in time.

As it was, the missile was more than thirty miles ahead of them. And it would certainly fall below their altitude before then.

But if they started dropping now, then all hopes of an intercept would be lost.

So there really was only one thing they could do. . . .

"So what are you packing back there?" he called to Delaney.

"It looks like we've got four air-to-air missiles and you've got a full cannon up there—or maybe it's the other way around."

Norton eyed the RMB-1750 again, and then tried to project an invisible point in the sky where their paths might cross under ideal conditions.

This was not an easy thing to do. They were still climbing and the missile was beginning to fall very rapidly.

It was in that moment that he knew that despite his masterful flying, and despite the fact that the plane was giving all it had, it was all for naught. They just wouldn't get in range in time.

"Damn it," Norton just said anyway. "Fire everything you got and I'll do the same."

"That's my boy!" Delaney yelled.

Suddenly the MiG started shaking as if it was coming apart at the seams. In seconds four huge missiles went flying off its under-wing rails, leaving a quartet of massive smoke trails behind them.

At the same time Norton located and pressed the cannon trigger. Again the plane began jumping around like crazy. One long orange tracer stream lit up the sky all around them—it nearly blinded Norton it was so bright.

At this point he hardly cared, though. This really *was* a fool's mission. He really felt it now, deep in his chest. Everything they'd gone through in the past two incredible days—for it to end here, literally at the top of the world, in failure—it was almost too much for him to take.

And that was when the night sky suddenly caught on fire.

The blast that hit his retinas was so violent, he felt a burning sensation in them. There was no sound at first. No shock wave. Just an incredibly bright light, so intense Norton felt its warmth on his face.

No wonder he thought he'd died. . . .

•   •   •

When he opened his eyes again, the sky was lit up with brilliant clouds of orange and red.

"Jessuz, can you see that?" he called back to Delaney— but in the next second it was impossible for his partner to reply. That was when the shock wave hit.

It picked up the MiG-29 and turned it over like a leaf in a hurricane. The next thing Norton knew, they were going backwards, turning nose over end, absolutely out of control and falling, both engines flamed out, with the plane caught in the grip of a complete stall.

Again it was strange because Norton really didn't remember thinking about it—but as a test pilot he'd been in similar situations before. Purposely putting a plane into a spinning stall was bread-and-butter work for a test pilot. And somehow he knew exactly what to do next.

And that was nothing.

For ten long seconds he allowed the airplane to fall. Backwards, engines coughing, every light on the control panel blinking madly.

But then finally, gravity took over, and the nose of the airplane found its way pointing towards the ground. When that happened, Norton calmly restarted both engines. They coughed once, twice—but the third time was the charm. They both flamed on at once and with his last ounce of strength, he pulled back on the control stick and leveled the fighter off.

He would later learn he was but a thousand feet above the snowy ground when he finally recovered flight.

Once back at level, he began calling Delaney. It took a while, but finally his partner came to—swearing as usual.

"Jessuz," he said groggily. "What the fuck just happened?"

"I'll tell you later," Norton said. "Just look north and let me know if what I'm seeing is real."

Delaney did—and swore some more.

"God damn," he whispered. "Is that what I think it is?"

It was the remains of the explosion of the RMB-1750. It looked like a huge flower still—bright orange and red just hanging in the sky, the stars twinkling around it.

"Did *we* do that?" Delaney asked him in astonishment.

Norton looked at the ball of fire, and judged the distance again.

"Who else?" he replied.

24

The MiG was just about flying on fumes by the time Norton spotted the *Kuznetsov* through the clouds.

Despite the still-blowing rain and snow, it had been fairly easy to find the battered ship again. Every light that could be turned on aboard the carrier was now glowing brightly. But there was another reason the ship stuck out in the darkness as well: Hanging off the top of the Island, and off the bow and stern of the ship, were hundreds of bedsheets colored red, white, and blue. Some even formed very crude approximations of the American flag.

"Well, that answers a few more questions," Norton radioed back wearily to Delaney. He was referring to the "red room" he'd seen while crawling through the carrier vents, as well as the passageway that had been washed in blue dye. "I guess this was one way they were going to let their true intentions be known."

"Boy, these kids really got bit by the Old Glory bug," Delaney replied. "Not many real Americans are this patriotic."

"That's the problem," Norton radioed back. "You really don't know what you got until it's gone."

They could also see that the *Battev* had pulled up beside the carrier by this time. Every light on that ship was burning brightly as well. It had never looked so good.

They were ten miles out when the MiG began bucking. Both engines started coughing out big puffs of thick black smoke. In an effort to save fuel, they had shut off all nonessential items for the dash back. It really was a small miracle that they'd gotten back at all. But now, the Russian fighter was clearly running out of gas.

"We going to have to ditch?" Delaney called up to Norton.

"No way," Norton replied. "I don't want to get any wetter than I am right now."

He had one more trick up his sleeve. They could see the carrier, now about nine miles away. They were at about seven thousand feet and descending. They had maybe a minute's worth of fuel left. However, the carrier was at least two minutes away.

So Norton shut off the MiG's two engines.

Delaney felt twin bumps as the power plants shut down. Now the only sound he heard was that of the wind rushing by.

"Please tell me you did that on purpose," he called up to Norton.

"Old test pilot trick," Norton radioed back. "You'd be surprised how far you can go on just a glide and a prayer."

Flying so high, so fast with no engines was a bit eerie.

"Well, I got that prayer thing cornered," Delaney reported.

Down they went, through many layers of clouds, always trying to keep the carrier right off the nose of the airplane. Once they reached two thousand feet, Norton crossed his fingers and tried to start the engines again.

Both power plants ignited on cue, shaking the airplane

down to its rivets, but giving them just the push they
needed to reach the ship.

"Great stunt, Jazz!" a very relieved Delaney called up
to him. "I owe you a beer."

"Make it a case," Norton told him. "Better yet, a
keg . . ."

Landing was perilously routine.

Norton did not have the luxury of a go-around. So he
simply put the MiG's nose down, banked steeply around
the back of the carrier, and crossed his fingers. They came
down hard, snagging the last available arresting wire. The
huge fighter jerked to a stop—and the engines went dead
a second later. Both were out of gas.

Delaney let out a whoop. He was breathing again.

Norton lifted the canopy and they climbed out. Delaney
shook his hand, but then said: "Next time we save the
world, I'll do the flying, okay?"

"You got it," Norton told him without a blink.

There was a welcoming committee of sorts waiting for
them. Chou, his Team 66 guys, Smitz, Gillis, and Ricco
were all on hand, each one looking like he desperately
needed a bath, a shave, a hot meal, and a change of
clothes. The two National Guard pilots surprised them
with warm handshakes.

"I've just got one question," Delaney said. "Have all the
nukes in the basement been disconnected? Because if not,
we're flying right off again."

"They are being disconnected as we speak," Smitz replied. "Should take about another two hours."

"I guess I can wait a little longer," Delaney said.

"You've got to see this guy Kartoonov," Smitz told
them as they walked away from the airplane. "He's like
someone from a bad spy novel."

The CIA man escorted them up to a small anteroom
next to the bridge. On the way they saw many members
of the *Battev* crew moving about, some doing so very

quickly. They were distinctive in their drab gray uniforms, and it was as if being aboard the carrier had brought them back from the brink of terminal boredom. The pilots also saw many of the carrier's original crew as well, including the sailor Seklovski, the man they had taken prisoner, who was now helping to run the bridge. Like him, the *Kuznetsov*'s crew had come out of hiding, the long nightmare finally over, to reclaim their ship again.

They reached the anteroom and there was Kartoonov, obviously with a few vodkas in him, rambling in stern Russian with a few of his Nahimoutsi gathered around him.

"Gillis was right," Smitz told Norton and Delaney, closing the anteroom's door a bit. "He wanted to defect all along. They all did. They thought we were Russians the whole time. That's why they were launching the RMB-1750's. But give them credit. They battled the Sharks and took us on for good measure."

"Yeah, but what about the guy with all the medals hanging from the rope?" Delaney asked. "Kartoonov got a twin brother?"

Smitz just shrugged. "He says they came upon the body of a guy the Sharkskis killed early on, someone his height and weight—minus the head, of course. He figured with the staff officers killed off, if the Russian Northern Fleet thought he'd been chopped up too, they'd never suspect he was behind the scheme to get to America. So they put the guy in the admiral's clothes and over he went."

"So it was Kartoonov and the kids all along who sent the radio message to the Northern Fleet?" Norton asked.

"As best we can determine," Smitz replied, looking back at Kartoonov. "Though I think we'll have to let him sober up a bit before we can really get a good debriefing. It might take a while."

"It's a hell of a way to defect," Delaney said. "But at least it livened up my holiday season."

"Strange thing is, all the kids really *are* orphans," Smitz said. "But with Kartoonov as their den mother, they're just one big happy family."

"Yeah, but what the hell happens to them now?" Norton asked Smitz. "I mean, seriously fucking up the biggest ship in the Russian Navy? When they get back home, they'll hang Kartoonov from the nearest tree and probably shuttle the kids off to some gulag for the rest of their lives."

Smitz smiled slyly. "Let's just say I have some alternative thoughts on that," he said.

"Good, let's hear them over coffee," Norton said, pausing before adding: "There *is* some coffee on board this pig, right?"

But Smitz wasn't listening. He was looking at his watch instead.

"Well, what do you know about that?" he said.

"Takes a licking and keeps on ticking?" Delaney asked with a straight face.

"No, the time," Smitz replied.

"What about the time?"

"Well, we just crossed it," Smitz said. "The infamous Zero Red Line."

A silence came over the room.

"Is anyone working on turning this boat around," Delaney finally asked him.

Smitz smiled again.

"As we speak," he said.

Lieutenant Commander Andy Rogers was wide awake again.

He was in the *Skyfire*'s officers' mess, pouring out what had to be his fifth cup of coffee in just the past hour and rummaging through the condiment drawer, numbly searching for a packet of Sweet'n Low.

He found one—it was old, stained, and hardened—but Rogers didn't care. He dumped the clump of artificial sweetener into his brimming cup and stirred the concoction with his finger. There was a plate of Christmas sweets set next to the coffee urn. Sugar cookies with red and green sprinkles on them. Rogers picked one up and tasted it. It was stale, hard as a rock. He ate it anyway.

He sat down at the table and found himself staring at the pathetic holiday decorations strung up around the small compartment. He was sure he'd be home for the holidays this year. He'd missed them the last four years—missed seeing his kids on Christmas Day. Missed opening presents with his wife; watching the football games, drinking beer.

He sipped his coffee. Would he even be alive this time next year to try again?

Would he be alive an hour from now?

That was when a young sailor hurried into the mess.

"Excuse me, sir," he said. "The skipper wants you forward. He says the target has been sighted."

•

By the time Rogers made it up to the main deck, Captain Bruynell was hanging on the periscope, eyeglasses pushed up on his head.

He heard Rogers approach.

"Take a look," he said soberly.

Rogers got on the periscope and focused it for his eyes. And there it was. A huge aircraft carrier dead in their sights, twenty thousand yards away.

But it was strange. The ship was aglow—not with the usual running lights. Instead, every light on its hull and superstructure was illuminated. Plus he could see some small fires and smoke columns twisting up into the snow and wind. And he could see banners of some kind, hanging all over the place. They were all red, white, and blue.

"I don't have any idea what is going on aboard her," Rogers said. "But obviously that ship is in trouble."

"What do you recommend?" Bruynell asked him.

"Turning around and going home," Rogers said.

Bruynell pretended he didn't hear the comment.

"Your counsel, please, Number One?" he asked instead.

Rogers thought a moment. There was an air of unreality to what they were doing. This seemed more like an exercise—a simulation—than the real thing. They'd been running without any of their electronic gear turned on. No sonar, no underwater radar. No radios. Nothing. Especially strange were the reports that said they could expect no resistance to be put up by the carrier. It was a huge sitting duck.

"I'd say a spread of four would do it, sir," he finally replied. "Fused for twenty thousand yards. Even if she isn't wired with nukes, they will take her down very quickly. And God help anyone still aboard her. . . ."

He paused a moment, then added: "God help us as well."

Bruynell gave the orders and seconds later, four MK-48/6A "can't miss" torpedoes were on their way toward the carrier.

Rogers still had his eyes on the periscope, but they were closed. He just couldn't watch as the torpedoes sped to the target. He thought of all the lives they were about to take. Of what might happen if the ship's nuclear weapons detonated when the MK-48's hit. He thought of his family. His wife. His kids. This time tomorrow, they might be fatherless.

Only a miracle could save them all now.

He counted off the minutes and seconds in his head, and then finally looked into the periscope again. He was certain that he would see the impacts on the big carrier by now.

He got a surprise instead.

The carrier was still in one piece, still very much afloat. In fact, it was fading into a snow-enshrouded fog, turning back east, disappearing rather peacefully from view.

But where were the torpedoes—the four "can't miss" Mk-48's? It was as if they'd simply vanished.

He got off the periscope and just looked at Bruynell.
"What happened?" the captain asked him.
Rogers just shook his head.
"I really don't know," he said.

25

Somewhere in Nevada

The two techs who manned the small hangar on top of the secret mountain had never heard a Beta-Six radio call before.

They had to look it up in the operations manual before they realized that the secret transmission was telling them that the Aurora hypersonic aircraft was inbound and that it had sustained "battle damage."

The two techs couldn't believe it.

"What the hell has he been doing out there?" one asked, astonished.

They didn't know and would not find out until the airplane returned.

So they set about preparing for its arrival. It was over Utah right now, moving very fast, but not as fast as it could. They took this as a bad sign.

While one tech prepared the landing platform and readied the roof to open, the other hunted down the small hangar's trio of fire extinguishers. He also retrieved the first-aid kit.

The aircraft arrived over the mountain five minutes later.

The roof opened and it came down slowly, almost painfully. The two techs were appalled. The precious aircraft had scorch marks running up and down its fuselage. It was bent in some places, chipped and smoking in others.

It landed with a bump. The canopy opened and the weary pilot tumbled out.

"What happened?" both techs asked at once.

"You can watch the tape," the pilot said. "But before you do, patch it up—I have to go up again."

The techs just stared back at him.

"Go back up?" one said. "You've practically ruined this thing. You can't go anywhere. Not for at least a few weeks."

"You forget what this thing cost; what it is made of," the other tech said. "We can't just patch it up."

The pilot they called Angel just stared back at them. They had never seen him look quite that way before. His eyes were like twin blue lasers—and that was no exaggeration.

"I said patch it up," he repeated simply.

There was a very long silence.

And then both men just nodded.

"Okay," one said. "Grab a Coke—we'll see what we can do."

Thirteen levels below

"Have we ever celebrated with champagne before? Do we even have any around?"

"Champagne? Are you nuts? The carrier is back on the other side of the Zero Red Line. The North Pole is safe once again. And we didn't wind up killing several hundred of our own men—on Christmas Eve. I think that we should get a bottle of Kentucky sour mash whiskey and start pouring!"

A button was pushed, and in a few minutes a bottle of Kentucky sour mash appeared on the huge conference table.

"Can we see that intercept video again, please?" one voice asked as the drinks were being poured out.

The huge TV screen on the room's far wall blinked to life.

"Begin sequence . . ."

Suddenly the screen came alive with a three-shot view of the RMB-1750 missile being intercepted over the Arctic. The MiG being flown by Norton and Delaney was prominent in one shot. The missile itself, spiraling wildly, was centered in another. But in the third shot all that could be seen was a whitish blur. It was an object going so fast, it was nearly impossible to discern what it was.

Unless you knew already.

Just as the last of the MiG's cannon shells and air-to-air missiles, falling far short of their mark, faded from view, the white blur entered the field where the missile's downward track was depicted. Suddenly there was a long beam of red light—and in the next frame, the missile exploded into a million pieces.

Then the sequence ended.

"A thousand bucks says that those two chopper pilots still think that they KO'd that missile. Any takers?"

"Let them think it. In their minds, they just saved the world. After what they just went through, why ruin that illusion?"

"Okay, but we must have a talk with our angel-winged friend," another voice said. "That is a priceless aircraft he is flying. You could not replace it for a trillion dollars. He seemed a bit reckless with it this time."

"*Reckless?* He's the one that really *did* save the planet—from a huge catastrophe. . . ."

"True—but you know the origin of that aircraft—we can never build another one like it again."

"Okay—let's give him a speeding ticket then. All's well that ends well, I say."

"Can we see the former target, please?"

The screen blinked again, and soon they were looking at a heat shot of the *Kuznetsov* under tow by the listing but ever reliable *Battev*. The storm had finally dissipated and the seas were relatively calm.

Three all-black CIA-run Ospreys were just taking off from the carrier's deck. One headed west, one east. The other south.

"Looks like those ships are making about five knots combined," one voice said. "If that . . ."

"That means they'll make it back to Murmansk in about two years."

There was laughter around the table. A rare event.

"Maybe they'll be in another heat wave again by then. . . ."

More laughs.

But then someone said: "May I bring up one last enigmatic topic?"

There were no objections.

"Is there anyway we can find out *why* those torpedoes did not go where they were supposed to?"

A dead silence in the room.

"Maybe we can just put it down to a little divine intervention on Christmas Eve?" someone suggested, only half in jest.

"Maybe we should just not speak of it at all," someone else said. "Some things are better left unknown."

There was a murmur of agreement in the room on that.

"Okay then, one last detail: How will they explain Kartoonov's disappearance? I mean the orphans—no one will be looking for them. But someone might be curious as to the whereabouts of Mother Russia's highest-ranking Naval officer."

"Look, he was going to get sacked anyway," came one reply. "As far as the Russians are concerned, officially at least, that was his body dangling at the back of the carrier—and not just some cook who ran into the Sharkskis at the wrong moment."

"Besides," another voice added, "they'll need a new bartender at Seven Ghosts. He'll do just fine."

Then another silence came over the room.

Then, as one, the seven men raised their glasses.

"To Artie Rooney," one said. "A damn good guy."

"To Artie . . . may he rest in peace."

Triple Shot Key

The light appeared from the east this time.

It was moving faster as well, and was much higher in the sky than the first time.

Alex was asleep by the fire when Mo first spotted it. She wanted to make sure before she woke Alex up. There had been several false alarms in the past forty-eight hours. Lights in the sky, moving strangely. Each time they had watched them, hoping that the promise Norton and Delaney had made to them before leaving—that they would return soon—would come true. But each time they'd been disappointed.

The reason for the two women wanting to see Norton and Delaney again was twofold. They had concerns, of course, that wherever the two mystery men went, they'd be safe and would return unharmed. But there was also another more practical concern. The women had no way to get off Triple Shot Key. No way to call anyone. No way to flag down a passing boat or airplane.

They had come by helicopter; they would have to leave the same way.

Or so they thought.

•   •   •

But now the light was turning amber and huge, and that was just how Mo remembered it to be two nights before. So she began shaking Alex awake.

"I think this is them!" Mo was shouting.

By the time Alex opened her eyes, the Osprey was overhead, already translating into a hover mode just above the beach.

Alex jumped to her feet and hurriedly ran her fingers through her hair. She had thought a lot about Norton in the past two days—after the anger at him leaving her high and dry had passed, that is. The truth was, she was surprised that he had affected her so much.

The Osprey finally set down with a typical hurricane whirlwind. Once again, it blew out the fire and mussed their hair.

As soon as it hit the sand, the side door opened.

Alex straightened out her clothes and tried to fix her hair again. She was wondering if she should run to Norton's arms—or play it cool.

But as it turned out, Norton was hardly the first one off the strange aircraft. Instead, when the doors opened, a long stream of very ragged young boys began falling out.

They looked like refugees who had just gone through some terrible war—which, of course they had.

After the thirty or so boys had filed out, a large man in shorts and a T-shirt emerged. He was at least seventy years old, appeared to be quite drunk, and looked, well . . . Russian.

Only after he deplaned did Norton and Delaney finally tumble out of the odd airplane.

No sooner had they walked away than the Osprey took off again. It was up and gone in a matter of seconds.

After gathering the Nahimoutsi in one spot, Norton and Delaney asked them to sit on the sand for a moment, which they were quite willing to do. Blue water, palm trees, a beautiful sunrise coming up over the ocean. They'd never seen a place such as this—neither had Kartoonov. They were all mesmerized by its beauty.

Finally Norton and Delaney walked over to Alex and Mo to face the music.

To the surprise of all, the females included, they fell into each others' arms. Norton naturally so.

"You're in trouble, mister," Alex whispered to him. "*Big* trouble."

Norton smiled for the first time in two days.

"That's just what I want to hear," he replied.

Smrzy, Bosnia

It was raining hard in the Gryzenk Valley.

Huddled inside a hut next to the main road were six members of the Blood Red unit.

These men were terrorists within their own country. Their leader, the man known as the Vulture, had taught them well. They were the scourge of the countryside, so much so the Serb-Allied forces alternately avoided them or chased them if they happened to slip out of their small zone of influence.

Rape, robbery, murder. The Blood Red unit wore these things like badges of honor.

And tonight, despite the rain, they were especially upbeat. For tonight, as soon as the Vulture arrived, they would, at last, see the cache of plastic explosives that he'd recently purchased. Then the planning for what these powerful explosives would be used for would begin in earnest. Killing American peacekeeping troops was certainly the first objective. That was, after all, what the Vulture was being paid to do by a myriad of foreign governments starting with both Iraq and Iran.

But using the hideous explosives on civilian targets, to spread more terror, set up more rapes, and pull off more robberies—these things too would be done up and down the Balkans.

And then they'd have even more money, even more power.

But none of this could begin until the Vulture arrived—and he was already twenty minutes overdue.

"This is very strange," one terrorist said, looking out at the muddy roadway down which the Vulture would travel.

"He's never been this late before. . . ."

Portsmouth, N.H.

Ryan Gillis woke up early on Christmas morning, but he did not jump out of bed right away.

He'd had the strangest dream. He was in his room, and an angel had come to him. This person was dressed all in white except he had a fighter pilot's crash helmet on, one that was way too big for him. And he was wearing sneakers, Keds, just like the kind Ryan wore, except they were black.

In his dream, the angel had told him that he knew why he was worried about his father. But he said that he had it "on good authority" that Ryan's dad would be home soon. Very soon. In fact, he'd be home by Christmas.

Ryan remembered the dream as seeming very real. But then there was the part about the flying saucer. That seemed real too, but really, why would an angel need a flying saucer to get around?

He almost laughed now when he thought of it. He could have some pretty funny dreams some times.

Then he got sad again, because now it *was* Christmas morning, and even though he knew there was a bunch of toys waiting for him downstairs, he just didn't feel like getting up and looking at them. Not without his dad.

So he looked up at the ceiling of his room instead and felt the rocks in his stomach return. Though he'd felt okay after seeing the light in the sky, now he was back to thinking his dad was never coming home, that he would never see him again. That he'd been killed in a plane crash.

He almost started crying, but held back the tears, and considered praying instead.

If only his dream was true, he thought. If only the funny-looking angel with the sneakers and flying saucer had *really* come to his room during the night and told him that his dad *would* be home real soon—what a happy Christmas this would be!

But Ryan was old enough to know that things like that just didn't happen in the real world.

So he finally decided to get up and go down and look at his crummy toys and at least try to make his mom feel better. But just as he was about to climb out of bed, he felt his right hand hurting him a little.

He looked at it and realized that he'd been holding it in a fist ever since he woke up, and probably longer than that. His fingers were almost locked together, he'd been holding them so tight.

And then he remembered that in his dream, the angel had given him something—something that he said would prove that his dad was okay and would be home soon.

Ryan felt excited and scared at the same time.

He looked down at his hand and opened it very, very slowly.

Inside was the tiny silver key to his money bank.

The next thing he knew, he was out of bed and running as fast as he could down the stairs.

He reached the first floor, and then he stopped. He heard a very strange sound. Was it someone snoring?

He slowly opened the living room doors, and that was when his eyes went very wide and the rocks disappeared from his stomach for good.

His dad was lying on the couch next to the Christmas tree, his clothes still on, his flight bag thrown beside him, sound asleep.

Somewhere in the North Atlantic

Approximately two thousand miles east of the Gillis family's house in Portsmouth, New Hampshire, there was a particularly deep part of the Atlantic known as the Mid-Ocean Shelf.

This was essentially an underwater mountain range, one whose valleys could run five miles deep or more.

Lying at the bottom of one of these valleys, not to be discovered for another thousand years, were the remains of the stealthy-quiet, deep-diving, nuclear-powered submarine *Okerzo*, one of its holds filled with fifty million dollars in cash and gold, and four unexploded but nevertheless deadly Mk-48 torpedoes sticking out of its hull.